STORMY WATERS
ON THE Sagebrush Sea

STORMY WATERS ON THE **Sagebrush Sea**

Richard Howard

Stormy Waters on the Sagebrush Sea
Copyright © 2022 by Richard Howard

Art by © Rachel Teannalach. No art may be reproduced in any form or by any means, including digital storage and retrieval systems, except by explicit prior written permission of the artist. Cover art: "Spring Storm Over Foothills." Section dividers: "Sunrise Over Payette Lake," "A Drive Through Long Valley," "Lost River Range Sunset," and "Thunderhead Over the Boise Front."

Author photo portrait © Allan Ansell. All other images as credited.

Cover and book design, typography, and editing by Meggan Laxalt Mackey, Studio M Publications & Design, Boise, Idaho.

Editing by Patricia Entwistle, Boise, Idaho.

Print ISBN 978-1-0881-2258-7

First Edition May 2022. ISBN 978-1-0879-2341-3
Second Edition January 2023, with updated stories, new chapters, and more photographs. Printed in the United States of America.

Published by ELKSTONE PRESS McCall, Idaho

Dedicated to

For Dr. Richard and Alice Howard,
understanding parents who became great friends.

Best of all, he loved the fall, the leaves yellow on
the cottonwoods, leaves floating on the trout streams
and above the hills, the high blue windless skies . . .
now he will be a part of them forever.

—Ernest Hemingway, Idaho, 1939

There is no such thing as bad weather,
just bad clothing.

—Stacey Gebhards, Idaho, 2016

Acknowledgments

Along the way, I have met and worked with fascinating people who contributed in their own way to the creation of this work. Sometimes it was through a comment or a joke, or sharing with each other a tragedy or a triumph from our lives. It was living off the edge with people in places where coffee, tea, breakfast, and dinner were made over an open fire. It was meeting them in the classroom, field lab, or conservation rally at the Capitol, at the local pizza parlor, the Manhattan Café in Shoshone, Elevation 486 in Twin Falls, Pickle's in Arco, the Flying M in Boise, and at my book designer's studio in Hidden Springs.

It is to my family and friends that I dedicate the contents of the book. They have given life to it in a way that could not otherwise have been invented or inspired.

I would like to thank my family: Marcia; Eric, Lindsay, Kash, and Karter; Anna, Brett, and Weston; Gunda Hiebert; Fran Cheney; Tim Freeman, Dawn and Henrik; and all the rest.

Also, I thank Meggan Laxalt Mackey and Dennis Mackey, Rachel Teannalach, Pat Entwistle, Jan Derrington, Dennis and Cheryl Harms, Scott Sawby, Doc Mullin, Wayne Melquist, Jay Gore, Roy Heberger, Dan Herrig and Jeri Wood, Herb Pollard, Stacy Gebhards, Bert Bowler, Bill Horton, Bill and Colleen Mullins, Sam and Dorothy Mattise, Alan and Lois Sands, Bob and Sally Reichert, Dave Hayes, Bob Collins, Phil Bucher, Paul Mascuch, Ed Pitcher, Bruce Haak, Jon and Elizabeth Kittell, Cathy Rogers, Jim Clayton, and Sherry Schubert.

—R.H.

Contents

Preface

THIS BOOK IS A COMPENDIUM OF MOMENTS that span 50 years of living through diverse experiences and is a product born out of family history, Idaho culture, and Northwest lifestyle. These compositions, some illustrated with photos by the me and artwork by Rachel Teannalach, distill the tangents of my mind. Between the covers of *Stormy Waters on the Sagebrush Sea* are adventures, raw commentary, and humor that will entertain, educate, and move a reader to step outside and see the Northwest with fresh eyes. I've taken care to bring the novice along with the expert into the fields of fishing, falconry, and yoga.

Come with me as we discuss Northwest conservation; wrestle trout and salmon from big rivers; and lakes; journey to Alaska and Australia to hold hands with the planet; examine diverse subjects such as malicious parent syndrome, eulogies and obituaries, ballet dance, restored hats, petroglyphs, and tributes.

While some of these short stories border on being biographical, others are entirely fictional. Gordon Walker is an alter ego to the author. The distinct meaning of which is found in the literary analysis used when referring to fictional literature. Walker is a key character in many of the stories and gives me as author literary license to mold a character from his history, talents, and family background. Look for him in such diverse stories as the "Mulchatna Kings," "Cadillac Expeditions," "Too Many Notes," "Mortality Storms," and "Lost Weekends at Elkstone Cabin."

I call the tales "green tea contemplations"—inspired narratives that came to me while making tea over an open fire, pondering the fractal symmetry of dancing flames. These compositions surfaced from a life filled with summits and sunsets, anguish and doubt, courage and adventure.

—*Richard Howard*
Elkstone Cabin, McCall, Idaho
December 21, 2022

I: Stormy Waters

"Sunrise Over Payette Lake" by Rachel Teannalach

Stormy Waters on Hank's Lake

BESIDES FISHING GEAR, GORDON CARRIED his backpack and the yellow Helly Hansen rain jacket and pants to the boat. John only brought his fishing pole and tackle box. No rain gear. They climbed into the 16-foot Alumaweld drift boat.

Gordon took the captain's chair in the rear of the boat, lifted the motor up from the floor, and eased it onto the transom in the back of the boat. He tilted the motor into the water and heard the latch click, which firmly locked the motor. Now, the three bladed propeller was ready to push water. John sat in the cross-seat near the bow of the boat and set the folded boat tarp on the floor.

Gordon was a hunter and fly fisher who always checked the weather conditions before venturing outside. His hand-crafted three-piece fly rods were exceptional for their strength and durability. Gordon's friends admired his self-reliance and his skilled craftsmanship. They cherished his moments of generosity when he would give away a fly rod for no other reason than to see it perform when in someone else's hands.

He double-checked his backpack for the rain gear and looked at John. "Weather could turn on us today, John," Gordon said. "I'll take my chances," said John. "I'm more interested in catching big fish than what the weather holds."

Gordon pulled the starter cord on the 6.5 HP Mercury engine. The motor coughed. He pulled again. The motor turned over in a false start. On the third pull, the motor vibrated, then sucked fuel from the five-gallon gas tank into the cylinders. The sound of the motor reassured Gordon that it was running smoothly.

John thought to himself, *It's goin' to be a good day to fish; with the barometer falling that gets fish excited.*

Goin' out in Gordon's boat is always lucky. He is a "highliner," a term he heard often in Alaska used to identify fishing guides or commercial fishermen who caught the most fish.

Last year on Henrys Lake (often referred to by fly fishers as Hank's Lake), John caught a 7-pound 12-ounce hybrid rainbow/cutthroat trout while out in Gordon's boat. At the end of the day, in the big cabin at Wilderness Edge Resort, the other ten guys who were staying at the cabin toasted John with beer glasses held high. This was their ninth annual Fly Fisher's Rendezvous.

Each year, they reserved the last week in May at the resort to enjoy camaraderie, intense humor, music, and Cordon Bleu meals. Four guys brought drift boats, and one guy, Herb, brought his big Crestliner boat. Trolling big flies for big fish at one of four nearby lakes, including Hank's Lake, tied it all together.

Gordon navigated the boat to the middle of Hank's Lake, about one mile from shore. He switched on the portable sonar. It began to scan and almost immediately showed fish on the screen beneath the boat.

They let their fly lines trail into the water about 40 yards behind the boat. Tied to the end of each line were red wooly bugger flies decorated with sparkling micro-ribbons. Twenty minutes went by without a strike. All John wanted to hear was the cry, "fish on," and to see a five-pounder jump out of the water behind the boat.

Fierce storms can roll in from the west through Red Rock Pass and churn Hank's Lake into a maelstrom. They are amplified by the U-shaped valley below the 10,000-foot peaks where Hank's Lake is located. The combination of physical geography, plummeting barometer, thunderheads, and accelerated winds makes for an exaggerated fetch on the lake that few boats can survive.

John's brown eyes grew round like two full moons as he saw the huge thunderheads building to the west. The wind started to ripple the water.

"Boy, am I glad you told me to bring the boat tarp," John said.

Gordon pulled out his Helly Hansen gear and struggled to pull it over his sweater and blue jeans. John grabbed the tarp and wrapped it over his shoulders as the first raindrops splashed on his head.

"This is going to be a real cloudburst of a storm," John said. John thought about the fish research job he held 20 years ago at the Great Lakes Science Lab located at Ann Arbor near Lake Erie. He worked on the "Osprey." The 32-foot ship, outfitted for conducting deep-water fish and plankton counts throughout the Great Lakes, was known for its superb performance during fall and winter storms. It was not uncommon to be caught in 14-foot white-capped waves on Lake Michigan that took the boat into the peaks and troughs of huge rollers. He never lost confidence in the boat's performance. However, there were moments of fear when he thought it might go pitchpoling down a roller. It never did.

As the wind whipped up to 40 miles an hour on Hank's Lake, Gordon and John quickly retrieved their fishing lines and prepared to seek the nearest shore. Gordon calculated how long it would take to return to shore. The calculation was simple: not enough time to reach the shore with the rapidly changing lake surface conditions. He now wished he had put his 15 HP motor on the boat this morning.

Foaming white-capped waves tend to reduce a boat's buoyancy just as it does when a raft goes through high rapids on a river. Water is less dense when laced with a high density of air bubbles. The cresting waves on Hank's Lake produced these conditions.

Gordon's boat survived the first seven waves. Drift boats are revered for their capacity to ride high rapids and big waves. However, they don't do well if the stern plug near the bottom of the boat is removed. The pressure of the eighth wave popped the stern plug out which went clanging under the boat's floorboards. A gush of water came pouring from the hole into the craft.

Gordon kept the boat pointed toward shore. John was scrambling to keep the boat tarp wrapped around his shoulders and over his head. The boat motor stopped after the tenth wave hit the boat. It was then that Gordon realized that water was gushing into the bottom of the boat from the stern. He quickly surmised that the stern plug had popped out. He reached down trying in vain to find the plug and replace it. Water was now up to his ankles and still he could not find the lost plug.

"We're goin' down," Gordon said. "Put your life jacket on, John . . . quick."

A 16-foot aluminum drift boat weighs 280 pounds empty. Three air compartments are built into its structure. The compartments will keep an empty boat afloat. A boat loaded with 350 pounds of fishermen, a 70-pound boat motor, 60 pounds of boat gear, a 40-pound tank of boat fuel, and four peanut butter sandwiches, with 40 mph winds and a missing stern plug is a sinking ship.

John thought momentarily about the safety of being on the "Osprey" in the Great Lakes. The galley had plenty food and hot coffee where one could get warm from the four-burner propane cook stove. Hot showers were a bonus on the boat.

As water poured over the gunnels from all sides of the drift boat, Gordon felt abject panic as it sank beneath them. The aluminum hull reflected dark green and blue rays of light from the sky as it settled on the bottom, 20 feet below the lake's surface.

Now Gordon and John were bobbing in the waves, held up by their orange life jackets. They yelled in vain as their voices were lost in the shrieking wind.

"Need some help?" called Herb and George. Herb gunned his 19-foot Fishhawk Crestliner toward Gordon, headed into the wind, and then drifted downwind so he could throw him a safety rope bag. It took both Herb and George to pull Gordon over the gunnels and into the boat. John was carried farther from Herb's boat by a big wave. He tried to swim toward the boat, but was held back by the drift boat tarp wrapped around his legs. Herb gunned his boat again, turned upwind and drifted by John, then threw the safety rope bag to him. They retrieved John just as they did Gordon. George and Herb smiled at these wet muskrats in the bottom of the boat—then looked concerned at the distraught bodies. "Are you OK?" asked George. They both nodded OK to George, but everyone knew differently.

Both Gordon and John were suffering from shock and hypothermia. George gave each of them old wool Army blankets for some protection from the wind and rain. Herb headed the Fishhawk toward the protective harbor.

Cutting through the waves, Herb braved the rollers, the surging wind, and the penetrating rain. After 20 minutes of bucking waves, he rounded the boat into the protected peninsula and the safety of the boat harbor. He tied the boat to the dock cleats.

He and George assisted Gordon and then John to Herb's truck. Herb turned the heater on full blast, drove 12 miles to Wilderness Edge Resort, and roared to a stop in front of the big cabin.

They helped John and Gordon through the doorway and to a sofa in front of the fireplace. A toasty warm fire in the fireplace turned purple lips and skin to a rosy-red color. The trembling fear soon turned to a calming relief for both. Hot chocolate laced with schnapps (or was it schnapps laced with hot chocolate?) warmed their tummies and brought life to their limbs. Dry clothes did the rest.

Gordon was suffering inside from reliving the loss of his boat and the near-death experience of almost drowning. "Thanks, Herb . . . George," he said.

"Good to know we were there to help out," said Herb.

At hearing this, John smiled, lit his pipe, and tossed down a double jigger of schnapps while thinking about tying more flies and his next big fish.

Back at Hank's Lake, an empty green tackle box popped to the surface while an orange lifejacket rolled on top of the waves. Twenty feet beneath them, an 11-pound cutthroat trout refused a red woolly bugger fly suspended at the end of a submerged fly rod.

The Henrys Lake "Fusion of Fly Fishers" during the 2017 encampment at the Wilderness Edge Ranch. Photo by Richard Howard (timed shutter-release mode).

Epilogue: Six stone obelisks mounted with brass plaques are located on the north shore of Henrys Lake. Just outside the circle of stones, a 12-foot pole supports the American flag. On each plaque is the name and date of a person who "passed over the great divide." The obelisk monument commemorates the 43 fishermen who have lost their lives from drowning or weather exposure from being caught in storms on Henrys Lake.

Monument dedicated to fishermen and women who have lost their lives while fishing on Henrys Lake. There are 43 names on the monument— maybe 44. Photo by Richard Howard.

Mulchatna Kings

THE DEAD BUMBLE BEE SLOWLY ROLLED upward from the dashboard of the Cessna 185 Skywagon as it hit a downdraft and dropped 1200 feet in 14 seconds. We had just completed the north section of the route through Rainey Pass in the Alaska Range. Our flight originated from Fire Lake north of Anchorage and was bound for the Mulchatna River confluence with the Koktuli, a 320-mile flight. Gordon, Elaine, and Terry, the pilot, had said their "goodbyes" to Cheryl who lives at Fire Lake just north of Anchorage. She is the wife of Dennis who owns Alaska Trophy Safaris.

The 185 Skywagon mounted on pontoons was packed with fishing gear, food, sleeping bags, cots, three wall tents, and 46 rolls of toilet paper. Add a full 50-gallon barrel of avgas into the package and Skywagon was officially grounded because it was overloaded. It was so heavy that it took Terry almost the full length of Fire Lake just to lift the first pontoon, followed by the other pontoon, off the lake to be able to gain enough flight speed. He pulled the stick so hard the plane barely cleared the birch trees at the other end of the lake. Terry was a good bush pilot, who flew by instincts unknown to "outside" pilots. He also mixed scientific dexterity with Minnesota farm mechanic know-how.

Two hours later with Rainey Pass and 30 miles of snow fields and glaciers behind them, the plane flew over the Koktuli Hills, the headwaters of the Koktuli River. (This is where the proposed open-pit Pebble Gold Mine was to be built. Thankfully wisdom prevailed and stopped the EPA permit process.)

The Mulchatna and Koktuli Rivers confluence was 45 minutes due northeast. Thirty minutes later, with a perfect tailwind, the party was flying over 18 wall tents and 11 "Jon" boats. This was the famous Mulchatna River fish camp, whose reputation had grown immensely from its modest beginnings in 1979 when Dennis established the first summer fish camp. In 1979, there were only seven wall tents. One was a cook shack and dining hall; three tents with two sleeping cots in each for fishing clients; two for guides; and an equipment storage tent for food, fishing tackle, extra rods and reels, aviation oil, and a first aid box.

But Dennis had plans to build a fishing lodge on this ground leased from the state. In 1980, extra cargo trips were made to Naknek and Bristol Bay to pick up lumber, paint, shingles, nails, carpenter tools, shovels, and beer. With this stockpiled, construction began in earnest in the spring of 1981. Guides were asked to come two weeks earlier than previous years and stay for two weeks extra after the fishing season.

Layout of the lodge began with Terry, the sky pilot and master mechanic also known for his Minnesota farmer carpentry skills. He organized the guides to clear brush and define foot paths from the lodge to the sauna, to the "two-holer" commode, and to the storage shack. With the physical tundra blueprint in place, construction began on the lodge. Two-by-fours and two-by-six braces for walls, roof, and floor were hammered out into component parts and laid out on the tundra.

One guide was assigned to dig a five-foot-deep hole, six feet long and three feet wide, then cover the bottom one foot with tundra brush. Over this hole was built the finest fish camp commode on the Mulchatna. When one was through with his business, the door opened to a vista of the confluence of the Koktuli and Mulchatna Rivers. One could, if they sat there long enough with the door open, see grizzly bear hunting for salmon, moose feeding on willow, and Terry landing the Skywagon on the river. The door handle was carved out of a birch limb, another fine touch by master carver Terry. There were no locks on the door, but inside there were two tiers of toilet paper with four rolls on each tier. No one was gonna' run out of toilet paper in this camp and have to call management for help.

The other buildings went up at the end of the fish season. First the sauna, the storage shack, and then the lodge. The sauna and shack were easy and were built in two days, working 14-hour days, since the sun only went down for a few hours and was back up again during the summer solstice months. The lodge took longer. The floor went down easy enough, but fitting the walls to the floor and to the framed roof required some serious engineering. High winds from the Bering Sea 40 miles away could turn from a calm breeze to a near-raging hurricane in an hour. Anchoring the walls and roof so they wouldn't blow away during a Bering Sea blow required quarter-inch steel cable looped over the roof, down the walls, and secured both to the lodge floor and to stakes pounded into the permafrost.

Just two days after completing the six-room lodge with kitchen and dining hall, a Bering Sea wind tested the design quality of all the buildings. Forty mph winds, with gusts to 60 mph and rain blowing sideways, let us know the work by Dennis and the guides under the supervision of Terry's construction management skills were superb.

All the buildings held firm, with no water damage or leakage. We could rest in peace that the Mulchatna Lodge would weather the arctic winter winds and snow. It would be there in 1982 to welcome Dennis, Terry, the guides and the clients. This was a huge upgrade from wall tents and dirt floors from previous years.

Disaster hit the Mulchatna Lodge in the spring of 1982. While flying over the Mulchatna and Koktuli confluence looking at the spring migration of Caribou, Dennis was shocked to find the lodge missing from the skyline. He circled down and aimed the nose of the Piper Super Cub so it would take a course directly over the lodge. From an altitude of 200 feet, he peered down at the remains of the black timbers, window frames, and the half-burned commode. He wondered, *Did someone leave a gas stove on or a lantern lit that would have caused this?* He banked again and confirmed that nearly all of their work from the previous year had burned. He landed on a gravel bar located on the Mulchatna River, hiked and waded to shore, then climbed the steep bank to the bluff. There was clear evidence that three people had been there at the lodge. They left footprints of their deed. Nearby, he found empty propane bottles with attached hoses and nozzles that were used to set the buildings on fire.

Later, he heard tundra rumors that the lodge and other buildings were torched by guys who lived at Stuyahok, a village located 23 miles downriver. To recover from this disaster and still have a season for fishermen who had already paid good money, Dennis and Terry flew in wall tents, wood, and propane stoves. When the guides arrived in late May, their first assignment was to erect the wall tents, assemble sleeping cots, insert stoves, and rebuild the commode ... and while they were at it ... build a sauna. The transformation was impressive. The wall tents, commode, sauna, and kitchen tent looked like a civil war encampment with a capacity for 30 people: 14 fishermen, seven guides, two cooks, a pilot's tent, Dennis' tent, and storage tents for equipment.

On the 14th of June, the first chum salmon made their way up from Bristol Bay, through the Nushagak to the Mulchatna, then to the confluence of the Koktuli and Mulchatna. A day later 14 fishermen were flown into camp via two big de Havilland DHC3 Beavers, who followed Terry in the Skywagon to the camp. The Beavers landed on gravel bars while Terry landed on the river because the Skywagon was equipped with floats.

The gravel bar had been carefully selected for its length, the size of the gravel, and its firmness. Flags were used to outline the landing strip and the no-go zone beyond where if planes rolled to a stop, they could sink their wheels in sand and be there for a while, maybe a long while. There were no incidents this time, but several years later a Twin Otter, fully loaded with passengers and gear, flown by a rookie pilot, rolled the plane into the no-go zone. It was stuck there for a week. The rookie was flown out by Terry the next day and told to look for a job washing dishes. An experienced pilot flew back with Terry. He cleverly used the counter rotation of the turboprops on the Twin Otter to back out the plane, turned it around, revved the engines, and took off as though he were General Doolittle flying a B-25 off an aircraft carrier. It was impressive.

During the next week, there was rapid orientation and adjustments by the guides to accommodate the fishermen. Each guide was assigned two fishermen. They went out during the day in "Jon Boats," 16-foot flat-bottom aluminum boats that a person could stand up, without the risk of turning the boat over. The boats had 15 HP gas engines mounted on the transom. This enabled the guide to go up or down river up to five miles from camp. A shore lunch was fixed by the cooks and placed in each boat. Added to the shore lunch was the morning's catch. The guides would meet up on a gravel bar, bring out a grill from the boat, gather wood, and campfire-cook fresh salmon fillets. This enabled the guides and fishermen to stay out all day up to 12 hours and return to camp in the evening for dinner. Oh, and a visit to the sauna before dinner or maybe afterwards, depending upon the liquor intake.

Each day was a search-and-report mission. The guides would share best places to fish at the end of each day. This allowed for tracking migrating salmon coming up the Mulchatna and finding huge concentrations of these fish in big eddies, at the confluence of rivers and streams, and mid-channel holding areas. So, the target fish list included resident trout to seven pounds in size, northern pike up to 28 inches long, the iconic arctic grayling, and three species of salmon (chum, sockeye, and king). The chum started to arrive in early June and weighed up to 11 pounds. When fresh, they were ok to eat if smoked; otherwise, they were returned to the river. King salmon weighed up to 35 pounds and on rare occasions up to 45 pounds. These were the main attraction for fishermen. The sockeye weighed four to eight pounds, the males being somewhat bigger than the females. Sockeye were the last to migrate upriver, arriving the 10th of July, and had their peak run about the 18th through the 23rd of July.

What made the Mulchatna a special place was the huge numbers of fish in the river. We are talking hundreds of fish per river mile by mid-July. Fishermen were dazzled to see the numerous raindrops on the surface of the water—only they weren't raindrops. They were salmon swaying their dorsal or tail fins on the surface of the water. Casting a lure into a big eddy pool with numerous raindrops rippling the surface made for tense moments. One didn't know just what species of fish would be hooked to a lure or well-cast fly? It might be a grayling or trout because they follow the salmon to their spawning redds and then feed voraciously on those salmon eggs that don't settle into the interstitial space of the gravel redds. It might be a nearly spent-out chum or an ocean-fresh sockeye that gently takes a fly but explodes in 20-yard runs when it is hooked. A double tug on the fish line usually signals a king salmon. The second tug lasts for microseconds before the brake ratchet on the fishing reel whines, smokes, and 30 yards of line is gone downriver with a 30-pound king on the other end. This feeling, the anticipated pulse, never gets old to someone who has a passion for fishing big fish in rivers or oceans. A good friend of Gordon's called it "shaking hands with the planet."

One day while flying food and fuel into camp, Terry spotted a set of moose antlers that had been shed. He noted the location. When there was a free day between clients flying out and new ones flying into the Mulchatna camp, he, Gordon, and two other guides took two Jon boats and went up the Koktuli River to find the antler sheds. It was six miles upriver and a half-mile walk across soggy tundra to the sheds. When they got there, they were surprised to find two huge moose antlers and skulls locked together in what was a fatal bull moose courting struggle. They must have been courting a cow moose and fought over the right to breed her. Both lost. Terry and the guides dug the antlers out but struggled to lift the 200 pounds of skulls and antlers and carry them back to the boats. Finally, after three hours, they got them into a boat, tied it to the other boat and motored back to the Mulchatna camp.

The next set of fishing clients to fly into camp saw the locked antlers of the moose sitting outside the cook tent. One guy was the CEO of the Caterpillar Company. He offered

Terry a thousand bucks for the antlers and told Terry he had a perfect place in his trophy room back home in Texas. Terry turned him down. The antlers and skulls were attached to the wing struts and pontoon floats of the 185 Skywagon and flown back to Anchorage.

One morning, very early before the cooks got up to prepare breakfast, a grizzly bear visited the camp. It walked past the

33

This remarkable photo shows the locked antlers of two bull moose that were found half-buried (white antlers above ground; dark antlers below ground) on the tundra near the Koktuli River Alaska. Photo by Richard Howard, 1983.

clients' tents where, 14 fishermen were "sawing logs" from having put in a 12-hour day fishing and a four-hour Texas "hold-em or fold-em" card game, lubricated by three fifths of Pendleton Whiskey. The bear walked by the pilot's tent where Terry and Gordon were sleeping . . . well where Terry was. Gordon read books early in the morning. It was free time, his time to read books like *Death in the Dark Continent* by Peter Hathaway Capstick or *Working on the Edge* by Spike Walker.

This morning was different. A sheet of #8 tent canvas was all that separated Gordon from a wild 600-pound grizzly. The bear prowled around outside the tent for ten minutes. He made no attempt to enter the tent. Had he done so (and by now Terry was also wide awake), the bear would be confronted with two .44-magnum Blackhawk revolvers loaded with hollow-point slugs, held by Terry and Gordon. The bear moved on, but not before devouring a ten-pound sack of flour, four pounds of bacon, and two dozen eggs from a storage box in the kitchen tent. He also wandered down to where the 185 Skywagon was tied down and chewed on five cans of motor oil. He didn't drink it but just pierced the cans with his huge canines and incisors. Then he left the area. It was a lively topic of discussion at breakfast that morning. Both clients and guides went home that year with a vivid bear story to tell.

Two of the clients, a son and father from San Diego, California, hit the sweet spot during mid-July. They arrived when all the species of salmon were at peak numbers in the Mulchatna. They were steel workers who worked at the Diego shipyards building ships for the U.S. Navy. Gordon liked taking them out each day because they always had great stories to tell about their work and their families. Luke, and his son Matt, took pictures of their trophy fishing trip. Gordon guided them to all the top fishing holes during the week. They caught all the sport fish species found in the river. By the end of the week, they caught (and released) a record number of 84 salmon, trout, grayling, and pike. At Christmastime, a package arrived in the mail for

Gordon. When he opened it on Christmas morning, he was pleasantly surprised to find a big picture of himself in his yellow Helly Hanson rain jacket, wearing his Eagle, Idaho, fishing hat, holding a 42-pound king salmon. It was caught by Matt. On the back of the picture was taped a note:

Gordon:

Sorry the picture has taken so long, but the first enlargement they cut off the tail of the fish. You can't have a picture of a king salmon without a tail so I had to send it back through again.

My Dad and I had the vacation of a lifetime—one we will never forget. I want to thank you again for your fishing expertise and your friendship.

—Matt

The 42-pound Mulchatna Chinook salmon caught at the confluence of Old Man Creek and the Mulchatna River, 1982. Photo by Matt Parker.

Two seasons later, on a cold mid-January evening Gordon reluctantly phoned Dennis to tell him he wouldn't be returning to the Mulchatna next summer. Dennis thanked him for letting him know early in the year so he could recruit another guide for the summer. He also asked Gordon if he would be interested in a caribou hunt at one of Dennis' other camps out at Ugashik River near Katmai National Park. "When?" Gordon asked. "This fall or in the fall of 1984," Dennis replied. "Eight-four is a good date," said Gordon.

In September of '84, Gordon flew to Anchorage, was picked up at the airport by Dennis' wife, Cheryl, overnighted at their home on Fire Lake, and flew out with Dennis to Ugashik the next day. The camp was located a mile from an abandoned fish cannery that had been active 40 years earlier. Twenty Chinese men and five white supervisors ran that cannery during the huge sockeye salmon runs that came up the Ugashik River to the Ugashik Lakes, ten miles east of the cannery. At one time, the cannery produced over 180,000 cans of salmon per year. But like so many other natural resources, the river and lakes were over-fished. After 15 years, the cannery closed.

Terry was in camp and so were two other guides from the Mulchatna. They all had Caribou permits for the Katmai Hunting Unit. Two of them had already filled their permits and were assisting client hunters with their gear and providing guidance on how to hunt caribou. On the first afternoon, three of the clients and Gordon went out to sight in their rifles. It took Gordon an extra half hour to sight his scope accurately to where he was satisfied with the fist-size grouping of shots within the bullseye of the target at 100 yards.

The next day, three clients were flown out in the morning, accompanied by one of the guides, to hunt caribou migrating out of Katmai National Park. When Terry returned, he gave Gordon the thumbs up to get his gear together. An hour later, they took off from Ugashik and landed on a tarn (a small lake) about two clicks from Mother Goose Lake and about 30 miles from Ugashik. On the way out to the tarn, Gordon noticed the remains of two planes on a prominent ridge. Their wings and fuselages were spread over the ridge like broken angels. It was eerie to think about what happened and whether the passengers and pilots survived the crash. Terry said, "Fog caused the pilots to lose it. The ocean is just ten miles from here and forms dense fog. I nearly lost the Skywagon last year when I hit this fog. Pulled up over the ridge. Missed by 30 feet."

They landed on the tarn, taxied up to the shore, and unloaded Gordon's gear. Terry gave Gordon a radio phone. "See you in three days," he said. "Don't phone unless you have to: it costs 40 bucks a minute out here."

Gordon set up his Kelty four-man green tent about 100 yards from the shore of the tarn. He had three days out there, all alone with about 5,000 barren-ground caribou on migration, numerous arctic foxes, dozens of ravens, and an unknown number of grizzly bears. He walked to the nearest ridge about half a mile from the tent, sat down, and glassed the huge open tundra plain with his binocs. From his vantage point, he spotted four herds of caribou: each had about 20 animals. Only five bulls in the four herds. He was hunting for a bull with a sizeable rack of antlers with complete shovels (a pair of smaller antlers that stem from the base of the main antler but face over the brow of the caribou).

The next morning, he fixed breakfast, organized a day pack with .270 ammo, two knives, a survival blanket, first aid kit, gloves, lunch, two cans of Coca-Cola®, extra socks, a pound of black pepper, and three packages of Twinkies. He grabbed his Ruger .270, inserted cartridges tipped with Nosler bullets, checked his shoulder holster for the Blackhawk .44 magnum pistol, and ate the last of his oatmeal breakfast. He returned to the ridge where he had spotted caribou, foxes, and ravens.

There were only caribou in the area this morning. One herd of about 40 animals was walking towards him, following a well-worn path in the tundra. He spotted one old bull in the herd.

Not what he was looking for. Then just as he was about to get up and leave, he saw a caribou rack turn 20 degrees. It looked like a candelabra with 12 tines. The bull was not more than 120 yards from him, lying down, looking the other way. Gordon was downwind from the bull. All the thoughts about hunting caribou came into singular focus. Gordon repositioned himself so his rifle was braced on his day pack and he was lying prone with the scope just three inches from his left eye. He took two deep breaths, whistled loudly, the bull stood up, and the impact of the 280-grain Nosler bullet set him back down. Gordon shot once more and saw a tuft of hair fly off near the bull's shoulder. It was done. Echoes of the rifle shots rang in Gordon's ear. His heart felt immediate tachycardia, then slowed as the adrenalin abated.

He lay there for five minutes not wanting to move as he drank in the morning's events that led up to this moment. The small herd of caribou he had seen earlier ran down a valley and disappeared. Two ravens circled overhead, calling loudly. The vastness of the tundra, the smell of thimble and lingon- berries, the snow-capped peaks of the Katmai 20 miles in the distance: all became a captured moment for Gordon.

He looked around and suddenly felt alone—not loneliness, but alone. No one knew exactly where he was. The morning blue sky was cut by a jet contrail. Passengers on the Boeing 737 Alaska Airlines jet flying at 43,000 feet overhead were just finishing their breakfast of coffee, orange juice, hash browns, and scrambled eggs—their destination, unknown to Gordon.

He got up and walked over to the bull caribou. Both shots were lethal: one through the shoulder into the lungs, the other cut into the heart. He began the process of field dressing the animal, but not before attaching the permit tag to the antlers. The bull was in his prime, probably five years old, and had nearly perfect symmetry of his antlers except for a misshaped shovel antler. It took Gordon the rest of the day to butcher out the animal and remove the antlers by cutting off part of the skull cap. He took out the quart of black pepper from his pack. Shaking it on the meat prevented flies from laying their eggs in the meat. He wrapped the five quarters of the animal with muslin cloth and tied two of the 30-pound quarters to his backpack.

By now, two foxes and seven vocal ravens were circling around the kill site. This was a signal to any grizzly bear in the area that the dinner bell was ringing. Gordon lifted his backpack onto his shoulders and packed the quarters back to his camp. He returned to the kill site three more times for more quarters, then positioned the antlers across his shoulders and hiked back to his camp. "Whew. Time for a beer and a twinkie," he said. It was all set in a pile about 40 yards from his camp and covered with a piece of old wall tent canvas. If a bear did visit his camp, he would go to the meat pile and not to his tent first! Fortunately, that night Gordon did not have any bear visits.

He woke up the next morning and made a breakfast of fresh caribou tenderloin fillets, hash browns sprinkled with black pepper, and coffee. He cleaned up his camp then took a walk along the shore of the tarn. About half a mile from his camp, he came across fresh grizzly bear tracks in the mud along the shore. They were headed for the kill site another mile east, where the gut pile was being picked apart by foxes and ravens. Soon they would have to contend with a 500-pound grizzly.

By prearrangement, Gordon used the radiophone to signal Terry that he was ready for Terry to pick him up. Terry was on another assignment when the signal came in. He was intending to ferry a load of fuel and food from Dillingham to the Ugashik camp. He called Gordon and told him to hang on but could not come right away. Weather had prevented Terry from flying back to Ugashik, so Gordon would have to wait it out until the next day. Gordon was out there in the company of ravens, foxes, and unseen bears. He was alone with his prized caribou and the animals that wanted to eat the meat quarters wrapped in the canvas. He spent the night, full of apprehension about bears but he also enjoyed moments of elation absorbing the hunt, replaying all the scenes in his mind.

The next morning the weather cleared. It was a "Willy Nelson" day with blue skies shining for Gordon . . . and for Terry. Gordon heard the reassuring sound of the 185 Skywagon's engine before he saw the plane. Just for fun, Terry came hopping over the nearby ridge where the broken wings and fuselages of planes lay on the ground. He was just 60 feet over the ridge and coming in for a hot landing on the tarn. He splashed down, feathered down the prop speed, and drifted into shore.

Gordon ran over to the plane. "Good to see you, Terry," he said. "Ten minutes ago, I saw a grizzly about one click out headed toward my camp. No doubt about his intentions." Terry helped Gordon pack up his tent, gear, and caribou meat quarters. He taped empty 12-gauge shotgun shells on each of the tines of the caribou antlers. This prevented them from being broken off or poking someone in the butt or arm or eye. He then tied the antlers to the wing and float struts. It was a 30-minute flight back to Ugashik but before leaving, they circled the area where Gordon had hunted two days before. Two grizzlies were in the area—one at the remains of the gut pile and the other still headed toward Gordon's camp site.

Three days later, Gordon said his goodbyes to Dennis and Terry. After a short while, he left Anchorage, flying at 38,000 feet in a Boeing 737, and eating a breakfast of scrambled eggs, bacon, and hash browns. His Alaska Airlines flight touched down six hours later in Seattle. A dual-engine turbo-prop Bombardier took Gordon home to Boise.

Two weeks later he picked up the caribou antlers at the Alaska Airlines baggage terminal. He also took delivery of 180 pounds of frozen, cut, and wrapped caribou meat for the winter. Three days later, he left Boise with his drift boat in tow. Steelhead season had just opened on the Salmon River.

Breached Dams:
What should be done after coffee break?

A N INSPIRATIONAL LETTER WAS SENT last November to the federal agencies that manage the lower Columbia and Snake River system. It focused on the removal of the earthen portions of four dams on the lower Snake River in the State of Washington. This would restore 210 miles of the lower Snake River that flows through eastern Washington. It would also be a strategic step in restoring the magnificent salmon and steelhead trout species that inhabit the Snake River drainage and its tributaries. So one must weigh whether this is a letter of fiction or a vision of hope and conviction.

"Dear folks who work for the Bonneville Power Administration, Corps of Engineers-Northern Division, and Bureau of Reclamation (the Agencies). The Environmental Impact Statement (EIS) the Agencies proposed in 2017 under National Environmental Protection Act concerning the Columbia River System operations for 14 federal dam projects in the interior Columbia River basin will be flawed should the option to breach the lower four Snake River dams not be included in the EIS.

"The federal projects that should be included in the breach option are Ice Harbor, Little Goose, Lower Monumental, and Lower Granite federal dams. This breach option (de-authorization of the four lower Snake River federal dam projects) should be treated as the preferred option in the EIS.

"To justify this, an independent cost/benefit analysis should be done, which considers: the past and present mitigation costs (1971 to 2019, or about 48 years) for federally-listed anadromous fish and their habitats; maintenance and implementation costs of these mitigation strategies (i.e.; fish ladders and dam modifications);

federal and state hatcheries; loss of megawatts due to flow augmentation régimes; barging of fish; habitat improvements and land easements and purchases upstream; costs to monitor declining Orca populations and other ocean species dependent upon salmon; and finally—costs to the agencies that are presently involved in related lawsuits.

"It should also consider the future beneficial costs of dam breaching for the next 50 years (about one human generation) to the anadromous fish and the watersheds they depend upon; the tangential benefits to the lower Snake River riparian habitat, and all the main and tributary habitats of the Snake, Clearwater, and Salmon Rivers; to sport and commercial fishing families of the Columbia Basin and west coast from Oregon to southeast Alaska; to the villages and towns where these families live; to the human health benefits of frequently including wild anadromous fish in human diets throughout the northwest and the nation; to creating alternate sources of green energy, especially solar and wind with backup storage batteries and the use of existing power line distribution infrastructure.

"To summarize, the Agencies should include a breach option of the lower four Snake River dams in the proposed EIS. Or . . . use common sense and the existing 2002 EIS as the legal enabling document, (2002 EIS, Alternative 4, page 25; which has a breach option, but the cost/benefit analysis is flawed), to get started now on the Lower Granite Dam.

"Get started now; like next Monday, December 5th after staff meeting and coffee break about 10:45 a.m. with three D-8 Caterpillars, two dump trucks, and a front-end loader.

"The Agencies and the folks who make this decision will leave an intelligent legacy for having done this."

/s/ Gordon Walker

Middle Fork
Salmon Odyssey

AN WROTE IN AN EMAIL: "HOW WAS THE the MFSR trip?" Gordon tried to keep his response modest. "Dan, the short story . . . excellent. The longer story . . . it had all the drama of a rafting adventure: rain, wind, rafts marooned mid-river on sneaker rocks, tight paths through turbulent boulder-strewn rapids, nearby strikes of lightning followed by the echoes of thunder that sounded like Thor's artillery on the offensive, more rain, even more wind, followed by the blessed sun."

This was an epic trip down the Middle Fork of the Salmon River.

There was great karma among the eight people who floated the river. No tears—just tons of laughter and stories throughout each day, then more laughter and stories around the evening campfire. Tibetan prayer flags fluttered from tents, sending out their Buddhist prayers at night.

Turbid water resulting from cloudburst storms within the Middle Fork drainage caused tributaries to flow like the color of a chocolate latte from the Flying M Bistro. Fly fishing for cutthroats was made impossible. A day later, the water cleared some, but only to a light green tea stirred with soymilk.

Mixed cereal, V-8 juice, coffee, tea, and Aleve for breakfast jump-started the day. Blackberry preserve jam and peanut butter sandwiches for lunch with sugar-charged Coca-Cola® and a handful of mixed nuts got one through the afternoon. Hors d'oeuvres and superb main course cuisine served in the evening, with Black Box Malbec or gin & tonics, sparked more stories around a dry-pan campfire.

Our 14-foot rafts made by AIRE were our lifeline each day. We launched them in the morning after packing our kitchen gear and sleeping bags and tents, with the confidence they would still be dry and in one piece at the end of the day. They took us through the heart of Idaho on a 97-mile journey from Dagger

Falls to the confluence of the main Salmon River. From south to north, we traveled 10 to 15 miles each day through soaring mountain canyons of granite, quartzite, and basalt.

We woke up to forests of green conifers for the first few days. But as we continued, we encountered altered landscapes of burned-out forests looking like huge vertical matchsticks with an undergrowth of refreshing native bunch grasses. There were galleries of green ponderosa pine along the edge of the river that survived the fires, which presented excellent campsites for both the Native American Sheepeaters (*Tukuduka*) of the ancient past and for our humble band of rafters of the present.

My rafting partner, Todd, an oarsman extraordinaire, had negotiated all the major rapids in fine style except Pistol Creek, the last rapid on the evening of the third day. We got stuck on a boulder at the top of Pistol Creek Rapid, a Class IV rapid. A rafter 40 yards ahead of us yelled, "Go river left!" when he saw that the passage to the right was very narrow.

We went river left and got wrapped on a partially submerged boulder. It was abject fear for 28 seconds. I had to get out on the downstream side of the raft, stand on the boulder and push the raft. If this failed, not even an Olympic swimmer could survive the caldron of water 12 feet below me. With teamwork and an adrenaline-charged push, we spun our raft off the rock, into the whitewater caldron, and microseconds later we were clear of the fearsome rapid.

On the morning of the sixth day at 8:50 a.m., we made it to the Main but still had three miles to go to takeout at Cache Bar. Cramer Rapid on the main Salmon River is a rapid fortress that one needs to confront before reaching Cache Bar. Its huge standing wave is caused by water pouring over Hummer-sized boulders strewn across the entire width of the river. It has only two places that allow for safe passage.

We dropped into one of those slots and at the bottom were swept back into the water cauldron but only momentarily; then, stroking hard, Todd pushed out using the deeper currents to his advantage. We were clear and floated down to the other rafters who were waiting in an eddy of quiet water, observing our progress.

Ah! But there was one more raft that had to clear Cramer. We watched as Steve and his brother John came down the same slot that we had just cleared. Their raft was at an angle instead of sitting straight just at the upper edge of this huge rapid. In slow motion, we all watched as they dropped into the white cauldron. Their raft hesitated, the back of the raft slipped under tons of cascade, the front half rose into the air, higher and higher, then flipped over into Cramer's grasp.

It held them for a few seconds and then pushed them out and down river. Much to our relief, we could see that both men were holding the safety ropes on the side of the blue raft. We observed some equipment floating downstream. The rest was well-secured to the raft. Todd rowed out toward the equipment while I got out my fishing net to retrieve it. Eleven Payette Brewery beer cans, all empty, were retrieved. Nothing like an IPA to knock the morning into high gear.

Todd back-stroked out to the men. He shouted, "You OK?" They signed back they were OK. Wet, but OK. I grasped their raft and Todd stroked both rafts into the eddy below the rapid, and finally to shore.

With Gordon's help, Steve and John turned the raft rightside-up. With no real concerns, we all rowed down to the Cache Bar take-out. Our river trip was complete after six and a half days.

Ten o'clock a.m. beers for everyone.

Celebration of Life at Thirsty Dog Cabin

"THANK YOU, MARTY, FOR ARRANGING this *Celebration of Life* for Charles. We appreciate your good work making this possible and inviting us to Thirsty Dog Cabin for this occasion.

"As to what will transpire this afternoon, we have no written program, but what I intend to do is to make a short introductory statement and then read excerpts from some of those eulogies that were sent to Marty. While I'm reading these excerpts, I invite the audience to think about what you may want to share with us today about your friendship with Charles.

"After reading the excerpts, I will read two poems that capture some of the essence of these high-mountain valleys that were so much a part of Charles and Marty and their lives well-lived.

"There is a common theme by those who took pen in hand to write about their friendship with Charles. All these authors recall when and where they first met Charles. Some are brief recollections; others are well-crafted essays. But they all speak to the legendary qualities of a man who impacted their lives and who helped them define who they are through his insight, his passion for outdoor pursuits, and his companionship.

"He was an inspiration to all of us as to how to live each season to its fullest: raising gyrfalcons at Thirsty Dog Cabin in the spring; trout and salmon fishing in the summer; pursuing elk, deer, and pronghorn in the fall; reserving the fall and winter seasons for frosty grouse hunts. There was always time for renewing friendships and telling twice-told stories around the kitchen table.

"The authors of these eulogies include: Bruce Haak, Barry Pharaoh, Rich Howard, William Smith, Nancy Cowan, J. David Remple, and John McIltrot."

BRUCE HAAK

On March 9, 2016, Charles H. Schwartz, age 71, lost his battle with cancer. For four decades, he was married to Martha Browne, who shared his passions for falconry, captive breeding of falcons, fishing, and travel. He is also survived by his son Alan and daughter Greta from his first marriage. A lifelong outdoorsman, passionate reader, and consummate falconer, he led a unique life and left friends and admirers throughout the worldwide falconry community.

Charles grew up in Ohio. He earned a degree in zoology with a minor in chemistry from Ohio State University, where he also played trumpet in the marching band. After graduating, he became a game warden in Ohio then moved to Idaho to pursue a Master of Science degree at Idaho State University.

The reins of destiny were lost, and for some time Charles had to make tough decisions as to which road to take. He regained the helm of his destiny when he met Martha Browne, married her, and took his interest in falconry beyond just another level.

Charles and Marty built a log home along the West Fork of the Big Lost River and named it "The Thirsty Dog." Their retirement sanctuary has a magnificent, constantly changing view of the Big Lost River Range and of Mt. Borah, Idaho's tallest peak, framed by the picture window. Towering mountains, rushing water, and broad sagebrush flats are all accessible from this isolated retreat.

Charles joined the North American Falconers Association in 1971, and served as Secretary in 1978 and Mountain Director in 1989. He was also a founding member of the Idaho Falconers Association (IFA), holding several offices, including president. Charles was the principal author of the IFA constitution. In addition, he contributed articles and photographs of falconry and hunting dogs to *NAFA*, the *IFA International Falconer*, *The Pointing Dog Journal*, and *Dog World*.

I met Charles while on a hawking trip in September of 1980. He and Marty opened their Pingree, Idaho, home to me, and showed me aspects of falconry that I had yet to witness. This was the first of many educational experiences that I would glean from their company.

BARRY PHARAOH

I met Charles in 1975 when he came to work for the chemistry section at the Idaho State Health Laboratory. We connected right away and a friendship developed that lasted over 40 years. We began hanging out together after work and sometimes on weekends, and before long he had me hooked on falconry. With Charlie's help and guidance, successful game hawking became a reality for me. Many great days were shared hawking and trapping. One of the most memorable times was camping near Mud Lake for a week in the winter of 1979-80. Our agenda included catching jacks in the mornings, sage-grouse in the afternoons, and pheasants in the evenings. My respect for Charles as a falconer, captive falcon breeder, and all-around outdoorsman is at the highest level. He was always enthusiastic and had a positive attitude, which made him fun to be around. Along with hawking, we also enjoyed hunting upland game in Owyhee County, deer hunting north of Fairfield, and antelope hunting at The Thirsty Dog. Sometime in the mid-80s, we both started fly fishing and began floating and fishing rivers together.

RICHARD HOWARD

When you know a person for 40 years and create good times on the rivers and across the high deserts of Idaho, it's hard to recall any one significant experience. They were all good. But let's start with the South Fork of the Snake River. Fly fishing was another side of Charles that he pursued, preferably from a drift boat.

The South Fork supports native Yellowstone cutthroat trout (YCT). They respond to dry or soaked wet flies when a hatch is swarming. From two-inch salmon flies to tiny grey-blue duns, these hatches can make a fly fisher's day.

Charles loved to float the river in his drift boat with friends from across Idaho. Once in a while, I would get a call from him that the South Fork hatch was hot and drive over ASAP. I would hook my drift boat up to the truck and drive with Barry Pharaoh from Boise to meet Charles. We spent good days floating the South Fork, keeping our boats 15 to 25 yards from the shoreline, casting to microsites behind rocks that held YCTs.

Other reaches would be productive where there were mid-river gravel bars. The bars dropped into eight-foot pools. It was Charles' favorite fishing structure. He would anchor the boat, step out and wade in the cool waters, and cast flies into the shallow water above the pools. It was so predicable to see a racing fish come out of the deep pools and hit the fly as it floated into the magic riffle caused by shallow water hitting smooth deep pool water. It was a hyper-feeding station.

Charles would get a hit on his lightly casted fly, let the fish run, reel it in, and then gently release it. Only then would Charles lighten up from focused concentration on the line, fly, and fish—and break into a broad smile. And then there were steelhead . . . but that's another story.

WILLIAM SMITH

I first met Charles in 1977. I had just moved back to the West from Virginia, where I had become good friends with Alva Nye, and had developed an intense interest in taking up falconry when I got out West. Alva gave me Charles' name, and I looked him up in Pingree when I took a job and settled in Idaho Falls. I asked Charles to be my sponsor, and he (somewhat patiently—Charles didn't suffer fools gladly) helped me through all the steps to study intensely, get facilities built and inspected, pass the test, etc., to become a licensed apprentice. We spent many real cold winter days cruising all over southeast Idaho in my truck to find a red-tailed hawk to trap, but it was so late in the year, and it was so cold, they were too few and far between. Charles found a "hand-me-down" red-tail over in Eagle, Idaho, and I took her on to learn how to handle and manage a bird and how to catch stuff. Charles and Marty were my best friends, and we'd talk pretty much daily while I figured out what I was doing. Charles also introduced me to many other Idaho falconers, all of whom I still call friends today. To my recall, in about 1978, Charles, Jesse Woody, Rich Howard, Barry Pharaoh, and Todd Shepard dove into founding IFA. They did all the contacting and communicating homework, drafted all the original legal documents, filed all the applications and papers, and made IFA a legal and operational organization. I contributed whatever Charles asked—drafting and reviewing documents, and then I designed the original IFA logo.

NANCY COWAN

This morning a good friend I never met went over the "Great Divide," as Morley Nelson would say. I met Charles via telephone connection over 20 years ago when I wrote a piece for *Dog World* magazine about raptors and dogs working together. I met and interviewed some illustrious and some lesser-known falconers across the U.S. and in Canada for the piece. Charles' was one of the names I was provided as likely being a very good source of material. He was more than that (even tho' I called him in the middle of watching an important football game and he asked that I call back after the game, and according to time zone differences as I was in New England and he was out in Idaho). Charles contributed some photos to the story that ended up with him being a paid photographer for the series. Charles had great stories, and the patience to explain things to a neophyte.

J. DAVID REMPLE

True falconers are a brotherhood of individuals bound together and driven by an obsession for birds of prey. Falconry defines the way one lives from the lifestyle one chooses to the place one chooses to live. In this respect Charles was a true falconer. He not only was a master of the hunting/sporting aspect of falconry, he also made major contributions to the welfare of the sport through techniques he developed in the area of captive breeding. It was through this breeding expertise while he was stationed overseas that I first met "Charlie."

In the late 1970s Charles Schwartz took over as Director of the Sulman Falcon Breeding Centre in Bahrain in the Arabian Gulf. A few years later my wife and I went to Dubai (a few hundred miles down the coast from Bahrain) to establish the Dubai Falcon Hospital, the first veterinary hospital in the Middle East devoted to the care of falcons. Shortly after our arrival, Charles called to welcome us to our new "home away from home," roughly halfway around the world. As mutual "expats" with common interests and being from common geographical areas, he and his wife, Marty, quickly formed a friendship with us.

We were bringing much-needed western veterinary medical expertise to a region of the world that had none, and Charles was quick to avail our services. We were delighted, as several of the falcon patients from the Sulman Falcon Breeding Centre were the first ones we treated, which helped establish the Dubai Falcon Hospital. And the friendship was reciprocal: as the "new" expats on the block, Charles (and Marty) provided counseland comfort, helping to guide us through our introduction to this unfamiliar culture. They also provided a reassuring shoulder to cry on during periods of extreme frustration (which was common among expats during those early days in the Gulf.)

JOHN McILTROT

Charles Schwartz would be eulogized best by his dogs. They were his intimate friends. All of us, his friends, sought out his companionship and wisdom, and enjoyed good times with him in the field and around the kitchen table. But Charles and his dogs simply shared each other's enthusiasm for life and the hunt, and they brought great joy to each other.

I have a heart full of memories of Charles: 20 years' worth. Memories of fishing and hunting, falconry, cooking, and whiskey, but my favorites are dog memories. One stands out. It was after dark, winter, driving across the snowy desert after hawking. Mac, the black-headed pointer, slept on the front seat between us. We had been driving in silence for a long while. Charles put his hand on Mac's head and told me, "You haven't been loved until you've been loved by a bird dog." I didn't know it at the time, but he was right.

RICHARD HOWARD

"So now to conclude this part of the *Celebration of Life* for Charles, I will read two poems. One is titled "Pahsimeroi" by Dr. Edson Fichter, Professor of Biology at Idaho State University. For 30 years, he studied the lifecycles of pronghorn and sage-grouse one valley to the east of Thirsty Dog Cabin, called the Pahsimeroi Valley. The other poem comes to us from Trail Creek Valley just west of here. It's more of a Haiku and was written by Ernest Hemingway. It is immortalized on a stone monument located on Trail Creek Road east of Sun Valley."

Pahsimeroi

No wilderness of my remembered years
As sweetly sang to me—
As this possessive land—
The night-sad voices of its haunting winds
That only searching hearts can understand.
Too late I came to consummate a bond
With every sensuous meaning
of its sage and mahogany,
its brooding slopes and secret valleys that
will never feel my shadow moving there.
Too late for total being. Yet I know
These hills will never let me go.

—Edson Fichter
Pahsimeroi, Land Beyond Words
Blue Scarab Press, 1988

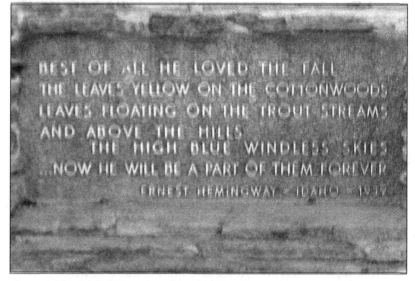

One of Charles Schwartz' preferred authors, when he was not
reading books about falconry or fly fishing, was Ernest Hemingway.
The Hemingway Memorial is located just east of Sun Valley, Idaho,
on the north side of Trail Creek. Photo by Richard Howard.

A Tribute to Idaho Falconers

THE WEATHER AROUND ARCO, IDAHO, WAS perfect in late October, 2018. Some breeze but not too windy; a cobalt-blue sky; superior visibility of 60 miles; the Grand Teton summits in Wyoming visible to the east; high temperatures in the low 70s during the day and in the 20s at night. For three glorious days, the Idaho Falconers Association membership met in Arco, Idaho. No complaints about ambient conditions, but boy—was the hawking tough!

Last winter's deep snows and frigid temperatures served to significantly knock down the rising population of jackrabbits and cottontails just as we were seeing an exponential increase. Some coveys of grouse were found, but only one was taken by Jack Oar's white goshawk—not by falcons.

Several of us witnessed a spectacular flight by Phil Bucher's intermewed peregrine when it hammered a huge sage-grouse and bound to it only to be kicked off microseconds later. The grouse headed for the horizon, and the falcon was left with a fistful of feathers.

In another episode on Friday, a very aggressive wild female adult prairie falcon insisted on keeping other falcons out of her territory. While flying at wild barn pigeons, Ed Pitcher's tiercel falcon, that had gained terrific height, was held at bay by this resident prairie falcon. A superb flight gone bad because of this brown falcon with a black belt in karate.

Later during the Saturday evening IFA banquet, I heard stories about two successful flights on ducks and that was *it* for the entire meet! While the hawking was good, the success-ful flights were few—kind of like fly fishing can be: "The fishing was great, but the catching was troublesome."

Early Sunday morning, there was a frantic cell call from the field. Someone had tried again to hawk ducks in this prairie falcon's neighborhood. A peregrine hybrid had been taken to the ground by the prairie. Fortunately, the hybrid was saved by some quick thinking by the falconer who ran up and separated the two like a referee at a World Wide Wrestling match. The prairie released the hybrid with only minor damage.

The frantic call to those having breakfast at Pickle's Café was to warn others to not hawk in the vicinity of this resident hen prairie. Later, some discussion around the table at Pickle's about this tenacious prairie falcon lead to the conclusion she may have been there for the past three years during the fall. She was probably a local bird defending wintering and nesting territory and may not even migrate. A GPS system placed on her tail would reveal lots of interesting information about this bird.

The annual IFA meets in Arco have become a tradition during the past ten years or so. We enjoy three social events during these meets. The first event is the Arco Park lunch picnic on Friday. Steve Buffat, his wife Sky, her mother Colleen Huffaker, Phil Bucher, Paul Mascuch, and Dave Smith have helped to establish this event. The main course includes huge pots of excellent home-cooked chili and chowder prepared by Sky. In addition, there is a potluck of dishes brought by falconers and friends, including smoked salmon, spinach/water chestnut dip, Stacy's® bagel chips, and two kinds of dessert. It is a picnic not to be missed! Then we try our skills at throwing hand axes, knives, and atlatl darts at targets to burn off the calories. To wrap up the picnic, we do the annual group photo.

All of this is held on Arco's green-grass park. I emphasize green grass because there are only two patches of it in all of Arco: one at the park and the other at the weathering area at the DK Motel. The rest is sage, gravel, and cheatgrass stubble scattered throughout the town.

The other two social events include a breakfast by the Guild of the Ladies of Arco, who cook up a fine breakfast on Saturday morning. Then, there is the IFA banquet and auction held on Saturday night at the Moore, Idaho, town hall and fire station. Steve Buffat contracts with local BBQ Master Chef Brady and his team at Grub Hub, who serve up a $30-dollar dinner for 15 bucks. It includes BBQ beef brisket, pulled pork, delicious BBQ chicken, an Idaho baked potato (served with sour cream, butter, and pepper), salad, and a tasty dessert. Sky and Steve also are linebacker cooks for this banquet feast.

During this particular banquet, Troy Taylor took the helm for the auction, and with Dave Smith's help and a few others, about 40 auction items were laid out on the table. Red auction tickets were sold, and bidding became intense for key items like Steve Chingren's book about grouse hawking, *In Search of Sage Grouse*, and Ed Pitcher's opus magnum, *The Flying of Falcons*, about training falcons to wait out of vertical sight.

57

The auction helps IFA's bank account immensely, and gives it the flexibility to put on quality falconry meets, contribute to The Archives of Falconry, and join alliances that are favorable to falconry in Idaho. The final tally on the number of red tickets sold for this effort was huge: about $1,800. (Congrats to Troy and Kelly Martinez for their good work organizing a successful auction; and thanks also to all those who donated auction items.)

Since 1976, the strength of IFA and its endurance lies in its membership and those willing to step up and volunteer for many things, such as organizing a falconry meet, becoming an IFA officer, heading up a conservation project, or helping friends search for lost birds or dogs.

The baton had been passed to new officers in 2017. Former officers were commended for all their good work. Mike Garets, then the President of IFA, passed the baton to Brad Smoot. Mike then took the baton from Jim Hanson (who had served for four years) to become the Southwest Regional Director for IFA. The other Regional Directors remained. Phil Bucher, IFA Treasurer for four years, stepped down and handed that baton to Paul Mascuch. IFA has good reason to be thankful for Phil's steadfastness and reliability. Our secretary, Carol Wambolt, continues to keep IFA membership informed by circulating timely updates and making sure email addresses are current. We salute all these good people.

With these changes, IFA remains in good hands and will continue as an active and dynamic organization. The membership is bound together by the type of falconry one can practice across the Idaho landscape. It also is associated with the North American Falconers Association (NAFA), that is bound together with 110 countries through the International Association for Falconry and Conservation of Birds of Prey (IAF).

Top: The core group of the Idaho Falconers Association at their annual meet in Arco, Idaho, in November of 2013. Some members in this photo helped organize IFA in 1974. A few have since gone over the "Great Divide." Photo by Richard Howard (timed shutter-release mode).

Bottom: Jack Oar, famous for his iconic hats and pipe, and his international contributions to falconry heritage. He is a great guy to be with in the field, hunting grouse, ducks, or jackrabbits with falcons and goshawks. Photo by Richard Howard.

On his way home from this IFA Arco meet, Gordon Walker stopped between Cary and Shoshone, Idaho, to get another breath of sage and to sense the open shrub steppe where grouse live. High overhead, in the cobalt-blue skies, he saw a V-shaped flock of about 300 snow geese cackling as they flew south. That made his day as he drove back to Boise.

It was a good day in Idaho that year. If you come here or live here, take care of its landscape as best you can.

In late October 2022, after the "Covid Years of 2020 and 2021," the IFA membership met again. Dr. Afshin Mofid took the baton as the new IFA president. One of his first tasks was to organize the annual meet. He pressed for revisiting his old haunts around Picabo, Idaho, when he lived in Ketchum, Idaho. So, we established base camp for the meet at the Silver Creek Hotel in Bellevue, Idaho, just south of Ketchum.

Rich Howard described the meet to his friends. He wrote, "Gents, it was a real pleasure to see some good hawking, throw some atlatl darts, and share in the IFA camaraderie that brings us together to practice the king of all field sports. Compliments to Afshin and Gary Moon for finding the Silver Creek Lodge with its heated saltwater pool and Jacuzzi hot tub, weathering yard for the birds and animal friendly attitude.

Thanks to Mike Garets for finding an insurance company to back the liability for the meet and being the four-way connector/facilitator for meet details."

Richard continued to write, "This was my 38th IFA meet. Each one has been different—and full of the unexpected. As I mentioned in my newest book, *Stormy Waters on the Sagebrush Sea*, the strength of IFA and its endurance since 1976 lies in its membership. I previously detailed some items that those who volunteer for IFA accomplish in my book, plus other important tasks such as building conservation bridges with agencies such as the Idaho Department of Fish and Game or other organizations, and working on conservation projects for raptors."

Newly-installed President Dr. Afshin Mofid and former IFA officers are to be commended for all their good work this past year (2022). Secretary Carol Wambolt continues to keep IFA membership informed and connected by circulating timely updates. She and Treasurer Paul Mascuch work to ensure that email and Facebook addresses are current, which is a big job. We salute all of these volunteers.

The view behind the Silver Creek Hotel that fall was perfect. Looking west over the Big Wood River, we could see deciduous trees that were full of a dozen fall colors. Beyond the trees, we saw tawny-colored sagebrush hills, speckled with deep pine green and light grays of rabbitbrush. The cool, crisp fall mornings encouraged falconers to weather their birds in the morning sun before taking them up and preparing for the day's hunting foray. E. Hemingway would have approved of all that took place this weekend.

The hotel accommodated us as we held our "safety meetings" in the lobby or the dining room after a day's hunt, to discuss how it was out there on the Sagebrush Sea. Not many grouse were flushed—and those that were, turned the hunt into what fly fishers call a "catch and release" episode. Those grouse are tough birds!

The habitat in many places looked like great shrub-steppe haunts for grouse. But in other areas, there was a vast landscape of monostands of wheatgrass, mustard, wild rye and cheatgrass. We did find several 500-acre islands of habitat that supported 50-year-old stands of sage that were three to six feet high. Within these islands were numerous cottontail and jackrabbit trails. Fresh rabbit pellets were indications this is how the landscape used to be.

The Harris hawks had their field day hunting rabbits that ran familiar trails and hid in protective coves. One rabbit was taken on the first slip by Mike's Harris hawk named *Arya*. We continued to hawk with Arya after she caught her first rabbit, but to no avail. She had about a dozen slips at other bobbing tails.

We returned to the trucks in time for lunch. We shared a few pilsner beers from the local brewery. Rich got out his atlatl and darts. During lunch we all took a crack at throwing darts out to about 50 yards. He told the falconers that 6,000 years ago in that same area, paleo-men were hunting bighorn sheep and bison with atlatls. Archaeological sites nearby were excavated in the 1970s and verified these events.

Three rabbits were taken during the meet, but more than a two dozen slips were initiated by their white bobbing tails. While the meet and banquet had a more modest turnout this year of about 30 people, we applaud all who joined.

Top: Mike Garets, former IFA President, and his Harris hawk, after a successful hunt for cotton= tail rabbits. Photo by Richard Howard.

Right: Mike Harris' hawk, Arya, on a T-perch ready to hunt. Photo by Richard Howard.

Thanks to those who donated quality auction items, including a big IFA Halloween pumpkin with a carved-out face highlighted by a black marker. Framed prints of a soaring eagle and bull elk by Erica Craig appeared on the auction table. There were also custom-made knives, falconry gloves, and falconry equipment for the auction.

Special auction donations were made by Nancy Whitehead and her daughter Laurie Summis, the owners and editors of *Sun Valley Magazine*. Laurie, the present editor, donated several editions of the magazine. Nancy, a brilliant photographer, donated a copy of her photo book, full of pointing dogs, and a framed 18" x 24" color photo of two English Pointers.

We said our goodbyes, took different paths, and wandered home on Sunday morning. I felt profoundly thankful for having the privilege to live in Idaho. I took yet another road I had not traveled, just to see what was over the hill.

Along that route, I could see that fall elk and deer hunts had already begun, as hunting camps with trucks and trailers were circled like tipis every three to four miles. The road went over a divide and down a drainage covered with summer habitat for sage-grouse, and fall habitat for deer and elk. I exited the back country road at Fairfield and headed west to Boise.

The 2022 Idaho Falconers Association banquet in Hailey, Idaho. The event was attended by 24 members from around the state. Photo by Ashley Neubrand.

Overhead and 500 feet above in the cobalt-blue skies, at least 200 Canada geese flew in their customary V-formation pursuing their route south.

As I have said before, it was a good weekend in Idaho. When you come here, or if you live here, take care of the landscape as best you can.

Gary Moon's gyrfalcon hybrid in the weathering yard at the Silver Creek Hotel in Bellevue, Idaho. Photo by Richard Howard.

II: Stetsons

"A Drive Through Long Valley" by Rachel Teannalach

The Stetson

WHILE WATCHING THE MOVIE *INDOCHINE*, admiring the acting talents of Catherine Deneuve as Éliane Devries and Vincent Perez as Jean-Baptiste, I looked out the window of Elkstone Cabin. The first snowflake of the 2003 winter season settled on the solarium glass attached to the cabin. Several hundred more snowflakes fell nearby, leaving micro water craters as the flakes melted on the glass. It was 2:38 in the afternoon. Winter was born. The day was covered with a penetrating cold, enhanced by the wind and raked by snow squalls. Near the cabin, the tamarack pine needles that had turned brilliant yellow had fallen to the ground, defining an oval-shaped yellow circle.

Sage, my border collie, stared outside the second story of Elkstone Cabin. This structure, built from high-altitude, dense, lodgepole pine 36 years ago, had south-facing windows on the second floor. The windows extended from the floor to the ceiling. Sage basked in the warm sun that radiated through the windows. A fox in a thick, light red winter coat, trotted through the back pasture, eliciting sharp barking from Sage. If the slider door somehow opened, he would run through the door, across the balcony deck, down the thick wooden plank stairs, under the Tibetan prayer flag strings, and out to the south field to chase the fox. Instead, he remained on his hind legs, with his front legs pressed against the window, looking at the fox that finally disappeared behind a ponderosa pine.

Nothing was certain at Elkstone Cabin. It could be hot in the summer—sometimes 15 degrees below zero in the winter, with five feet of snow guaranteed on the level by mid-February. One could savor a comfortable temperature regime only in the months around the spring and fall equinox transitions. During the rest of the year, the cabin and the surrounding five acres on which it was located, demanded "recreational maintenance." It was surely "recreational": power-washing the cabin and then applying coats of Cetol to preserve the logs, replacing the barn roof, trimming limbs from aspen and pine trees, mowing a firebreak, and shoveling snow off the roof.

Nine miles south of Elkstone Cabin, in Donnelly, Idaho, Randy Priest brushed the final restoration touch on a grey-tan beaver felt Stetson hat. He owned the Priest Hat Company—a business he started 43 years ago. His reputation as a superb haberdasher who made and restored hats grew by word of mouth from cowboys, Mormon farmers, rich folks, and collectors from all over the northwest. He was from Pocatello, Idaho. He graduated from high school with my sister Frances and a bunch of other talented folk in 1958. The student crop that year was like good Malbec wine. They were remembered for their achievements in sports, academics, and having fun.

Randy learned the hat trade from his uncle who made felt hats and sold them to Mormon farmers and local ranchers to supplement his income. Randy liked living in remote areas—and while Donnelly was not a perfect town, the men and women who lived there shared most of his values. They survived the long winters and became a part of its earth and sky.

The band inside the Stetson was sweat-stained from years of use. A near-perfect hat again, Randy had worked hard to make it wearable. Inside the crown of the hat was printed in blue ink: "Dr. Richard Howard, 544 South 7th, Pocatello, Idaho." On the trademark label inside the hat was a date and place: "1948, Lubbock, Texas, official Stetson."

John Stetson started his hat company in 1865, and was a huge success in that his hats became known around the world as the "cowboy hat." Cowboys riding the Chisholm Trail from central Montana to Lubbock, Texas, rode herd on thousands of free-ranging cattle from the 1860s through the 1890s, where they were sold, slaughtered, and devoured by hungry men and woman who were rapidly taming the west. Their choice of hat was the Stetson.

A Stetson was weather-resistant; a shield from sun and rain; and resilient to being blown downwind, stomped on by horses and cattle; and always ready to assume its original shape when properly cared for.

Through the years, Stetsons became fashionable in the West. They were worn by businessmen in black suits with gold watches, lawyers with silver watches, and doctors with pocket watches. Ten different designs were available for custom-made fitting to these men of the West. They were sold in ranch and farm shops and department stores throughout the country.

The hat Randy Priest was restoring was originally purchased at Fargo's Department Store in downtown Pocatello, Idaho. It was the "Bozeman" model. It cost $31 dollars in 1951. Alice, Doc Howard's vivacious wife, bought it for him to celebrate their 20th wedding anniversary. Around town, the hat became Doc Howard's iconic feature. He would always place it on the top arm of the six-arm hat stand in his office on the second floor of the Carlisle Building in downtown Pocatello.

Doc Howard wore his Stetson when went out on house calls to see patients, to social events, and to the symphony. Doc liked the symphony at Idaho State College. It was small, maybe 30 musicians. It was directed by Professor Harold Mealy, an Oberlin College graduate. Mealy challenged his musicians to play advanced pieces from Grieg, Bach, Scarlatti, Mozart, and Chopin. Doc liked Chopin pieces the best.

On weekends, Doc would make house calls on the Shoshone-Bannock Indian Reservation to help Native American patients at Fort Hall. He tipped his hat when greeting Native American women. Many times, a call from a patient or from the nurse at the small infirmary at Fort Hall informed him that he left his Stetson hat on the chair. They would keep it for him to retrieve when he returned that way. While many Native American men on the "Res" cherished owning the hat, none would ever be so dishonest as to steal Doc Howard's Stetson hat. It would, however, look good with a bright beaded band around the hat and an eagle feather hanging off the back.

Doc carried on the tradition that his mother, also a medical doctor, started in 1906 when she cared for Native Americans on the

Reservation. Both had the sense to work closely with medicine men who had their own ways of curing people. When tribal medicine didn't work, western medicine was tried in order to heal a patient. Many times, a combination of both would bring about a full cure.

I inherited the Stetson when Doc went over the "Great Divide" in 1994 at the age of 93. I put it away for a time and then began to wear it on occasion while attending an archaeological conference or going out to band ferruginous hawks. Because of its age, the hat didn't hold up well. Its wear patterns told me the hat would be just a museum artifact if I didn't take care of it. So I stopped wearing it. The Stetson sat in the closet with a dozen other hats I had collected from fishing lodges in Idaho, Washington, and Alaska; falconry meets; The Peregrine Fund; and one hat from Czechoslovakia that my brother-in-law gave to me. Three official U. S. Fish and Wildlife Service hats were provided to me to wear while on official duty. I wore them outdoors for fieldwork, on a wildlife refuge, or at interagency meetings. One was a baseball hat, another was a wool hat for the winter, and the other was a dark brown Stetson cowboy hat. There was no obligation to wear any of these hats at the Fish and Wildlife Service.

So, one day after retiring from the Fish and Wildlife Service, I was driving north to Elkstone Cabin. I drove through Donnelly, which is about 12 miles south of my cabin, and saw the sign, "Priest Hats—New and Repaired" above a corner store. It made me slow way down. As I drove by, I looked through the windows. I saw many hats on the shelves, and a few in the window, which compelled me to turn around and park.

I went into the store. A bell jingled when I opened the door. Inside, I immediately knew I had come to the right place to have my dad's Stetson refurbished so that it could be wearable again. I talked to Randy for a while and learned that he had gone to high school in Pocatello with my sister Frances, and knew her other friends: Carol Elle, Steve Anderson, Saundra Harrison, and Floyd Andersen. Randy was especially interested in how Saundra was doing. I told him not so well—she had been in a car accident and her leg had to be amputated, but her beautiful Irish face and red hair had remained untouched. He was pleased to hear she was still alive and hoped one day to see her again. He recalled that she had a radiant smile and an infectious laugh.

I told Randy about the Stetson hat that belonged to my father and the other brown hat that was provided to me by the U.S. Fish and Wildlife Service. He said, "Bring them in and we will see what can be done." I thanked him and left. Weeks later, I remembered to bring the two hats to his shop. I told Randy, "No hurry. Just see what you can do to restore them and refit to my head size, please."

A month went by, and the snowflakes that began this story had become two-feet deep at Elkstone Cabin. I stopped at the Priest Hat Company to check on the status of the hats. Both had a bright glow about them as if they were new and had just been taken out of the hatbox. Randy had me put each of them on my head and made some minor adjustments with his hat-stretching tools. They rode perfectly on my head. Each was very comfortable to wear, as they were fitted to tilt at a slight right angle while on my head.

I paid Randy for his professional work. I was silently amazed, as was every other customer, cowboy, or farmer who had their hats refurbished by him.

Before I left the store, I had to give Randy the sad news that Saundra had passed two weeks previous. Randy never did get to Pocatello to see her.

Author Richard Howard, wearing Dr. Howard's Stetson. The doctor wore the hat on house calls both in Pocatello and to the Shoshone–Bannock Indian Reservation at Fort Hall, Idaho. Inside the hat, the famous Stetson company logo reads "John B. Stetson, 4x beaver." Photo by Allan Ansell.

71

Huntsville Pilgrimage

HEY GORDON, YOU INTERESTED IN GOING on a special retreat during semester break?", asked Gary. "Come with us for a week to Huntsville, Utah."

Gordon, a junior in anthropology and a Lutheran agnostic who attended Idaho State University, didn't know what to do during semester break. His grades were good. He had just broken up with a girlfriend. He was unsure about continuing his effort earning a degree in anthropology. Life was a like a dull paned window that hadn't been washed for months. Also it was late January: Gordon was suffering from an acute bout of seasonal affective syndrome (SAD). The only bright light at that moment was for him to join a Catholic student group on the Huntsville retreat. Gordon said, "Yes," to Gary's invitation.

Gary was enthusiastic about this group of students. Most, like himself, were recent converts to the Catholic Church. The Catholic Student Center had installed a new priest the year before: Father Echeverria. He was a charismatic and talented man whose heritage was deeply influenced by his Basque traditions, language, music, and dance.

Father Echeverria learned early in his life that music was a universal language. So, at the age of seven he started his journey with a mid-sized, six-string guitar. By the time he was 12 years old, he was in demand for concerts at church, the Catholic schools in his hometown of Boise, and sometimes at Mormon and Lutheran events too. His forte was playing folk songs that were sung in the native Basque (*Euskara*), Spanish, and French languages that were filled with vivacity.

Later after pledging his life to the Catholic priesthood, he was influenced by the social trends of the 1960s when "hooten-annies" were popular. With his talents and background, Father Echeverria made creative contributions to these song fests, locally and regionally. His priesthood order was shaken by these songs and the people who were attracted to the crowds when "hoots" were organized. They thought, and wisely so, that he might best serve the church by being placed on a college campus.

Weeks later, Father Echeverria's destiny was determined by an opening at Idaho State University's Catholic Student Center in Pocatello. This appointment also determined the destiny of more than a few non-Catholic students who were encouraged to join the Church because of this charismatic priest—and because the students needed some faith, relevant music in their lives, and a foundation of social stability during a period of chaotic change.

74

Gary had met Father Echeverria two years earlier in September, just after he returned from his job as a back-county wilderness ranger in the Sawtooth Mountains. It had been a good job, full of challenges. With his string of pack horses, he would trail into this wilderness for five days at a time. It was not solitary work. He met many hikers and climbers along the trail. Most of them were good about putting their campfires out and packing out their garbage.

Some, however, had no respect for wilderness etiquette. This became Gary's mission. He packed out garbage by horseback; put out untended fires; and erased the presence of wild beer party camps littered with Oly, Coors, and Budweiser cans. Trail maintenance was another part of his job. Rock falls, minor landslides, and winter avalanches would erase sections of trail. Packing picks and shovels on his horses, he enlisted hiking or climbing parties to help him repair trails. Often, he would join them at their campsite when the days' work was done. Gary, like Father Echeverria, had a talent for music; and while his forte was playing trumpet in high school, he found that guitar and songs fit together a lot better than a trumpet at "hoots" gatherings or around a campfire.

A year later after attending conversion classes at the Catholic Center, Gary pledged his soul to the Church. He and 16 other students found some peace and certainty knowing they were bonded by the ritual aspects of the Church, prayer time, confession, meditation, and the sacraments. It was new to them, but reassuring.

Gary, one of the older converts, became enchanted with Basque culture after he had met Basque sheepherders when he was on wilderness patrol. Father Echeverria, who was Gary's gateway to Basque culture, sometimes would take students to Boise to witness the colorfully exuberant Oinkari Basque Dancers. Gary was first in line on these trips. This also gave Gary an opportunity to talk to Father Echeverria during the four-hour bus ride to Boise. He prodded the Father to teach him Basque songs and novel cording on the guitar. He excelled at this.

The Oinkari dancers are sponsored by Boise's Basque community, even today. They play an important role in preserving Basque culture and traditions, including their unique language, food preparation, and personal histories—while serving as ambassadors of good will at the same time. The vitality of the dancers and their costumes is marvelous to witness. When invited to join in their dance routines, it's even better.

Gordon had little idea of what to expect when Gary had invited him to go on the retreat in Huntsville, Utah. They would spend a week at a monastery eating good food, taking long walks, attending chapel, and maybe get to know one or two of the monks that resided there. The idea sounded good to Gordon, considering that the alternative during semester break was to work in the museum on some dull, repetitious project, identifying bones from digs and falling deeper into his own SAD issues. He told Gary to put his name on the "go" list to Huntsville, knowing it was only two days from then, and he'd better get his gear together.

Well, there is not much to pack for this retreat, he thought. *Throw in some winter clothes, gloves, toothbrush, razor, some vitamins, two changes of underwear, and an extra pair of pants.* He withdrew $200 from his checking account, although he wasn't sure how he would spend it. *Buy some sandwiches, chips and cokes at rest stops along the way to Huntsville.* He knew he would do this.

Father Echeverria didn't go with them. They were on their own for this retreat. He needed to cover services for a priest at St. Anthony Catholic Church on North 7th Street in Pocatello who had become violently ill. He was in the hospital and was not expected to recover for several weeks.

The day before they were to leave, Father Echeverria called the students together for an hour-long orientation of what was expected of them when entering the monastery grounds. First and foremost: the observation of "strict silence." There was to be no talking after they entered the grounds, except when in conference with a monk. One would learn to be creative with communication, using body language, and hand and face gestures—all day long, from 5:30 a.m. rising until 8:30 p.m. bedtime. They would sleep in a Quonset hut that had bunk beds, bathrooms, and showers. After getting dressed in the morning, they would all walk to the chapel and participate in services conducted by the monks.

Breakfast would be next. Father Echeverria assured them that they would enjoy this. All the food served at the monastery came from the 1,800 acres on which the monastery was located and owned by the Trappist Order. It was pure organic and hearty. By the end of the retreat, they would have a spiritual awakening just from the delicious food alone. Loaves of bread; ten kinds of jam; honey; eggs; meat from chickens, sheep, pigs and cows; garden vegetables; milk; six varieties of cheeses; five types of juice—freshly squeezed from fruits of the orchard; and cold spring water gave sustenance to the monks and their visitors. All of this bounty was provided by monks' handiwork throughout the four seasons of the year.

Their daily routine would include prayers, bible and book readings, and meditations guided by Brother Jerome, a 56-year-old monk who was a World War II Marine veteran. Most of the older monks, like Brother Jerome, were veterans from WW II and the Korean Wars. Other younger men from all walks of life were attracted to this way of life as the world became more complex—and stillness was a luxury. Mindful qualities could be found here, unchanged in the Trappist spirit that has followed the Rule of Saint Benedict since the Middle Ages. In the 1960s, about 80 men were part of the Huntsville monastic community.

Father Echeverria was at the bus at 8:30 a.m. to see the group off and to wish them a safe journey. Gary, Gordon, and the other students then climbed on the bus for their five-hour drive on Highway 91 from Pocatello, Idaho, to Huntsville, Utah. On the way there, they had three stops.

This first stop was for a break at Red Rock Pass, Idaho. There, they read a highway kiosk sign about the significance of the pass. This was where old Lake Bonneville broke through its banks and flooded the Portneuf and Snake River Valleys about 15,000 years ago. It lowered the lake level by 331 fee, creating basalt scablands along the Portneuf and 300-foot canyon channels in the Snake River. It was like the Columbia River scablands that were formed by Lake Missoula in northwestern Montana. The Clark Fork, a tributary to the Columbia River, broke through glacial ice dams sometimes 1,000 feet high near Clark Fork, Idaho, during the late Pleistocene.

The second mid-morning stop was in Preston, Idaho, at one of the Jackson's Truck cafés. Jackson advertised his cafés by placing a series of small red signs, each with words of a longer, full message. These "Burma Shave" signs were often placed along more remote stretches of highway. The familiar red signs were also found throughout southern Idaho highways. One Burma Shave series there said:

1. *Angels*
2. *Who guard you*
3. *When you drive*
4. *Usually retire at 65*
5. *Burma Shave.*

The Jackson's Truck stop was a combination store, café, and gas station where travelers could stock up on snacks, Burma Shave, or nourishing meals. Gordon looked for snacks.

He found his favorite food, Twinkies. He bought three packs. He loved the yellow-orange bread and whipped cream taste. Gordon devoured two packs of them while at Jackson's and another one on the bus.

By noon, they arrived in Logan, Utah, to visit the Utah State University campus. Some of the students were considering it for graduate school. Little did Gordon realize at the time, but six years later he would be accepted into the Natural Resources College at the university where he would earn a master's degree in wildlife ecology. Gary was also accepted into the graduate school and earned a degree in wilderness recreation management. Their degrees would determine their future professional destinies and intertwined personal stories.

By mid-afternoon, the bus came to a sign on the highway that said, "Monastery Road." Another sign gave the location as defined in Mormon coordinates, "S. 9500 E." A half-mile-long winding gravel road, with rows of trees along each side, led to a parking lot where there were nine buildings of various sizes. One was obviously a barn, and another a huge Quonset-shaped building with a blue stained-glass window of a cross on its front. This was the monastery chapel of the Abbey of Our Lady of the Holy Trinity of the Cistercian Order of Trappist Monks. They had arrived.

The students got off the bus and were led by a monk to their Quonset quarters. It took about 30 minutes for everyone to get settled. The monk pointed to a daily routine register posted near the door. They were to be in the chapel in just ten minutes, where they would take Holy Communion, follow the retreat opening ritual, and then recite evening Vespers.

They walked into the chapel and sat down. At the head of the chapel was the 25-foot-high blue stained glass window. The evening sun shone through it, making an image of the cross on the aisle floor of the chapel. Sixty monks arrived in the chapel, walking down the aisle single-file and then sitting on the

A tree-lined road leading to the Trappist Monastery near Huntsville, Utah. Photo courtesy of The Salt Lake Tribune.

pew benches. They wore light brown robes with hoods that were set back around their neck and shoulders. The robes were made by skilled tailors within the Brotherhood. Evening Vespers began with Holy Communion, and then moved into a 30-minute recitation from the Scriptures in Latin given by one of the monks. After the recitation, 20 of the monks intoned a 16th century Gregorian chant. Gary and Gordon were awed by this introduction to the monastery. Here was a spiritual transition from street clothes into a mindful Catholic contemplation.

Morning Mass at 6:20 a.m. and evening Vespers in the chapel became part of the 16-hour daily retreat schedule that the students followed. After Vespers, they broke bread and shared dinner together with the monks in the 80-seat dining room, but in strict silence. This was followed by individual student consultations with a monk for an hour, and then to bed.

The consultation was where Gordon first met Brother Jerome. During this consultation, Gordon realized that here was a man who had considerable wisdom regarding the human experience. He found out that Brother Jerome was from a small farm town in Iowa who had joined the Marines just out of high school. He was a WWII veteran who had fought in the war and witnessed terrible battles against the Japanese—and returned home, looking for peace and sanctity. In 1947, he became a novitiate of the Trappist Order (Order of Cistercians of the Strict Observance—the *Ordo Cisterciensis Strictioris Observantiae*, or OCSO) at the Huntsville Abbey. Six years later, he took his final vows.

Gordon listened to Brother Jerome's life story and how he came to be a monk. Brother Jerome told Gordon, "There is so much cacophony in the world today that the subtle, divine voice is not heard. Listen to your heart and be compassionate first to yourself and then to others. Meditate on these thoughts during your retreat."

Thomas Merton, another Trappist monk, from the Abbey of Gethsemane located in Bardstown, Kentucky, brought a lost tradition back into the Trappists. He lived apart from the abbey in a hermitage the final four years of his life. He wrote profoundly about social justice, contemplation, and the silence of thoughts based on his European background and Catholic service. His most famous book, *The Seven Storey Mountain*, sold millions of copies. He published 60 books during his lifetime. It's no wonder that the small cabin located near the Aabbey became a pilgrimage for many who were influenced by Merton's writings. Some of the monks at Huntsville adopted this tradition of hermitage. They built a small one-room A-frame cabin near Bennett Canyon on monastery property.

It was a place where Trappist brothers could go for several days of individual prayer, reading, and solitude. It was also a wildlife sanctuary where, during the fall rut, bull elk could be heard bugling—their grunts and trumpets echoing off the walls of Bennett Canyon.

In the springtime, a pair of goshawks would frequently fly by the cabin after hunting for birds and ground squirrels to take to their young. Their three-foot-wide stick nest was located high in a cross-branch of a 70-year-old aspen tree half a mile into Bennett Canyon. After fledging, the young goshawks would soon find the Uinta ground squirrel colony near the cabin. When on hermitage, Brother Jerome took great delight in observing the young hawks improving their hunting skills trying to catch young ground squirrels. By the end of August, the hawks had dispersed, and by the end of September, they had begun their migration south. It was all a part of the miracle cycle of life that absorbed Brother Jerome's thoughts during meditation.

Gordon heard about this hermitage from Brother Jerome one evening during consultation. Brother Jerome sometimes spent days at the cabin after he finished with the harvesting of hay and tending to the gardens, beehives, and orchards. It was there that he pondered the simplicity of mysticism and how evasive and yet universal to mankind the mystical experience was.

His own personal color of light was lilac. He had discovered it when one evening, as he sat cross-legged on the porch of the cabin, the setting sun reflected through a small colored-glass cross that hung on the porch. The lilac-colored light turned into a column directed at his chest. Soon, Brother Jerome felt enveloped by this light and the love it emitted. It lasted for half an hour until the sun set. He sat there transfixed on the porch until the next morning, not wanting to disturb the inner presence of this magnificent energy. He never shared this experience with anyone. It was his alone to cherish, but afterward his behavior and actions did not go unnoticed by all the monks at the monastery.

His presence was rewarded by becoming the public face of the monastery for decades. For years, Brother Jerome greeted those who came on retreats to the sanctuary. He was their first exposure to the Trappist monks at Huntsville. He guided them through orientation, ritual, and consultation. Many were forever changed by his humor, humility, and compassion.

Brother Jerome also was rewarded with the honor of blessing the annual cycle of agriculture on the 1,800 acres of Catholic land located in Ogden Valley. In the springtime, he would bless the 12 fields of the monastery, each named for a prominent Catholic saint. Walking to the northeast corner of each field, he would intone the blessing by asking for a productive harvest.

"Oh God, by whose help we cultivate the earth and all that will grow by the effect of your power, grant that what we know to be lacking in our labors may be supplied abundantly by you." During the blessing he would take a cup of holy water and sprinkle it in each of the four cardinal directions.

All of this was timed to occur with the first spring migration of sandhill cranes returning to Ogden Valley. They wintered in southern Colorado and northern Arizona. Some pairs would remain in the valley to nest, while many other pairs would head north to Grays Lake National Wildlife Refuge and into numerous other southern Idaho valleys. But it was late January and the cranes wouldn't arrive until late March.

The retreat week for the students went by fast. They drank from the well of rejuvenation with their exposure to the monks of Huntsville. The prayers, communions, and consultations had opened doors of perception that would forever be gifts to their lives. They packed bags, cleaned their Quonset hut quarters, walked into the chapel for one last prayer, and were blessed by the abbey patriarch. They climbed on the bus, drove down the tree-lined road to the highway, and traveled back to Pocatello.

Except for one student who remained behind: Gordon. He had decided this was too inspirational. He had told Brother Jerome the night before that he intended to stay for a while. Gary and the other students didn't learn of Gordon's decision until just before climbing on the bus. Gordon told Gary to tell his parents about his decision to remain at the monastery. It would mean giving up a semester of school, but Gordon needed to explore the deeper aspects of the men who made this lifelong commitment to become Trappist monks. Gordon would decide whether to remain just after the sandhill crane migration at the end of March.

He was assigned to work in the dairy to learn the process of making cheese. Also, because of his youth and strength, he was assigned to feed hay to the 16 dairy cows that were the source of milk for the cheese. Both were everyday tasks without relief. The eight-hour days passed quickly. The snow in the valley disappeared. The first harbingers of spring were blue, red, and yellow crocus flowers and vivid green shoots of pasture grass. Enormous thunderheads would appear to the west over the Wasatch Mountains. Spring rains, combined with snowmelt runoff, nourished the valley.

Gordon studied the Catholic Catechism in preparation for conversion to being a Catholic, with baptism. In two months, he had finished chapters of the catechism and committed them to memory—normally that would have taken four months. It surprised his Trappist monk mentors that he was so astute at absorbing Church Doctrine. It didn't surprise brother Jerome. From his discussions with Gordon, he knew this student had exceptional insights into religious scripture that went far beyond his age. As Gordon stood on the brink of baptism and conversion in late March, Brother Jerome took Gordon to the hermitage for a three-day retreat. Aspen leaves were beginning to leaf out. The goshawks had returned. On the second day of the retreat in mid-morning, as they sat cross-legged on the porch of the cabin, they both heard it: sandhill cranes. There were about two dozen, foraging in a nearby field, calling to their mates. Brother Jerome and Gordon watched the cranes from the porch for over two hours until they finally flew across the valley and landed out of sight. They completed the three-day retreat, joyful at having seen the return of the cranes. They walked back to the main abbey to resume their work and religious commitments.

That evening was a somber one for Gordon. He attended prayers, took evening Communion, and because it was Sunday, he heard yet another Gregorian chant as only the monks could intone. He recited the Latin chant to himself. When he returned to his room, he kneeled at his bedside and said a prayer. He then wrote a note to brother Jerome from his desk. It read:

> *Brother Jerome,*

> *"I must explore my spiritual destiny beyond the Catholic Church. You have given me a foundation on which to make that exploration. The exposure to your fellow monks, studying the scriptures and taking Communion, reading the books by Thomas Merton while here at Huntsville, and taking the exceptional hermitage retreat these past few days will be cherished for my lifetime. Someday, I will return and know that this was the right decision."*

> *—Gordon Walker*

The next morning before the bell for prayers in the chapel was rung, before other monks rose to complete their morning dress, before the cock rooster crowed, Gordon walked into the chapel and left the note on the altar where the abbey patriarch would see it. Wearing his Filson jacket and hat, an old pair of Levi jeans, a pair of Vibram hiking boots, with his backpack slung over his shoulders, he walked down the tree-lined road to the highway. An early morning truck driver saw him in his headlights and stopped to pick Gordon up. He was headed for Boise, Idaho, by way of Pocatello. Gordon left his Trappist robes and a personal chalice on the bed at the monastery.

Postscript: The Abbey of Our Lady of the Holy Trinity closed in 2017. The aging monks were not able to recruit novitiates. John Slattery made a film about the monastery titled, *Present Time: Journal of a Country Monastery.* It chronicles the founding of the monastery in 1947 through 2017, with a focus on the last 15 years of its existence against the background of the dominant Mormon religion in the area. He also published a limited-edition coffee table book under the same title. It includes photos that were selected from over 2,000 images, given to him by the monks and visitors. Monastery lands are now held under conservation easements managed by the Ogden Valley Land Trust.

Trappist monks in the chapel at the Abbey of Our Lady of the Holy Trinity in Huntsville, Utah, recited daily Mass at 6:20 a.m. every day except Sunday, which was at 8:00 a.m. Photo courtesy of The Salt Lake Tribune.

Old Mr. Wilson
and the 544 House

MR. WILSON KNOCKED ON THE BACK DOOR of the red brick, three-story, Howard family home at 544 S. 7th Street in Pocatello, Idaho. When its painted gray door was opened, a visitor was presented with two sets of stairs. The first went up 12 steps through the covered back porch and into the kitchen. The other set led down to the basement that contained the coal furnace. It that warmed the home during eastern Idaho's icy-cold winters. It was deep winter and the temperature outside was only 10° when he knocked.

Sean Wilson usually took the back porch stairs up to meet Alice Howard in the kitchen. She would greet him with a cheery smile and sometimes a plate of sandwiches and cut carrots.

"How is the Misses this fine winter day?" he would ask in his guttural Irish brogue. "And how is the doctor too?" he would inquire.

"Oh, I'm doing fine; Rich is not here right now. He is out doing house calls around town," she said.

"Thanks, Misses Howard, for the sandwiches. This is the first thing I've eaten all day," Wilson said. "Do you want a little nip Misses Alice?" "I have some fine Irish whiskey in my flask."

"No," replied Alice. "Mr. Wilson, you had better get downstairs and shovel some coal before the fire goes out and the house cools down," she said. "But first, finish your sandwiches and I'll get you some coffee and hot chocolate."

Wilson thought, *Coffee and whiskey go together on a cold winter evening. I hope she brings me a big cup with room for a whiskey nip.*

She did. He poured about two jigs into his coffee. *I'll eat the sandwiches later . . . need some whiskey fire in the belly right now,* he thought.

"I'll be in the kitchen, so when you're through tending the furnace, just knock on the kitchen door and we can settle on what I owe you for the week," said Alice.

Wilson took the coffee and hot chocolate mugs as Alice closed the door and returned to fixing dinner in the kitchen for Dr. Howard and the three children, Gunda, Frances, and little Richie. His older sisters called him "Dickey Duck" even though he was 12 years old. He cringed every time they called him that.

Wilson took the staircase down to the basement with a rough, partially-crumbled, cement floor that was painted green. The basement smelled of burning coal and musty coal bags.

Wilson walked into the furnace room and took the hopper shovel and began to shovel coal from one of two three-ton storage bins. He filled the hopper bin with about 200 pounds of coal. The hopper bin, which sat about five feet from the Lennox Furnace Company fire door, would hold enough coal to heat the home to about 70 degrees for 48 hours. It had an eight-inch metal screwing pipe that augered the coal from the hopper bin into the furnace.

To stoke the furnace, he opened the furnace fire door and saw that the fire inside was bright yellow and burning good. He threw four hopper shovels of coal into the roaring fire and watched until the fire nearly turned blue. This boosted the temperature a few degrees inside the home and kept the Howard family toasty warm until bedtime.

He closed the furnace door, and checked the auger pipe to make sure it wasn't jammed with coal or other harder rock that sometimes got mixed with the coal. *Everything lookin' good,* he thought. He checked the flue pipes coming out of the furnace, all eight of them.

No leaks. The flues were 10 inches in diameter and snaked out to different rooms behind the walls of the home where they disgorged the heated air through the metal ventilators. Some were embedded in walls and others in floors.

The children had favorite places to stand or sit near these ventilators. The most favorite was the wall heat ventilator in the kitchen. Early in the morning, Gunda, Frances, or Dickey Duck would compete for this site so they could watch Alice fixing a breakfast of waffles and lingonberry jam. No one ever thought about who was keeping the heated house comfortable during the winter, except Alice and old Mr. Wilson—sometimes, Dickey.

On the evening that Wilson came by, Dickey went down to the basement to visit with him. Wilson called him "the master of the house." Dickey was always interested in what Wilson had to say because there was a sinister quality about him that made him laugh. Tonight was no exception. "So, are you keeping us warm?" Dickey asked Wilson. "Warm and a wee bit toasty," he replied.

"I have some sandwiches and some hot chocolate for you," Wilson said. "Are you hungry," he asked?

Dickey was always hungry and gulped down a sandwich.

"Are you thirsty," he asked?

"Here, I'll add a few nips of Irish whiskey to your mug of hot chocolate."

Dickey thought to himself, *What kind of adventure is this?* He drank the hot chocolate. It tasted bittersweet but was pleasant to the smell.

"Say, what kind of hot chocolate is this? I'll take some mor' if you got it," Dickey said.

The mug of hot chocolate was beginning to cool. "Warm it up!" implored Dickey.

Wilson poured another couple-o-nips into Dickey's mug. He took two more nips himself and . . . they began to laugh. Not about anything they had said. Just that the old octopus furnace that looked, well, like an octopus furnace . . . smelled like one too.

"Master Dickey, do you know what klinkers are?" Wilson asked.

Dickey replied, "Nope. But I'll bet they don't taste as good as this nip and hot chocolate."

"You don't drink or eat klinkers," Wilson said.

"You shovel them out of the furnace after the coal has burned up. It's what is left of coal after it has burned and heated the house," he continued.

"How'd they get that name?" Dickey asked.

Wilson replied, "Klinkers come from old Ireland, when after six nips of whiskey and a beer chaser, me pals at the pub would 'klink' our glasses until they broke and fell on the floor."

"And you'd get klinkers," Wilson added.

"Naw that ain't true, really?" Dickey asked.

The coal furnace at the 544 House was affectionately referred to as "The Octopus." Mr. Wilson would smile his Irish smile when the kids talked about the octopus. Photo by Richard Howard.

"Really. In Ireland we would do this on Saturday night after a rousing game of soccer," he said.

Dickey asked, "Let's have one more nip before I have to go to bed. OK, Mr. Wilson? Let's klink our mugs and call it good for tonight."

Wilson and Dickey finished their drinks. "Good night, Mr. Wilson. My stomach is warm, my mouth smiling, and my head is swirling from the nips and klinkers."

Wilson swept the basement floor of the coal dust that had spilled while he was shoveling coal. He took a dustpan and scooped it up, threw it into an ash can, hung his shovelin' gloves on a nail, put on his tweed cap, went up the backstairs, and opened the gray door.

A bitter cold wind penetrated his coat. He began to dread his walk back to the 3rd Street apartment where he lived. Wilson went upstairs and talked to Alice. "I'm done with the furnace and need to collect some dollars for rent and heat at me apartment," he said.

She gave him 18 dollars for the six times he visited the Howard House during the past three weeks.

His apartment was nine blocks from the Howard house. He walked half a block, finished his flask of whiskey, and re-wrapped his old Irish muffler around his neck and over his hat and ears. It began to snow. Wilson's shoes had holes in both soles. Not big ones, but they did let the cold and snow into his feet. By the time he arrived at his apartment, his feet were numb with frostbite and his hands had turned a cold gray.

He wished he were back in Ireland, with his whiskey friends at the tavern, telling stories, sitting by the huge fireplace in the Boarshead Pub. He would tell them, once again for the tenth time, about when he climbed to the summit of the highest mountain in Ireland, Mt. Carrauntoohil.

He was a younger lad and full of energy, but he did not have a lassie to court, so climbing mountains made him happy. The climb took four hours and he arrived at the 3,400-foot summit just before five o'clock.

He went to add a rock to the summit cairn near the cross that had been erected by the local Catholics. He heard footsteps, turned around, and there she was. He dropped the rock.

Emma came up to him, kissed him on the cheek, stood back, and smiled. Her red hair glistened in the afternoon sun. Her cobalt-blue eyes danced with happiness. Wilson knew that this young woman lived in a nearby village. He had seen her at annual Irish festival step dances. Now she was grown-up and as pretty as an Irish rose. He fell in love with her on top of the mountain.

They drank a bottle of wine that she brought with her. He kissed her rosy cheeks made rosier by the cold weather at the top of the summit. They talked about village life, of the

Carrauntoohil in the MacGillycuddy's Reeks, the highest mountain in Ireland, where old Mr. Wilson met Emma, his true-love lassie. Image retrieved online, copyright-free, photographer unknown.

peregrine falcons that nested on the mountain, the beauty of migrating geese, and how wonderful it would be to visit Dublin. Neither one of them had been there.

An hour later, while still on the summit, it began to snow on them. The storm clouds made it seem darker as the evening light began to dim. They began the hike back down to the village. She began to run, and the clouds and snow enveloped her. Wilson told his friends at the pub, "I never saw Emma again but I will always remember her blue eyes, her cheeks, and her smile."

Sean Wilson, cold and tired, and 71 years old, arrived at his apartment on 3rd Street. He walked down the outside stairs to the basement door, opened it, and entered his apartment hovel. The cold air found its way through the cracks and wrapped around Wilson.

He turned on the gas heater in his room for more warmth. He found his prized 16-year aged Jameson® Irish Whiskey on the bookshelf behind the books with Irish titles. Only one drink had been taken from it: that was two years ago on Donore Night, the night of the winter solstice.

He poured two nips into his favorite etched Shamrock glass. He swilled it in his mouth—it had the sweet taste of Ireland. Warmth, true warmth, came back into his body, and he nipped the bottle three more times. He began to hear his friends at the pub, laughing, and eating corned beef, stout pie, and boiled potatoes. It all felt so good he decided to join them. By then the Jameson bottle was empty.

Two days later, the apartment manager became concerned when Wilson had not shoveled snow off the walks. The police found Wilson wrapped in a blanket on his bed. The storm was still raging outside. He had passed over the "Great Divide" with a smile on his face, hugging a whiskey bottle like it was an Irish lassie with blue eyes.

The police informed the Howard family about Mr. Wilson's passing. Alice arranged for him to be buried near other Irish tombstones in the Mountain View Cemetery.

Now the cottonwood trees sway above Mr. Wilson's resting place. Once a year on Donore Night, fresh Irish roses are left at his gravesite, but no one knows who brings them. If one walks through the cemetery on this winter solstice night, and the wind is blowing through the leaves, one can hear an Irish whistle and Celtic harp being played—and can imagine Wilson's whiskey friends huddled around the pub fireplace listening to his story about Emma.

Historic photo of patrons in the John Mulligan Pub, which opened in 1854 on Poolbeg Street in Dublin, Ireland. The Mulligan family first established its pub business in 1782. Pubs like this might have been similar to where old Mr. Wilson would join his pals for a nip of whiskey, a pint of Guinness stout, and plenty of story-telling. Source: Wikipedia references and images, c. 1953.

Cadillac Expeditions

WEEKS AFTER WW II ENDED WITH JAPAN'S surrender, Charles Nordin, Gordon Walker's uncle, inserted the ignition key into his 1931 V-12, British green, convertible Cadillac. The car coughed and bellowed black smoke out the tailpipe. The Portland Storage Company cared for this gem for five years while "Chico" transported U. S. Navy and Army Air Force ordnance from Seattle to Hawaii and then to Guam. The wartime bonus he earned while being the ship's engineer on the Black Tern, a 9,500-ton freighter, enabled him to afford such a luxury car.

There was no place to spend money while on the ship, so during a one-week onshore leave, he stopped at the Park Price Cadillac dealer in Portland, Oregon. He saw the car on the exhibit floor and bought it for cash: four grand, plus some tax and dealer doc fees. It was a small reward to himself for the danger and terror he experienced while on the high seas. Four times, the ship had been damaged by Japanese Zero airplanes and twice by submarine torpedoes. He turned the ignition key again. The engine ignited fuel in the car's twelve cylinders. It sat there idling. His destination: Pocatello, Idaho.

On a sunny Saturday in August, Chico took the wheel and turned east from Portland onto Highway 26. The five-hour journey to Burns took him by Mt. Hood, over the 4,000-foot Bluebox Pass, across the Warm Springs Indian Reservation to Madras, and south into Bend. He stopped in Bend for fuel at a Sinclair gas station. The Cad fuel tanks took 11 gallons each and gave the car a range of 260 miles. Twelve miles per gallon . . . not bad for a two-ton vehicle. He would need this when taking Highway 20 from Bend, across the Alvord Desert to Burns, and on to Ontario, Oregon.

Twenty miles west of Burns, he ran over a jackrabbit. Five more miles put him in the middle of hundreds of jackrabbits trying to flee the oncoming car. A ten-year eruption cycle of jackrabbits had the locals wondering if the critters were a sign from God that they had sinned and should have gone to church instead of the rodeo.

Every ten years the Burns Rodeo fell on August 16th, the day of the Sabbath—and every ten years the rabbit population would explode to where all the haystacks and surrounding fields were vulnerable to being eaten by the furry critters. So, after shooting hundreds of rabbits, they went back to church and prayed for a hard winter. This seemed to work, for they usually got their hard winter. The next spring would blossom. Globemallow and Indian paintbrush flowers would flourish across the desert, but the rabbits were nowhere to be found. Prayer, church, holy blessings, along with .22 caliber rifles seemed to favor the ranchers who lived in the area. The Burns Rodeo for the next nine years would be held on Saturday, August 15th. No rabbit troubles.

Chico called ahead and secured a room at the Burns Sunrise Motel. It was not a Hilton, but rather, a refurbished barracks from WW II. Its only saving grace was that the hot water from the shower tap was plentiful, even though the wooden floors in the bathroom were soft and bouncy. The Burns Water Department had access to a natural hotspring, which enhanced the reputation of the motel. Cowboys and loggers from miles around would come to stay the weekend at the motel just for a hot shower or bath, and of course to pray and receive blessings on the Sabbath, and then, go to the rodeo.

There was something spiritual about Burns that Chico discovered, and so he stayed an extra day just to talk to cowboys and the local folk. Sunday, August 16th, was no epiphany. He attended an early church service, sang sweet songs from the hymnal, and heard the minister talk about the evils of holding rodeos on the Sabbath (but added forgiveness since it only happened once every ten years). Then they all recited the Lord's Prayer.

After church, Chico followed the cowboys to the Oxbow Café for a ranch breakfast of black coffee, two eggs sunny side up, hash browns with ketchup, homemade bread, and choke-cherry jam. They exchanged sea stories for range stories.

Later in the afternoon the rodeo took place at the stocking chutes where cows were rounded up for shipment east on Union Pacific railcars. Nobody broke bones that afternoon, but bruises and backaches won the day. The cowboys didn't complain though. They just picked up their hats if bucked off a horse or wiped their foreheads with neckerchiefs after bull=dogging a calf.

For dinner on Sunday night at the Horseshu Café, Chico ordered a 16-ounce T-bone steak, served with gravy, pepper, mashed potatoes, and a sun-dried cherry cabbage salad. Later, he drank two Maker's Mark whiskeys at the Horseshu Bar. He felt revived recalling his Sunday. It started with the early morning church service, followed by the rodeo, and then superb food and whiskey. It got even better with the late-night hot soak in the tub, lathering up with his own English Bradshaw soap that smelled like heather.

On Monday morning, the cowboys and some of the town folk crowded around to admire Chico's Cadillac. He told them the history of the car and smiled his Scandinavian smile. He then opened the driver's door, started the engine, and moved the floor-mounted stickshift into first gear. He waved good-bye to the good people of Burns and headed east.

Not much eventful happened from Burns to Ontario, Oregon. Just more sagebrush and lots of cows—and more cows. He stopped in Boise to see the famous Union Pacific train depot. He drove down Capitol Boulevard, which ended at the Idaho Capitol building footsteps. The he proceeded to Twin Falls, where he passed through miles of sagebrush desert. Along the way he noticed a series of signs. One sign read:
Petrified Watermelons. Free!
Take one home to your mother=in=law.
Fearless Farris Stinker Stations.
Sure enough, there were hundreds of rock-sized melons along the road.

Another sign read,
> *Nudist Area.*
> *Keep your eyes on the road.*
> *Cowboys please remove your spurs.*
> > *Fearless Farris Stinker Stations*

Just outside of Bliss, Idaho, were four Burma Shave signs.
They read:
> *1. His line was smooth, But not his chin,*
> *2. He took her out, She took him in,*
> *3. To buy some . . .*
> *4. Burma Shave*

Chico looked forward to a ten-day visit with his sister
Alice and her husband, Doc Howard, in Pocatello. As he arrived
in town, he was inspired by a friendly gesture and ordered two
cases of Miller Highlife Beer to be delivered to Doc Howard's
mother, Dr. Minnie Howard. Surely, this would be a pleasant
relief from the hot summer days of August.

Little did he know that she was a strong-standing member
of the Woman's Christian Temperance Union of Idaho. Upon
his arrival at Doc Howard and Alice's house at 544 South 7th,
he learned from Alice what he had done. Both nearly doubled
up laughing, but were quick to make extraordinary efforts to
stop the beer cases from being delivered to Dr. Minnie Howard's
house. They drove the Cadillac across town to Garfield Street,
where Minnie's home was located. They intercepted the delivery
truck just one block from Minnie's home. A potential family
disaster was averted. Alice and Chico drove the Cadillac back
across town to 544 South 7th, and kicked back to enjoy the beer
while recounting the episode to Doc Howard and a few friendly
neighbors. It was a great summer evening for a Miller Highlife.

Chico decided to leave the Cadillac at the Howard home,
since he needed to return to Portland to take on other shipping

assignments, as well as ferrying troops and equipment from overseas back to the States.

The car became a Howard family icon in Pocatello and was the main feature of Pocatello High School and Idaho State College homecoming parades. What regal transportation for the homecoming queen, who sat atop the back seat of the Cadillac convertible as she rode through downtown Pocatello. "Dollar-a-Car" night was a hit on Fridays at the local Sunset Drive-In movies: 12 people sitting in the car, which had three rows of seats. For one buck, they enjoyed Humphrey Bogart and Ingrid Bergman in *Casablanca* or *Gone with the Wind*, starring Vivien Leigh and Clark Gable. There was lots of popcorn and no end of entertainment at the Sunset Drive-In Theater.

Since the Cadillac was a touring car, the Howard family and friends would go on picnics to Scout Mountain. Three people could sit in the front seat, four in the middle seat, and four in the back seat. Scout Mountain is about 11 miles south of Pocatello.

The 1931 V-12 British green Cadillac owned by Chico Nordin in front of the Howard family's 544 South 7th Street home in Pocatello, Idaho. It was loaded with family and friends for Dollar-a-Car night at the Sunset Drive-In Theater. Photo courtesy Idaho State Journal.

There was a favorite family place called Table Rock, on the South Fork of Cherry Creek. Alice prepared the fried chicken, potato salad, celery sticks, black olives and gooseberry pie. When Chico was in town, he would bring his girlfriend, Jo Berryman, and a case of Miller Highlife. Jo was a classical pianist who taught music theory at Idaho State College. Jo and Chico were an unlikely combination: a piano player and a freighter ship's engineer. Nevertheless, good company and superb picnic food made for a delightful Sunday afternoon.

Good rancher friends of Doc Howard and Alice were John and Nida Augustine. They owned the Ybar Ranch five miles northwest of Blackfoot, Idaho. On another Sunday, Rich, Alice, Chico, and Jo toured by Cadillac out to the ranch, a 35-mile journey from the Howard house on South 7th. Alice and Nida rode horses while John and Doc sat in rocking chairs on the porch and talked about the history of the area. Chico and Jo went for long walks or sat in the shade and enjoyed their Miller Highlife.

The four travelers also enjoyed longer trips in the Cadillac. They traveled to Arco and stopped at Pickle's Café for apple pie and coffee, after which they headed to Ketchum. When in Ketchum for a weekend, Doc Howard was contacted by a local doctor who was working on a medical emergency. The patient had a heart murmur that couldn't be controlled. Doc Howard arrived at the hospital where he met the other doctor and the patient: Ernest Hemingway. The two doctors conferred after reading the patient's EKG. Doc Howard prescribed a medicine that he always carried in his doctor's bag. The key compound in the medicine was yarrow extract, from a common plant found in southern Idaho deserts. It's a popular medicinal among the Shoshone-Bannock medicine men. Like aspirin, Doc Howard prescribed two tablets then for Ernest and another two in the morning. By the next afternoon, his heart had reverted to a normal rhythm. Ernest was more than mildly relieved.

The travelers returned home through the Craters of the Moon National Monument. The Monument headquarters is located 17 miles west of Arco, Idaho, and attracts visitors who want to view its moonscape-like terrain. Its cinder cones are 400 feet tall, and there are underground caves, some with permanent ice deep inside; and the surface lava flows cover a 120,000-acre area.

They paid their two bucks to the National Park Service at the entry gate and started their drive through the Monument. Two miles into their drive, one sign, "Bear Skull Cave," attracted their attention. They stopped, got out, and hiked a half-mile over lava flows and clinker ash. It was rough on shoes and could quickly shred soft leather and tennis shoes. The trail led down into a lava tube cave. The cave was 30 feet high but it narrowed to about ten feet high and was 300 feet long.

An older Native American man and woman exiting the cave told them that a bear skull was in the cave, and that they would need "flashlights and some courage." Doc and Chico hiked back to the Cadillac with the couple. A vigorous discussion took place. Doc and Chico found two flashlights in the car. They looked around to continue their discussion, but the Native American couple had vanished. Doc and Chico returned to Alice and Jo, and all began the hike down to the cave entrance.

They switched on the flashlights. About 200 feet into the cave, they came to a side channel. It felt as though a portal had opened in the wall. Wanting to explore this, they walked about 90 feet. By now there was no light from the cave entrance and they lost all perception of space. One of the flashlights dimmed and blinked out. They took several more steps and explored the floor and walls of the side channel with their only remaining flashlight. They saw an alcove in the wall that was four feet from the floor and about six feet deep. To their surprise, there was not one—but two—bear skulls in the alcove. Sitting on top of the skulls was an old piece of paper held in place by a fist-sized rock.

Doc open the folded paper that had aged to a dull yellow. The note read, "The gold is hidden behind these bear skulls. Don't open the box. It's ours. Slim Reeves." Along the bottom of the note, "Goldberg Mining Company, Ogden, Utah" was printed. At first, the travelers discussed what they should do. Doc said, "Maybe we should just turn around and walk back out the cave entrance. This is adventure enough for one day." Alice spoke up with her firm opinion and said, "We need to find out how much gold there is, if any, and then decide what to do." Chico and Jo nodded their heads in agreement with Alice. Doc still had reservations.

Doc and Chico removed the skulls and set them down on the floor of the cave. They were huge skulls—Doc thought they might be grizzly bears. Deep inside the alcove, they found a wooden box about the size of a 20-quart Yeti cooler. It had a thick layer of dust on it. There was no lock, just a hasp and handle holding the box lid closed. They dragged the box out and placed it on the cave floor. Chico turned to Alice and asked, "Do you want to open the lid?" Alice nodded that she did and turned the handle and opened the hasp. The hinges were rusted, so the lid did not open easily. Alice applied more pressure and finally the lid opened. Inside the box was yet another note. It said, "Slim and Jimmy Reeves robbed the Oregon Shortline for this gold. We hid it here. Don't touch it. It's ours. October 1883."

Inside the box were 40 gold ingots wrapped in chamois leather. Each was weight and date stamped: 6 oz. 1883, G M, Idaho. It was apparent to Doc, since he knew Idaho history, that the gold ore had been mined at the Goldberg Mine on the east side of the Pahsimeroi Valley. It was probably brought to Mackay, Idaho, to be stamped and rendered into gold ingots for shipment to Ogden. The Oregon Shortline Railroad, built in 1881 to ship ore from the central Idaho mines, was the spur from Mackay, Idaho, that connected to the mainline that crossed the Arco Desert and terminated at Ogden, Utah. Doc told his traveling companions about the possible origins of the gold.

There was no turning back on this discovery. It was 1956—73 years after Slim had written the cryptic notes. Surely, Slim and Jimmy had passed, and the Goldberg Mining Company had closed. They quickly agreed that this was not Park Service business since it was dated before the Monument was established. The travelers drove through the Park Service gate after closing hours and returned to Pocatello with the box of ingots.

They needed a lawyer to file a quitclaim deed. The deed would publicly proclaim anyone with ownership of the ingots to come forward within 60 days. If no one came forward, the named individuals in the quitclaim would be given legal ownership to the gold ingots. They decided to see Gus Carr, an astute lawyer friend of Doc's in Pocatello.

No one was to know the story about the ingots or where they had been found, which was exactly the pledge made by the group until Gus Carr could file the quitclaim. They would wait for 60 days for a final ruling about ownership.

At the end of the legal waiting period, no legitimate claim had surfaced for the ingots. Oh, there were four claims made, but they turned out to be from beer buddies of Chico's who lived in the Whitman Hotel. They had heard parts of the story from Chico during a lively Saturday night at the Whitman nightclub. The quantity and weight of the ingots was important to support a legitimate claim. The beer buddies all guessed at the numbers and weights, ranging from 100 to 250 ingots and 12 ounces to ten pounds. They all had gold fortune dollars in their eyes. Their claims were dismissed.

Silver dollars were plentiful in the 1950s. When the final decision on the ingots was announced, Gus recommended that the ingots be appraised for their worth and converted to silver dollars. He further advised that the new owners should register the ingots and assume any liability. The travelers took his advice. The Red Hill Gold and Silver Exchange in Pocatello provided the appraisal. The 40 ingots were carefully weighed and tested for purity. Gold with a purity of .999 was worth $20 per ounce. The total value of the ingots was $4,820. It was not a fortune, but it would pay for gas, oil, and new tires for the Cadillac.

The traveling friends were bonded together by this experience. They traveled to Yellowstone for ten days and took Doc and Alice's daughters, Gunda and Frances, with them. Jo played classical music on the grand piano at the Old Faithful Inn and Chico carried both daughters out to see Old Faithful geyser. They saw lots of buffalo and two grizzly bears and crossed paths with the two Native Americans whom they had met at Craters. It was the best of times.

The Cadillac sat in the Howard family's garage for several years, neglected and collecting dust. In a nostalgic moment, Doc and Alice took the car out for an evening drive just to turn the motor over, lube the engine, and check the headlights.

A representative of an antique museum saw them driving in downtown Pocatello. He followed them in his own car and noted the address where the car was stowed. The next day, he approached Doc and Alice with a monetary offer the family couldn't refuse. The exchange was made, and later the check was cashed: it was from the Harrah's National Automobile Museum in Reno, Nevada. Today, the Cadillac is still in that automobile collection.

Dr. Minnie's
Petroglyph Stones

EMAIL: *Wonderful, Rich, what you have done. I love this train of emails and responses from relatives and friends about the possibility of returning the petroglyphs to the Shoshone-Bannock Tribes. Thanks to all who are a part of this train, which I read during the New Year's weekend. I think of Andrea, our recently "discovered" cousin who lives in Colorado, and how deeply touched she was to hear from you about the petroglyphs. It was so good of her during last summer's visit to Pocatello to find our grandparents' home located on land that Dr. Minnie and William homesteaded in 1901. It also touches my heart that Andrea visited our family graves at the Mountain View cemetery south of Idaho State University.*

Lots of love—Fran, Jim, and Buddy the Buddha Cat.

Dr. Martha Simpson retired from the Idaho Museum of Natural and Social History (IMNSH) after 30 years of diligent service. She kept the archaeological and paleontological archives and accessions in research-quality order. Without knowing it, she inspired a string of emails between family members. When I was notified of her retirement, I sent this email to her:

Congratulations on your retirement from the Idaho Museum of Natural and Social History. Hope you have plans to travel and will "look with wonder" to what is over the horizon. You have a standing invitation to visit Elkstone Cabin and to explore some of the sights and sounds in Long Valley. We'll leave the light on for you.

Dr. Simpson, I remember how you granted my request some years ago about looking at some stones stored at the museum. You said, "I will have them on private display for you in an hour. Come by the museum and we will look at them together."

The request was to view seven basalt stones that were saved from my grandmother's house that had been donated to the museum 31 years earlier. Each stone had an ancient petroglyph on it. When I arrived at the museum, I told Dr. Simpson the rest of the story about the stones.

Ninety years ago, Dr. Minnie Howard saved the petroglyph stones from certain destruction. At the time, she was a young medical doctor and Idaho historian living in Pocatello. When she heard about the pending destruction of these stones, she and a skilled stone mason took a horse-drawn wagon out to the site. They searched and found them on a huge boulder. With chisels, they chipped each petroglyph out of the large basalt boulder, wrapped them in light canvas, and placed them in the wagon. The boulder was destined to be dynamited so the existing road could be extended and a bridge could be built over the Portneuf River. The location of the proposed bridge was near the old Zwigart Meat Packing Plant in northwest Pocatello.

The stones were taken to Dr. Minnie's home on South Garfield, located just south of the Pocatello Library. They were embedded in an arched pattern just below the mantel in the face of the family room fireplace. They remained there for 52 years, admired and protected. Upon my grandmother's passing over the "Great Divide," the house was left empty, pending its final destruction. Windows were broken by strangers, birds roosted inside, and the back door was left open. Dust from spring windstorms had settled throughout the house.

The owners of the Bannock Hotel, the biggest and grandest hotel in Pocatello, bought the property. The hotel was located just a block away, and the owners wanted to convert the property into a parking lot. A decision by the hotel owners in 1972, however, changed the fate of the house and the property. The City of Pocatello purchased the property and the house was removed and transported to the country about 12 miles away. It was relocated to the homestead farm that Dr. Minnie and her husband had developed. The house was rebuilt and landscaped for a family who moved in—and they still live there.

Before this happened, late one afternoon in September 1969, a passionate student archaeologist who knew about the stones pushed his way through the back door of the house. It was dark and musty in the house. No electric lights. Only distant memories lingered Drs. Minnie and William Forest Howard's home, where they had raised four sons who also had become doctors. For decades, the stones were witness to many toasty fires inside the home during winter's frigid blizzards.

With a hammer and chisel, flashlight, canvas cloth, and duffel bag, the student chipped out the crumbly cement that held the stones. He carefully wrapped the stones in canvas and put them in the duffel bag and hefted the bag over his shoulder. As he retreated from the fireplace, across the living room to the back door, he shuffled to rub out his footprints. This treasure of ancient stones was stored in a dark room in the basement of another home located across town at 544 South 7th.

A few years later, the stones briefly saw the light of day again, transported to the museum on the back seat of a green Volkswagen. There, they were given a special collections "accession number," and stored in another dark room.

As to the petroglyph symbols embedded in each stone, one can only speculate as to what significance they had to the Native Americans who pecked them. Their imagery is abstract, but based on symbols of a similar size and rendition, and when associated with other similar-aged artifacts, they possibly could be over 2,000 years old. Given their location, it is highly probable they were rendered by heritage members of the Bannock Tribe, a prominent Eastern Idaho Tribe. They developed a horse culture in the 1800s and became independent of the Northern Paiute Tribe. In 1879, they fought the U. S. Army on the Camas Prairie in southern Idaho. It was to be their last encounter. Reluctantly, they surrendered and were removed by the U. S. Army to the Fort Hall Reservation north of Pocatello.

Ten years earlier, a much bigger contingent of Northern Shoshone were engaged in a fierce battle along the Bear River in southeastern Idaho. Two hundred Native Americans were killed. After their surrender, they too were removed to the Fort Hall Reservation. Gradually, over the decades, the Tribes combined to become politically known as the Shoshone-Bannock Tribes. In a 2010 census of the Tribes, 89 people claimed they were of Bannock ancestry, 38 full-blooded. The enrolled membership of Native Americans on the Reservation at that time was 5,310, mostly Shoshone.

So, one can take Dr. Minnie's seven stone petroglyphs and open a "stone book" that has fascinated archaeologists and amateurs alike. Symbols in stone, petroglyphs, have been found in 67 countries on every continent except Antarctica. The oldest are in Iran, which may have been made about 40,000 years ago. Petroglyphs are not to be confused with pictographs, which are images drawn or painted on rock surfaces. The antiquity of both is about the same, based on images found in 300 caves from southern France and northern Spain. Both belong to a wider category of images referred to as parietal art ("cave art") that is found in caves, rock shelters, boulders, and rock cliffs.

Collectively, there may over three million parietal images that comprise this "stone book library." To think about the images that were made prior to a written language is to know something about the evolution of man's collective consciousness as he emerged from the Pleistocene era, leaving behind records of his hunter, scavenger, and gatherer behavioral patterns. Domestication of wild grains, cereals, and animals about 10,000 years ago gave man a different economy—as he had the luxury of more time. Man invented alphabets that became a transition for written histories and collectively formed a different kind of library: one that could be passed on to future generations.

From just seven stones with chiseled images, a modest amount of curiosity—and a sense of preservation, Dr. Minnie saved a part of Bannock County prehistory. Together, each stone is a permanent part of the "stone book library" that is now a part of our written history.

Dr. Minnie Howard standing in front of the fireplace where the petroglyphs were embedded for safekeeping. The glyphs were outlined in white chalk to improve viewing when this photo was taken in 1953. Photo from the Idaho State Historical Society Archives.

In September of 2022, there was a significant update to the story of the stones. I attended an Idaho History Conference in Pocatello. I was most fortunate to meet a woman who was most familiar with the Special Collections Library at Idaho State University for Dr. Minnie. Her name was Kathryn Lopez Luker, a librarian at the Marshall Public Library in Pocatello. At the conference, Kathryn presented an excellent paper about Dr. Minnie. She even dressed in period costume at the conference to look like Dr. Minnie. Later, when I approached her, she told me about more petroglyph stones in the Portneuf River Valley.

Prior to the conference and meeting Kathryn, I wrote to Dr. Charles "Andy" Speer, an anthropologist at Idaho State University. My goal was to work with Andy to have the stones repatriated to the Shoshone-Bannock Tribes. Andy noted that he was already working with the Tribes on over a hundred items in Idaho State University's Museum of Natural History. The stones were included in this effort.

Collection of seven petroglyph stones that were embedded in Dr. Minnie's fireplace mantel. She rescued these stones from possibly being stolen or destroyed. Photo by Richard Howard.

This then gave life to a possible project beyond just repatriation of the stones. Before any public project around the petroglyph stones could be realized, however, we needed Andy Speer to validate that repatriation had some possibility—and the true origin of the stones had to be determined.

Andy had deciphered some handwritten messages on a dated postcard from 1951. There was a brief mention in the postcard about the origins of the stones: near the old municipal golf course in south Pocatello, not from boulders near the Zwigert packing plant in northwestern Pocatello. I told Andy that additionally, Kathryn Luker knew of several other petroglyph stone sites in the southern Pocatello area along the Portneuf River.

The new information prompted a discussion with Andy about creating a proposed short educational documentary, *Dr. Minnie's Petroglyph Stones*. The story would be written by Richard Howard based on same story in his book, *Stormy Waters of the Sagebrush Sea*." Because the film would be more anthropologically and culturally-focused, it could disclose the true physical origin of the stones, with images from the museum collections and information about other petroglyphs and pictographs in the Portneuf River Valley and Pocatello.

The documentary would include interviews with Andy and Tribal members, as well as a larger body of professionals who are vested in the history and culture of the area. Key members of this larger group of Tribal members and academic professionals from the Pocatello area could include: Nolan Brown, Shoshone-Bannock Tribal Representative; Jacqee Alvord, Chair of the Fort Hall Replica Foundation; Kathryn Luker from the Marshall Public Library; Dr. Elizabeth Cartright, Visual Anthropologist at Idaho State University; Ann Merkley, a local independent scholar, artist and historian; Dr. Linda Leeuwirk, Pocatello City Council member; Amber Tews, ISU Museum of Natural History Collections Manager; and Lynn Murdock, Special Collections Manager for the Bannock County Museum.

Above all, the film project would engage Tribal members in the production, to help preserve critical information about their heritage. This educational film would be used in schools to help young people learn about the significance of this heritage.

A formal ceremony of repatriation would be developed with the Tribes to commemorate the return of Dr Minnie's stones, and included in the film as a meaningful conclusion to the story. Another focus would be on the community of individuals and groups who work to preserve cultural heritage for future generations of Tribal and non-tribal students. The proposed film budget for a 45-minute film would be about $51,000, which likely would require grant funding and other contributions from private and professional organizations.

Richard Howard would provide seed money for film costs with a $10,000 donation. The *Dr. Minnie's Stones* documentary would fulfill a lifelong dream of Richard's to make a film based on one of his short stories. This film would also be a meaningful way to honor Dr. Minnie Howard and her brave and forward-looking actions to preserve and protect cultural heritage.

One–liners from AAPA and BCHA

LET'S START THIS BY GOING BACK TO ZAK'S Bistro in Austin, Texas, just one block down from the Hyatt Regency, where the American Association of Physical Anthropologists (AAPA) conference was taking place. I was guided to a table in the enclosed veranda by a friendly host at Zak's. She said the light brew of North Texas Longhorn beer was the best in the state. I ordered one. A friendly waiter delivered it and said he would bet me that I would drink two more glasses before lunch was over. I restrained myself and only drank one glass with lunch. He lost the bet.

Gazing around the veranda with folks at 20 other tables, I looked up at the umbrella over my table. It was placed there for protection from frequent springtime rains and unbearable hot summer temperatures. There was a message printed on the underside of the umbrella that kind of summarizes why people like beer. It read, "Beer speaks, people mumble." I had to agree since I don't hear so well and I really like lager beer. With lunch over, I wandered back to the conference at the Hyatt and to the paper presentations, poster papers, and exhibit booths.

More than 1,100 people had gathered there to talk and tell stories about their science-based discoveries for four days. The conference focused on the paleo-evolution and migrations of *Homo sapiens* and his precursors such as *Paranthropus, Australopithecines, Zinjanthropus, Heidelberg man, Neanderthals*, and *Cro-Magnon* men and women.

My first memorable moment (described briefly, or as I say, as a "one-liner"), was when I shook hands with Dr. Lee Berger, the most famous paleoanthropologist in the world whose work in South Africa has filled-in many of the blanks about the Hominid evolutionary tree. He takes his place alongside Richard Leakey, his father Louis Leakey, and Donald Johanson. I remembered meeting Dr. Berger for the first time in St. Paul, Minnesota, at the first AAPA Conference that I attended in 2012.

Memorable event number two was meeting someone from Idaho at the conference. Kari Prassack was the resident National Park Service paleontologist from the Hagerman Fossil Beds, located west of Twin Falls, Idaho. I was looking forward to talking to her because she had a poster paper about examining bird species found in the Olduvai Gorge in East Africa, where the Leakeys did so much of their work. Birds can tell you a lot about what the vegetative landscape looked like 1.2 million years ago (MYA) at Olduvai.

114

My third "one-liner" was Pauline, an undergraduate from a local Texas university who was sitting on a bench in the hallway outside the conference auditorium. She was distraught and over-whelmed by the meetings. She had a keen interest in anthropology and had taken a few courses in the subject, but she didn't know where to find her niche. I sat with her for a while and tried to cheer her up. Finally, I suggested that she should consider becoming a high school science teacher and volunteer to go on archaeology digs during the summer. It might be a good game plan for her future, where could bring the benefits of her work on summer digs to high school students. It seemed like a way out of her emotional dilemma and she thanked me for it . . . with tears in her eyes.

In the case of number four, I was going to a real Texas BBQ pit across the Congress Avenue Bridge from the Hyatt Hotel. Coopers BBQ is one of the most famous in Austin. It is no black-tie-and-tux place. Whether someone is on a construction job, or is a pinstripe-suited lawyer from District Court, or is someone attending an anthro conference, *everyone* waits in a long line at the rusty brick cavern restaurant. The BBQ pit is huge, which is where patrons choose meats based on how many *pounds* you want. A server with a generous smile carves off slices of meat from your choice of 12 different cuts, puts them on a plate, and delivers them to you. You are pushed down the line by the thrust of men and women behind you making their own selections: pinto beans, red potato salad, coleslaw, BBQ corn on the cob, fresh berry cobbler, and 20 beer selections. I selected a pound of pork ribs, with pinto

beans, potato salad, and a light lager beer from the North Texas
Longhorn Brewery. Well, it was as good as it gets for a BBQ
in Texas.

My fifth memorable event was after dinner when I walked
across the Congress Street Bridge. This bridge is famous for
the bats that roost under the bridge and come flying out in the
evening around 8:00 p.m. on their nightly hunting forays for
insects around the city and along the Colorado River. I watched
in wonder while nearly 90,000 bats flew from beneath the bridge,
and in a threaded formation, disappeared around the river bend.
It took nearly 30 minutes for all the bats to clear the bridge.
In late summer when the young bats join the adults, nearly
600,000 to 800,000 bats can be observed. Austin has the nick-
name "Bat City" because of this natural event.

The next day (and number six), I came down from my hotel
room and rejoined the conference. One of the first booths I visited
was the Texas A&M University Press booth. There were about
a dozen publishing houses with booths in the poster paper and
exhibit hall. Each day, the exhibit hall was open for about four
hours, and representatives from these publishing houses were
there to answer questions and sell books. From Berkeley Press
to Oxford Press, these reps from the U.S. and abroad are there
to showcase their most recent publications.

Well, I stepped into the booth of the Texas A&M Press
and immediately saw a book authored by Drs. Roger Powers and
Dale Guthrie who were professors at the University of Alaska at
Fairbanks. The book, *Dry Creek, a Paleo-Riverine Hunting Camp*, is
a synopsis of work over a 12-year period when they published five
papers about this key site. This was the first site that established
conclusively that people in Alaska 12,000 years ago were hunting
mammoth, bison, and other now extinct animals using Clovis
points. The site is even more significant because the tool assem-
blage is similar to sites found in Siberia. This means that people
who were living in and crossed the "Beringia Land Bridge"
between Siberia and Alaska 12,000 years ago were most likely

using very similar tool assemblages and hunting the large mega-fauna found there.

The collection of papers about this site was largely obscure and not readily available to archaeologists or the public. This book, edited by Dr. Ted Korbel from Texas A&M, who also was a graduate student of Roger Powers, was a real contribution because evidence from the Dry Creek site was then much more widely available to the public. The other story was that it caught the attention of the Texas A&M book rep at the booth. I told him I had gone to high school with Roger Powers. We enjoyed hanging out at the museum what was then Idaho State College (ISC).

We read reports that were stored at the museum about ISC-sponsored digs in Idaho. We got to know B. Robert Butler, a rogue archaeologist who never finished his PhD at the University of Washington. He was of Irish heritage and had an irascible sense of humor. Also at that time was Marie Hopkins, the paleontologist whose Paleo digs at American Falls and Hagerman Valley Horse Quarry brought international attention to southern Idaho.

I revealed another of Roger's interests that I followed: he played the base violin in a jazz band. Frequently, he and I could be found in the evenings at the Whitman Hotel nightclub across from the Union Pacific train station in downtown Pocatello. (We both had false IDs since we weren't yet 21 years old to legally gain entrance to bars and nightclubs.) After high school classes during the day, I would go at night to listen to the jazz band, drink Olympia beer, smoke Lucky Strike cigarettes, and ponder my next date with Michelle and what would happen after high school. It turned out Roger became infatuated with Michelle too, so it tested our friendship. She was of Italian heritage, and so vivacious.

Roger was one of the first high school students in Pocatello to earn college credits while still in high school. He took courses to learn the Russian language and introductory courses in anthropology. His mentor was Dr. Earl Swanson, the director of the Anthropology Department.

Nine years later, I returned to Pocatello to finish my BA degree. Dr. Swanson also was my mentor. By then, I had stopped smoking, but still drank Oly beer. I did my senior thesis work at the Lenore, Idaho, site along the Clearwater River. The Lenore site is significant because after several summers of excavation and lab analysis of its artifacts and soil samples, Dr. Swanson determined a 10,000-year span of human occupation there.

Little did I know at the time that 45 years later I would connect with Roger (on a posthumous basis, for he passed in 2003) and Dr. Dale Guthrie through this book at the AAPA meetings in Austin, Texas. But the story doesn't end there. Two years later, I joined my friend Dr. Wayne Melquist on a journey north to Alaska. Our objective was to travel the 500-mile "Haul Road" that begins in Fairbanks and ends on the shore of the Arctic Ocean.

I arranged to meet Guthrie in downtown Fairbanks at the Thai Basil restaurant. I had spoken with his wife by phone, and she told me to hold the visit with her husband to just an hour since his health was frail. Dale brought a geologist friend of his along and the three of us sat at a table, drank tea, and enjoyed Cha Gio egg rolls and Naam Thok (grilled beef with scallions, mint and fried rice served over cabbage). Four hours later we finished our last cup of tea. We had covered a wide range of topics about the Pleistocene from Siberia to Alaska to Idaho. I never did hear from Guthrie's wife about not adhering to the one-hour limit on our visit.

Then a year later, while at an Idaho Archaeology Society conference in Pocatello, I presented a paper about this chance meeting with Guthrie and his association with Powers. During my presentation, I let it be known that I was donating a copy of the *Dry Creek* book to the Museum of Natural History at Idaho State University. I ended the paper with the story about how, for six months while in high school, Powers and I dated the same ravishing beauty, a precocious Italian girl named Michelle. All of us being teenagers, it ended badly.

My seventh "one-liner" recollection was at another booth in the exhibit hall. There, I met Kristin Berger, Development Director for the Leakey Foundation, which has offices in San Francisco and Nairobi, Kenya, in East Africa. She talked to me about the foundation and how they raise one million dollars a year to sponsor students and professional archaeologists to work in East Africa. After talking to her for about 20 minutes, she gave me a ticket and said, "This will get you into the special Leakey Foundation dinner scheduled for this evening." About 20 people were to attend the dinner to listen to presentations about the foundation. She hoped I could attend and become a donating member to the foundation. What an opportunity! With regrets, however, I turned down the invitation because I had to fly back to Idaho that afternoon. She gave me her business card and told me if I was ever interested in visiting Olduvai Gorge in Kenya, to give her a call. She said would open doors for me so that I could visit ongoing dig sites.

After hearing a dozen paper presentations at the conference, visiting the exhibit hall, and pondering how to make number seven a reality, I sorted through the long line of tables where about 90 auction items were set out for viewing with bid sheets beside each object. The auction items included a bones-and-skull tie, a woman's silk scarf decorated with ancient Hominid teeth samples, a superb close-up photo of a gorilla face, numerous books, and a Masai Warrior Spear from Kenya, Africa. I bid on the spear. Later, after I had left Austin, I learned that I had won the bid. It stands against a bookshelf in my home office along with a bolas from Argentina and an atlatl dart that I hand crafted.

At that point, I needed to sit down in the exhibit hallway on a bench to rest before leaving for the airport. A portable desk was nearby, so I took out my composition book and drafted my "one-liner" impressions of the memorable conference while eating a banana.

It didn't stop there.

I arrived home to lasting memory number eight, when I remembered that another conference was taking place in downtown Boise for the Backcountry Hunters & Anglers (BCHA) organization. They are focused on keeping public lands public in the American West and help create cooperative access agreements with private landowners.

One of the speakers at the meeting was Yvon Chouinard, founder of Patagonia Clothing Company. There was an auction, and an exhibit hall in the Boise Center on the Grove. Over 1,000 people were gathered, waiting to attend the event. I met some friends outside and started talking to them. Then the crowd around us seemed to part—and there was Yvon.

He was about 5' 6" tall and carried a wry grin, topped with a balding head. He was 78 years old and I was 75, so we kind of stood out from most of the people in crowd, who were probably 20 to 40 years younger. I went over and introduced myself and told him I used to buy pitons and chocks from his climbing equipment company in the 1960s (before he turned the company into Patagonia outdoor clothing). He smiled that wry smile, and we talked about climbing and how much I had enjoyed his books and followed his adventures. We also talked fishing and falconry. He once was a falconer too and still has an interest in raptors, and also served on The Peregrine Fund Board of Directors for a few years. I thanked him for helping to underwrite the video production *Damnation,* a superb documentary film about the damage dams on key rivers do to fish, rivers, and their watersheds. He smiled that wry smile again, and then he was gone.

He spoke later that night before this huge audience of men and women at the BCHA conference. He told four amusing stories. The most memorable was about the time he was climbing in Africa, including this one . . . He and some friends wanted to climb to the highest summit of the Mountains of the Moon, which is located just west of Lake Victoria. He told us a little about the history of the area and how in the 1800s there were several expeditions from Europe that set out to find the source of the Nile River. Most notable was the story about the Stanley expedition. While Stanley found Lake Victoria to be the source of the Nile, Yvon explained that there were other smaller rivers flowing into Lake Victoria. The real source of the Nile began at the summit of the Mountains of the Moon. Yvon and his friends climbed to the summit of that mountain, and Yvon took a pee while at the summit. On the way down, the thought crossed Yvon's mind: *For one split second while I was at the summit, I was the source of the Nile.* This story had everyone in the auditorium rolling with laughter.

Rogue Ballet
at Pinkerton's

I T WAS A SHORT TWO-BLOCK WALK FROM my home on South 7th to Gladys Pinkerton's School of Dance. The school took up the entire second floor of her home. She was a commanding woman with a stern look that often broke into a smile when teaching her 40 students. The classical music that was emanating from the open screened windows late one spring afternoon motivated me to stop at Gladys' home in 1961.

Classes were divided into eight students per group, according to ability and age. I was one of eight students who were in her advanced class. In fact, I was the oldest and I didn't belong there. I was a rogue in a child's shop.

With two hours of practice in the morning at the barre by myself and two hours in the late afternoon with the class, I rapidly learned the five positions of ballet and how to plié and count steps, as well as sequences to steps. I was strong in the legs and arms and gifted with superb balance from mountain climbing, playing tennis, and downhill skiing. I would soon claim that I that was a ballet dancer too. Or, well . . . learning ballet or learning to dance in a different kind of social way . . . or just working out to keep toned up.

But then, my introduction to ballet had deeper roots—long before that, when my sisters were taking lessons from Gladys in the early 1950s. They were entranced with a movie titled *The Red Shoes*. These distant memories must have impressed me as a seven year old.

Frances, the younger of my two sisters, was a star dancer at Pinkerton's School of Dance. I mean, *she dressed up like a star,* with a crown full of stars, and she held a wand in her right hand with a star on the tip of the wand. And sister Gunda was not so much a star dancer in the school but a social butterfly who must have been impressed by all the piano scales and runs while she practiced pre-toe-shoe dance steps.

Frances and Gunda lasted a few years at Pinkerton's: Fran longer than Gunda. Some foot issues soon decided that Gunda was not going to be the social butterfly at Pinkerton's. Instead, she became a huge success at the local Lutheran church, playing the organ during Sunday morning sermons. Fran left Pinkerton's because a violin had no strings attached to the social aura at Pinkerton's. She became a top violinist in high school and was a student of Professor Harold Mealy, who taught at Idaho State College in Pocatello.

On to *The Red Shoes* and why this film so impressed me: well, I was all of eight years old. The film was released in 1948 and came to Pocatello in 1950. All of Gladys' students went to see it, with or without parental permission. It was really an adult film and had some very tragic scenes in it, but it was also about ballet and what it takes to become a ballerina princess. At about the same time the film was showing at the Chief Theater in Pocatello, the British Sadler-Wells Ballet Company performed *Swan Lake* at Idaho State College in Frazier Hall.

This immensely boosted both my sisters' interest in ballet. I was left swirling about as to which was the best road to follow: ballet, orchestra, or piano. At the time, I was taking piano lessons from Mrs. Griffith who lived on 12th Street. My best day with Mrs. Griffith was playing the entire piece of *Home on the Range* by memory at the semi-annual piano recital. Mrs. Griffith congratulated me with a big hug. I got a big hug from my mom, Alice, too. That was my last contact with Mrs. Griffith. I rode off into the sunset on my bicycle and never looked back.

But back to ballet and to the film, *The Red Shoes*. The film was based on a story by Hans Christian Anderson. The script writers of the film used the technique of creating a story within a story. Victoria Page (played by Moira Shearer) was a brilliant young ballerina who was caught in a love triangle between the creator of *The Red Shoes* ballet and the chief choreographer of the ballet company. The creator refused to let the ballet be performed anywhere, out of his frustration and love for Victoria, who had shown a preference for the choreographer.

While in Monte Carlo on the French Rivera with the ballet company, Victoria was visited by both lovers. She became confused and in desperation ram to the train station where one of her lovers was waiting to board an outgoing train. When the train started moving, she tripped on the red shoes she was wearing and fell in front of the train. Tragically, she was killed. The creator of *The Red Shoes* was distraught, but to honor her, he allowed it to be performed the very night she died. The ballet was performed with a spotlight on, aimed at the empty space where Victoria would have been the star ballerina.

123

The film made a frightful impression on me because of the train scene. I had nightmares about this event for months after my sisters told me about what happened in the film. I wasn't allowed to see the show at the time it played in Pocatello. So just hearing about it from my sisters sent my imagination soaring about how horrible it was. I became convinced that it happened at the Pocatello (not Monte Carlo) train station. I imagined a yellow Union Pacific streamliner coming into the station. The *Red Shoes* ballerina tripped off the station platform into the path of the train and had her legs sliced off. This was my first contact with ballet.

It would be years later when I finally sorted it all out. I saw *The Red Shoes* in San Francisco. All the tales about the movie that my sisters had told me—and all the nightmares—came back in a rush. I was distraught for a week about this tragedy. But, after all, it was only a movie.

Which brings me back to that spring day in 1961, when I heard classical music coming from the open windows of Gladys' School of Dance. This was a positive—unlike *The Red Shoes*. I walked across the street and listened. I heard a voice counting cadence for young dancers who were doing barre work and sometimes giggling to a run of piano music scales.

It compelled me to knock on the door and ask if I could watch. Gladys didn't seem to mind and invited me upstairs to watch. The second floor had an oak hardwood floor, open screened windows, a piano in one corner, a full mirror glass wall on one side, and around the other three sides of the room were ballet barres arranged at different heights for shorter and taller dancers. The dance wizard, if there is one, took her magic wand with a star at the tip and touched my head with dance dust. Within 20 minutes of watching young dancers do pliés and pirouettes, I was hooked.

I talked to Gladys about joining a class and she invited me to attend a class for older students. She told me to be there on Thursday at 4:30 p.m. Well, I quickly decided I needed some attire to make this commitment. I went to a clothing store and found out that. although they had tutus and ballet slippers for young girls, there were no stretch pants or slippers my size. I showed up Thursday in my black long underwear that I used for skiing and some black socks for my slippers. The other students in the class, five girls and two boys, all about three to five years younger than me, thought I was pretty funny.

Gladys was influenced by Harold Christensen, the teacher, choreographer, co-founder (with his brothers) of the Utah Civic Ballet, and also the founder of the San Francisco Ballet. As Alice, my mom, would say, "If she didn't study with him, she could have."

In six months, I had progressed from being a total novice to a star student. That fall, Gladys had ambitions of having her school perform the ballet *Coppélia*. She kept encouraging me to learn more advanced steps during those six months. The gleam in her eye shone brightly as I learned step sequences that integrated with other advanced students in her class. In late September, she brought us together and announced our roles in *Coppélia*.

Coppélia is a comic ballet originally choreographed by Arthur Saint-Leon with music by Leo Delibes. The narrative is about a life-sized dancing doll, made by Dr. Coppelius. Franz, a young man in town, becomes infatuated with the doll whose name is Coppélia. His real girlfriend, Swanhilda, becomes jealous. Then the story becomes very mixed up. In the end, Franz and Swanhilda are married and the entire village celebrates by dancing.

I became one of the star dancers in Gladys' version of *Coppélia,* along with Nicole and Nick, and two younger dancers, Kristi and Julie. We practiced hard. I became adept at catching the two younger dancers when they would leap for my braced legs set in a demi-plié position. I would catch them by their outstretched arms—more of a tumbling maneuver than a *jeté en l'air*. It was the grand finale of *Coppélia,* and we did it well.

The first performance took place in the old Pocatello High School Auditorium. I don't know how many people showed up but it seemed like a lot of people filled half the seats in the first tier of the auditorium. The music was played on 45 rpm records through the auditorium sound system. Somehow, due to Gladys' genius for choreographing little kids, bigger kids, and one rogue dancer from up the block, we put on a one-hour performance that seemed like, well . . . like a ballet.

From October through December, Gladys found places to perform our dance. With braced legs, I caught Kristi and Julie in their jeté en l'air during a dozen performances. Nicole and Nick and their dances were the foundation of the ballet. They performed wonderfully under all kinds of stage conditions. We performed at schools, at churches, and at two assisted living centers.

This set the foundation for me to move on to the Utah Civic Ballet Company. The company was founded by William Christensen and his brother, Harold Christensen. It later became known as Ballet West. In earlier years, Harold had founded the San Francisco Ballet. They knew ballet from top to bottom.

The brothers knew Gladys and sometimes accepted her more promising students as temporary dancers in ballets. They did this to see what trained talent was coming out of her school in southern Idaho. There was synchrony—and a future link for me between the brothers and Gladys.

While it was not my intention to move to Salt Lake City, I did like to commute from Pocatello to SLC for two reasons: fabulous powder skiing at Alta and Brighton. The ballet classes for apprentices were held in the evening. I was discovered to have some skill at learning the steps and keeping up with barre work, so I was invited to audition for a very minor role in *The Nutcracker* as one of the bigger elves.

The Nutcracker is a two-act ballet choreographed by Marius Petipa with the music by Peter Tchaikovsky. The story opens on Christmas Eve, when a big family and their friends have gathered to celebrate the festive occasion by decorating a Christmas tree. A local magician named Drosselmeyer joins the party and brings four life-like dolls to the party. The dolls dance to the delight of all, especially the children. He puts the dolls away and then brings out a special doll, the Nutcracker. A young woman at the party named Clara falls in love with the Nutcracker.

With the clock striking midnight, the magic of Christmas Eve takes form—and the Christmas tree begins to grow to great heights. The Nutcracker turns into a handsome prince. It begins to snow outside in the forest. There is a battle between warrior mice and the prince's army. Ultimately, the prince wins the battle and asks Clara if she will marry him. She consents. The prince becomes a king and he makes Clara a very happy queen.

I kept up on my barre work and dance practice, inspired by this invitation. They put me in this big elf role and I came on stage with about a dozen other dancers. This was the scene when in the ballet story, the Christmas tree got bigger and rose higher and higher. The little kids in the audience were just dazzled by this. All this work in front of mirrors and at the barre gave me two minutes on stage for six performances.

To dance at the barre with other men and women was reassuring, and my progress was being made by leaps and bounds. These people had real aspirations. They were dedicated to the toes of grace and performed in front of live audiences, accompanied by real orchestras. They made it work while keeping second jobs off stage. Only the soloists of the ballet were paid full time to dance.

Two years passed and I still had one toe in Pocatello and the other in SLC. One day, while talking with Bill Christensen, he mentioned to a few of us about stepping it up a notch to see if there was a future in San Francisco. I said to him, "Come on, I'm not that good. I should have started dance when I was eight—not eighteen."

Well, as luck and destiny would have it, I took a sabbatical from dance in the fall of 1963. I went to New York, first by freight train to Minneapolis and then by bus and car to the Bronx shipping yards. There I found a freighter, the "Black Tern" of Black Diamond Shipping Lines. I searched for the captain and found out the entire officer's crew was Norwegian. The yeoman's crew were from ethnic backgrounds of all sorts, some of which I'd never heard of before, like Caribbeans, Seychelles, and Corsicans. The captain looked like a twin of Nikita Khrushchev (Soviet State Dictator in the 1960s), including the mole on his left cheek. He took me on as an apprentice seaman. He put me to work with two other crew members, pounding paint off the gunnels and upper decks with big heavy ball pein hammers. I couldn't hear much by the end of the day. The job assignment improved when we started painting the area we had hammered.

We encountered one North Atlantic storm that lasted about six hours. I liked to ride the waves by standing at the bow of the ship during the storm. From there, I could see how the bow plowed into seven-foot waves, and the ship would ride up and down them like a bobbing cork. The Captain saw me and sent someone out to tell me to get back inside the ship. An hour later, tons of blue-white sea water washed over the bow as the boat slid through waves up to 12-feet high.

We arrived in Europe via Antwerp, a seaport in Belgium. I spent four glorious months wandering through ten countries. I attended ballets and symphonies at concert halls and churches; visited museums, climbed mountains, and went wine-ing and beer-ing while living in youth hostels. My BMW motorcycle got me from town to town. When it broke down I traveled by train until a Swiss mechanic repaired it. When I was finished with the European tour, I sold the motorcycle in Copenhagen, Denmark, to another vagabond.

Then it was home again via the passenger-freighter ship "Droning Alexandria." Five months later, it sank in a violent North Atlantic storm.

My legs took up the initiative to go to San Francisco and regain my skills in plié, pas de deux, and floor barre work. I had a letter from William Christensen that was addressed to his brother Harold, the director of the San Francisco Ballet. It was short and to the point: "Give this dancer two months in the apprentice program." He could have added, "Then kick him out." That was the tone of the letter.

I found a job working as a mail clerk and assistant copy-writer for the Richard Meltzer Ad Agency on Geary Street. The pay supported my room rent and food for three of the four weeks during the month. I liked the job, and the people who worked there were real pros in advertising.

Meltzer Ad Agency had accounts from companies all around the Bay Area and some in Denver, Chicago, and New York. It also had a most distinguished account with Carol Doda, a famous, well-endowed strip dancer who performed at the Condor Night Club in North Beach."

I soon found my pace in the city. I was up in the early morning hours to attend Buddhist meditation, then I took the bus to the ad agency. There, I worked an eight-hour shift and some overtime hours to make up for the other week of rent and food for the month. I attended three hours of dance school

in the evening four days a week, and four hours on Saturday.
Some of the dancers who I knew from Salt Lake City were also
in the apprentice program. They were showing promise of being
moved up to the Corps de Ballet of the San Francisco Ballet
(SFB). I set that as my goal too.

Two ballets that drew big audiences were performed by
the company. The performances kept the company financially
stable, but it still needed a lot of wealthy donors to maintain its
stature in the world of ballet. The *Nutcracker* was a favorite for
the Bay Area citizens during the Christmas holidays. The other
was a springtime favorite, *Swan Lake*. Both ballets drew from the
apprentice dancers to enhance the magnitude of the ballets and
to highlight the demi-soloists and soloists.

After two months, I had survived the initial scrutiny by
the SFB instructors. I enjoyed the rush of dancing while being
in the best physical and mental shape I had ever experienced.
It was just a natural high-high-high to enter through the
swinging doors and hear running scales of music as dancers
practiced and instructors counted cadence for step routines
and barre work. I left those practices in a shower of sweat—
exhausted, but ready to come back the next day and do it
all over again.

Harold took some notice and said to me, "Audition for
a place in the line of male dancers for *Swan Lake*." I took the
challenge, and placed as an alternate for the other line dancers.
I wasn't on stage but I was dancing the same steps, just waiting
for a chance.

*Swan Lake is a Russian ballet. The music was composed by
Peter Tchaikovsky and it was originally choreographed by Julius
Reisinger. The narrative was borrowed from a mixture of Russian
folk tales. Originally a two-act ballet, it grew into a four-act play
with many alternate endings. It tells the story of Odette, a princess
who was turned into a swan by an evil sorcerer's curse. A prince finds*

her and becomes involved in a very dark, complex, and convoluted plot. Ultimately, the prince finds the light of day again and can break the curse. Odette the swan is turned into a princess again and the prince marries her.

Swan Lake gave me high hopes of traveling that fork in the road for another year to see what was possible. I got the nod to dance in four *Swan Lake* performances. One of the better line dancers had a death in the family, and then he fell ill and never came back again. The nod was extended to eight performances. This put me on stage for three minutes in front of a live audience with a live orchestra. It was like a mountain climber's satisfaction upon reaching the summit of Mt. Rainer in Washington: breathless, but living totally in the present.

Then, one night after practice, Harold's assistant, Neil Satterfield, came up to me, and said, "We like what you're doing for us but . . . you will never be a Rudy Nureyev or a Mike Baryshnikov." *I knew what was coming . . .* "We've got to let you go to let other younger dancers make it here."

I really liked the candid part about not being another Nureyev. He was one of the ballet icons of the day. He had two attributes that I did not have: a shorter trunk and longer legs. Plus, he could jump, or rather hit, a jeté en l'air better than anyone in the business. There was no way I was going to change or compensate for that.

So, sadly, I took my ballet slippers off; got my gear out of the locker; and for the last time, listened to the piano scales tapping cadence and the soft breath of dancers as they worked at the barre. Then I walked out the swinging doors.

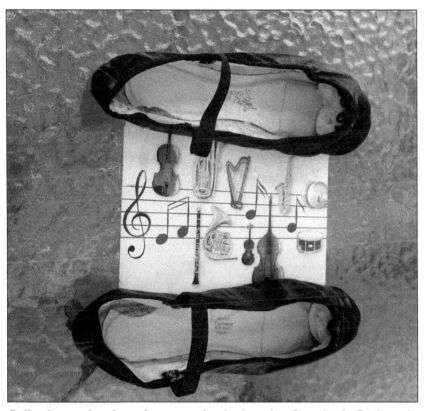

Ballet slippers that the author wore when he danced in Coppélia for Pinkerton's Ballet Studio. The dance studio was located at 343 South 7th St. in Pocatello, Idaho. Photo by Richard Howard.

Once Under
the Cockatiels

OUTSIDE THE WINDOW OF ROSEANNA'S Restaurant, the March 21st sun set between the cleavage of two massive rock pillars 400 yards off the coast. It marked the spring equinox, exclusive to the Oceanside village west of Tillamook, Oregon. Evening emerged from the sea. The moon rose just over Cape Lookout ridge. Later it became a full, round globe just before disappearing behind storm clouds.

Cecile Wettach and Gordon Walker walked through the door of Roseanna's on that Sunday evening, and to their surprise only three tables were occupied. The waitress seated them at a table beside the middle picture window. Roseanna's menu had a variety of seafood: creamed pastas mixed with shrimp and butter, razor clams, Dungeness crab, silver and king salmon, and the *pièce de résistance*—12 different dessert selections.

Through the window, they saw a green patch of grass, a round pot full of lavender phlox, and an unfinished raised garden box. The window framed the ocean beach and rock pillars. They watched with wonder as the high-tide waves broke onto the shore in a frolic of white noise.

Their eyes were drawn to the rock pillars. They witnessed the sun setting into the rock cleavage. How good it was that they could spend an intimate evening at such a beautiful place surrounded by a composition of natural rhythms.

Cecile and Gordon first met in 2010 in Zug, Switzerland, while working on the biomedical causes of tinnitus (commonly described as persistent ringing in the ears). The Auras Company was well funded to explore a promising new genetic approach to this condition that affects 16 million people in North America and millions more throughout the world. They each had two-year contracts to fulfill.

Their research resulted in the first known cure for tinnitus. The procedures passed with an 85% efficacy rate in all three trial

phases of the Federal Drug Administration (FDA) review.
This success launched their professional status into high gear,
but with different trajectories. Cecile went to Texas A&M
Medical Research Center. Gordon was hired by the Pfizer
Company in New York City to refine the tinnitus cure under
a co-contract with the Auras Company. The cure made millions
of dollars for both companies. Tinnitus patients were the real
beneficiaries of this, for they were able to enjoy calm, silence,
and a sense of tranquility for the first time in their lives.

Gordon and Cecile's careers brought them together again
in Portland, Oregon, six years later at an international conference.
Within hours of seeing each other again, they realized all their
personal feelings for each other had been set aside while working
in Switzerland.

Love in Portland overwhelmed them. Now they had a long
weekend after the conference just to themselves. Cecile decided
on a town along the Oregon coast called Netarts. They settled
into a rental cottage located one block from the ocean's edge.
It was late in the afternoon.

"Gordon, years ago when my family vacationed here,
my mother and dad would leave us at the motel and go to
Oceanside. It's a village just two miles up the coast. There,
they would enjoy an evening at Roseanna's. It was a great
restaurant known for its seafood, views of the coast, and
pictures on the walls," Cecile said.

"Let's go." Gordon said. "I'm starved for seafood and gin.
They do serve gin don't they?"

Cecile said, "I don't know, but let's go."

They found Roseanna's was still open. It was a slow day for
the cook and waitress but a good day for Cecile and Gordon.
They ordered an appetizer of fresh steamed oysters. Gordon
ordered the shrimp pasta entrée and Cecile, the salmon almond-
ine. No gin for Gordon, but they did pour superb local Oregon
Cabs, Syrahs, and Merlots.

After dinner, Gordon and Cecile looked at the pictures on the walls. They displayed a spectrum of the Oregon coast: storm waves, light houses, ship wrecks, and fishing boats. There also was a photo of Three Arch Rocks National Wildlife Refuge, the three massive islands of basalt rock located just offshore. It depicted the same scene that Cecile and Gordon had just witnessed: the sun setting between the pillars outside Roseanna's Restaurant.

Hanging on the south wall of the restaurant, however, was a large, almost obscure picture, framed in Eucalyptus wood. It was of two cockatiels. It was quite out of context and piqued their curiosity.

Gordon and Cecile wanted to make this a special evening, and so they asked to be introduced to the restaurant owner of the restaurant. Jackson, the chef, came out from the kitchen. Wearing a starched white chef's hat and an immaculate white apron, he talked to them about Roseanna. She lived in a cottage just two blocks up the street from the café.

After dinner, Jackson, who was Roseanna's son, took them up the street and knocked on the cottage door. "She is 83 years old and likes to tell stories," he said.

Sunset at Three Arches Rocks, taken from the west window of Roseanna's Café. Beyond the horizon is Australia where Roseanna saw her first cockatiel. Photo by Richard Howard.

The door opened. They were greeted by a warm smile from Roseanna, who invited Gordon and Cecile into her home and to sit at the table. She disappeared into the kitchen momentarily and came out again carrying cups and a pot of steaming hot green tea wrapped in an Australian wool tea cozy.

After short introductions all around, Jackson said, "I've got to get back to the restaurant and close up. Have a great evening with the Queen of Oceanside."

Gordon asked Roseanna, "Please tell us the story about the picture on the wall in your restaurant of the two cockatiels. It seems out of place with the others."

Roseanna looked out the window and said, "The short story is that I purchased the restaurant when I was 29 years old. The picture came later. There is nothing else to tell. Except . . . when I was 18, my father and I lived in Tillamook, nine miles east of here. My mother died when I was a child. It made me independent, aloof, and self-reliant. Father encouraged me to go to work at the Tillamook cheese factory to earn a cache of money and then travel."

Roseanna took a sip of tea and continued, "I worked at the cheese factory for six months. Making cheese and ice cream didn't suit me as a life-long vocation. It would be too much work and too little contact with people. I then applied for a position to be the manager of a local restaurant, The Pelican. This suited me just fine for two years."

"When did this happen?" asked Cecile.

"This chapter in my life unfolded during the Korean War in the early 1950s," Roseanna said.

"Taking my father's advice a step beyond his bounds, I quit The Pelican when I heard about a freighter that was bound for Australia, soon to depart from Portland. The jobs that were open included the head chef on the 9,000-ton freighter registered as the "Black Tern," owned by the Black Diamond Company. There was no hesitation about hiring a woman since all the qualified men were still committed to the war effort," Roseanna said.

She recalled, "We left Portland in March. The boat made ports-of-call in Hawaii, the Marquesas Islands, Easter Island, Bali, and Tahiti. The ocean weather was kind to us. We encountered no storms—just a huge expanse of water designated on the navigation charts as the South Pacific. The crew was good to me. I returned their respect by preparing the best menu entrées from The Pelican. Finally, after five weeks of sailing the South Pacific, the Black Tern arrived at Brisbane, Australia. I lived on the ship while it was docked in Brisbane. The ship was refueled and reloaded with freight. In a few days, it would leave for other ports in Asia."

Roseanna said she had tumbled her thoughts, wondering, *"Do I visit another port, fulfill my voyage, and return to Portland with the Black Tern, or stay in Brisbane?* I set my destiny by saying goodbye to Captain Jack of the Black Tern and found a hotel in Brisbane."

Roseanna took another sip of tea, and continued. "Daily, I would buy a *Brisbane Times* newspaper and scour the want-ads section for jobs. An ad for room and board in trade for work at a horse ranch 14 miles outside of Brisbane caught my interest."

She met the owner of the ranch, a Russell Crowe type of guy named Brendan Glasgow, who was 15 years older than she was. He hired her reluctantly and assigned her to sweep the horse stalls, clean the house, do laundry, and shop for groceries in Brisbane. At the ranch house, she was given a modest room downstairs. Brendan lived upstairs.

His wife had been killed during the Korean War, when as a nurse for the Australian Operations Command, she was captured and brutally mistreated by the North Koreans. She died of starvation and exposure in a POW camp during the harshest winter they had experienced there in 60 years. Brendan had tried to rescue her, with help from some of his mates with the Australian Special Forces. They were shot up badly, however, and forced to retreat before they could rescue her and 11 other Australians who had been captured.

Now, he only lived to breed stallions to mares and train horses for the Australian racing circuits. His other life was drinking whiskey and hanging out with his mates. The death of his wife settled his desire for women. They were kept at a distance. Until he met Roseanna, conversing with women was not on his menu.

Within weeks, she became a trusted friend and seemed to understand the grief he felt about the life that stopped after his wife was killed.

Brendan allowed Roseanna to exercise the horses. Within three months, Roseanna took to horses and racing like she had been born into the tradition. She did things that surprised even Brendan. She was a natural jockey, a rare woman who moved with ease among this closed society of men, horses, and whiskey.

Within six months she jockeyed her first race. Riding on "Handsome Willy," a strong black stallion, she won the 70-pound purse and an extra 40 pounds from her side bet at the window. Thus began her nine-year odyssey of training horses and working on Brendan's horse ranch.

One April evening, she was on the back veranda of the ranch house, feeding the cockatiels. It was her own personal way to display affection, as she had developed a tough emotional shell when approached by men who seemed attracted to her. But this evening was different. Brendan, who by now had known Roseanna for eight years, came around the corner, whiskey in hand. He helped her feed the 20-or-so cockatiels. He was feeling misty. She wanted to be touched.

She turned to get another handful of seed. It disappeared between her fingers as Brendan embraced and kissed her. They made passionate love on the veranda couch, then moved inside after it started to rain. During flashes of lightning, intense rain, and gusts of wind, they made more passionate love. It was a rare night for both of them. Pent-up emotions and desires brought them together—as though they were tasting water for the first time in months after crossing the Nullarbor Plain. Their drought was over.

They lived the next four days in tune with their emotional rhythms. This was happiness. It was a resurrection for Brendan and an immersion for Roseanna.

They enjoyed their blissful moments like a stallion covering his mare. After four days of loving and its afterglow, Brendan had to leave for Melbourne. He needed to secure lucrative horse training contracts from a mining magnate and two ranch owners. These would underwrite his ranch for three years and bring in more accolades about the quality of his horses.

While en route, the Melbourne Pas-Freight Airlines DC-3 plane crashed. A crack in one of the aluminum propellers caused it to disintegrate, exploding one of the twin engines. The plane fell almost vertically to the ground from 2,600 feet. The impact caused the gas tanks to rupture and the plane was engulfed in an explosion of orange flame. Everyone on the plane was incinerated.

"It took two days for them to give me the news about Brendan," Roseanna said. "I was devastated about the tragedy. My life and love were gone, vanished into flames and ash. I channeled my grief into organizing a memorial for Brendan and the other passengers."

The memorial was held at the crash location. First, a large trench was dug, and the ashes that remained at the site were shoveled into the trench. Flower wreaths were laid on the burial site. Folk songs about the Outback and the national anthem were sung. Then personal memories were shared with those who attended the sad, solemn ceremony.

"We drank a lot of Sullivan's Cove whiskey that afternoon," Rosanna recalled.

Unnoticed by the memorial attendees, a lone Aborigine was perched on a nearby hill standing on one leg, swinging a didgeridoo. He was a medicine man who had helped Brendan vanquish numerous diseases of the heart, mind, and body. He had foretold to Brendan that a woman from a ship would steal his heart after losing his wife in the war. Roseanna fulfilled this vision.

139

Coincidently, just after the last song was sung, a flock of cockatiels flew into a nearby eucalyptus tree. It brought more tears to Roseanna's cheeks, as she remembered that first evening with Brendan on the veranda.

Within a month, after the estate was settled, Roseanna left Australia to return to Tillamook, Oregon. This time she flew into Seattle and took the bus to Portland. She hitchhiked back to Tillamook. It had been nearly nine years to the day since she had left.

"While in Tillamook, I found I needed the seacoast to heal my emotional wounds," Roseanna said. "I would cry during the setting sun and the morning sunrise. Never could I find relief, but I thought about my aunt's vacant cottage in Oceanside and I hired an oyster farmer to take me there. He dropped me off on Seaside Street in Oceanside and then turned around to drive south to Cape Lookout Bay to his oyster harvest."

Roseanna took up residence at her aunt's place. Within a week, she found that a rundown café was for sale on Pacific Avenue in Oceanside. With her savings from working in Australia, she bought the place and renamed it "Roseanna's." It took a month to refurbish, develop a menu, and order seafood from the oyster farmer.

She hired two assistants, a chef, and a waitress, and then opened her doors for business. It was an instant success. Due to the great food, service, and location, Roseanna's reputation soared. Patrons lined up during weekends for lunch and dinner. She didn't take reservations. If you wanted to be served at Roseanna's you just showed up—and waited in line.

On Sunday, April 24th, as the sun was setting, Roseanna noticed the sun shining through the west windows of her restaurant. The windows faced the seacoast and Three Arch Rocks Wildlife Refuge. The sun set between the huge pillars of rock on the middle island. It startled her, and she became overwhelmed with emotion thinking about her past year.

The next day, a three-foot cardboard tube arrived in the mail. It was from Brendan's brother who lived in Darwin, Australia. She left it unopened until Monday, when the restaurant would be closed for "her" weekend.

She opened the tube. In it was a note from Brendan dated two days before he died in the plane crash. *My dearest . . . These are the best of times . . . Love, Brendan.* Another note was included from Garth, Brendan's brother. He told Roseanna that he had found the picture and the note inside the tube while moving Brendan's things out of the house before he sold the horse ranch. The watercolor was a full three feet long and two feet wide— of two cockatiels.

Roseanna looked outside of the restaurant window just as the sun disappeared between the pillars. It shone briefly on the south wall of the restaurant. Tears rolled down Roseanna's cheeks. She hung the picture on the wall where the sun cast an evening glow. She gathered flowers from the vases that were in the center of each table of the restaurant and made a wreath. She then left the restaurant and hiked along the shoreline to Netarts Bay.

The changing tide at the bay was flowing out to meet the offshore breakers. She set the wreath in the water and watched it float into the distance where it disappeared in the frolic of foam and waves. She sensed Brendan's spirit was out there just offshore and felt her tummy and the movement inside. She was five months pregnant with his child.

The spring moon rose over Cape Lookout ridge and cast its white-yellow light on the sandy shoreline. There was synchrony even in the tragedy of Brendan's death. It became her happiness, knowing that he would be with her through their son.

"My dears, it all happened 53 years ago, and now I'm so tired," Roseanna said.

Gordon and Cecile were astonished at how quickly the time had passed. Roseanna had finished her story about the cockatiel picture. It was 12:15 a.m. Now they found themselves looking at the spring moon outside the cottage window, two streets uphill from the restaurant.

Roseanna had fallen asleep.

Roseanna's Café. Photo by Richard Howard.

III: Summits

"Lost River Range Sunset" by Rachel Teannalach

Seven Summits
Meditation

GORDON ROLLED OUT HIS BLUE YOGA MAT, then took a set of yoga blocks out of a Trader Joe's bag and placed them beside the mat. It was going to be a good Sunday morning practice with Darcy Midnight, his yoga guide at Sage Studios in downtown Boise. He had already attended eight sessions with her as his teacher.

His early morning practice included Darcy and nine other men and women. It began in silence, standing, with three deep-drawn breaths through the nose and exhales through the mouth, with hands pressed together at sternum level. She then took her class through a routine of poses: Tree, Forward Fold, Downward Dog, and Standing Leg, and then repeated to include Warrior poses I and II. This prepared them for Lotus, Shoulder Rotations, Moon, Pyramid, Cobbler's, Rishi Twist, and Sage Twist. The 72-minute routine included other challenging poses, such as Standing Tree left leg, Standing Tree right leg, cleansing breath moments, and a Lotus relaxation pose while sitting with buttocks on two yoga blocks. It ended with a sitting meditation, two minutes of "Om" and "Zu," and silence for five more minutes.

Extraordinary focus was created with her routines. She had her own way of half-smiling after the completion of each pose, and projected a sweetness of sound in her inhaling and exhaling of cleansing breaths. Her bright blue eyes sparkled like waves on a mountain lake. *She was genuine*, Gordon thought. *She was authentic in every way.*

These thoughts caused him to reflect on his partnership with yoga. After retiring from the CIA, he needed to become recentered. A friend suggested yoga.

He began by setting a goal to visit ten of the 20 or so yoga studios in the Treasure Valley. This would give him exposure to teachers who approached yoga with different methods—different threads from the Far East.

After five years of yoga practice, how many times had Gordon sat on a yoga mat? More than 200? More than 400? The count didn't matter. He met his objective to visit ten studios. Sage Yoga was his first, followed by Yoga Tree, Yoga for Wellness, YMCA Yoga, Hollywood Market, True North, MUUV, Boise Hot, Dash, and River Time. Most practices lasted for an hour, yet some were only 20 minutes, and others, 40.

He had also developed his own routines and method of obtaining meditative focus. It wasn't Zen. It wasn't Tibetan Buddha or Indian Buddha practice. But it did have a central way of taking him into the immediate present through subtle breathing, followed by Hatha Yoga postures and movements.

Gordon followed the light. It became his "Seven Summits Meditation."

&

Begin the meditation with three deep breaths, hands placed together over the heart in a Lotus posture. Intone *Ohm* three times with eyes closed. Hands folded on lap and relaxed.

1. Next, visualize oneself on the summit of Mt. Borah, Idaho, looking east while the sun is rising. Visualize one of the four seasons. Prefer spring. Take five deep breaths . . . eyes closed.

2. Next, visualize oneself on the summit of Mt. Rainier, Washington, looking east while the sun is rising. Repeat five deep breaths.

3. Next, visualize oneself on the summit of Denali in Alaska, looking east while the sun is rising. Repeat five deep breaths.

4. Next, visualize oneself on the summit of Mt. Fitz Roy, (Cerro Chaltén), in Argentina, South America, looking east. Repeat five deep breaths.

5. Next, visualize oneself on the summit of Kilimanjaro, Tanzania, Africa, looking east. Repeat five deep breaths.

6. Next, visualize oneself on the summit of K2 in northern Pakistan looking east. Repeat five deep breaths.

7. Next, visualize oneself on the summit of Mt. Everest on the Nepal/Tibet border, looking east. Repeat five deep breaths.

8. Open eyes. Thank oneself for meditating on seven chakras (seven power centers of the body) in concert with seven mountain summits.

In 38 deep breaths, one has completed the Seven Summits Meditation and dwelled for a few moments on summits from around the world. This opens the mind to a sustained "peak experience" for the day.

&

Gordon began the meditation by visualizing a granite stone perched on a boulder. He became the stone. A picture then emerged of himself sitting in the Lotus position on top of the first of seven summits.

Mt. Borah, Idaho's highest peak at 12,662 feet, has a broad summit, enough area for an entire yoga class to share. Gordon noted that it was early spring, possibly mid-April, on the summit. Hard, compact snow, three-feet-deep, lay all around the summit and down the three main ridges. The wind was blowing about 15 mph. While the snow was compact, there was enough loose powder that it created a snow plume off the southeast ridge. The snow plume arched out beyond the ridge for more than 200 feet before plunging into the abyss. A cobalt-blue lake lay in a cirque 1700 feet below the ridge. The snow mist from the plume made microcircles as it settled on the surface of the lake.

Gordon watched this while breathing deeply and feeling the cool summit air fill his lungs.

Mt. Borah, Idaho. Image retrieved online, copyright-free, photographer unknown.

Gordon then moved his meditation to the summit of Mt. Rainier in Washington. This is a 14,417-foot dormant volcano. It holds the interest and the fate of 2.5 million people who live below its summit. They rely on its glacial ice as storage for water. People ski and climb on its glaciers. They fish its rivers for trout and salmon. The rivers flow into the Salish Sea. Gordon settled cross-legged on the summit cone near a sulfur dioxide gas vent. The wind blew the gas away from Gordon while he sat there motionless, and he reveled in the huge mass of mountain, snow, ice, and his own frailty. The season was still spring, and 120 feet of snow had accumulated during the exceptionally snowy winter. *This is replenishment,* he thought.

Next, Denali, the "Great One," took possession of his meditation. He rose through clouds and up the 6,000-foot west wall, while seeing climbers on the southeast ridge trudging toward the south summit. Gordon was immune to the minus-26-degree temperature at the summit. He sat on his yoga blocks while at the summit for what seemed like 20 minutes, enjoying the sun that didn't warm, watching snow plumes curl off the west wall toward Ruth Glacier. He reflected on the vertical environment of Denali. *Denali is the highest vertical ascent a person can climb on the entire earth. Everest is taller, but one starts the climb at base camp elevation of 17,600 feet and climbs to 29,029 feet—a vertical distance of 11,400 feet. Climbing Denali, one starts at Talkeetna, Alaska, elevation 348, and climbs to 20,310 feet—a vertical distance of 19,900 feet.* A good climber is cognizant of breath, and both lungs (right and left symmetry), as one steps upward. Inhale, hold for six; and exhale, hold for three.

Denali, Alaska. Image retrieved online, copyright-free, photographer unknown.

Fitz Roy, a granite column of rock located in the Patagonia province of Argentina, was Gordon's South American pilgrimage meditation. At 11,073 feet, it is the highest spire in the Parque Nacional Los Glaciares in southern Argentina. Before going to the summit, Gordon stopped at El Chaltén village on the shores of Viedma Lake. It is a trekker's paradise, with trails leading past the lake and into a dozen different mountain valleys surrounded by granite spires, hanging glaciers, lakes, tarns, and waterfalls. Wildlife is abundant. Cougars, guanacos, llamas, alpacas, and the iconic condor inhabit the park and the pampas that reach to the Atlantic coast, a hundred miles away.

No more than three square yards of stone and ice make up the summit of Fitz Roy, named after Robert Fitz Roy, who was Capitan of the HMS Beagle, the same ship that was used by Charles Darwin on his biological explorations of South America and the Galapagos Islands. Lionel Terray, a Frenchman, was the first to climb the peak. The first American to climb Fitz Roy was Yvon Chouinard, founder of the Patagonia outdoor clothing company. He and three friends began their six-month quest in 1968 when they left southern California in a VW bus and drove 6,000 miles to Patagonia to climb Mt. Fitz Roy. Yvon is credited with this quote about adventure travel: "It's not an adventure until something goes wrong."

Mt. Fitz Roy, Patagonia, on the border between Argentina and Chile. Image retrieved online, copyright-free, photographer unknown.

Gordon placed his yoga blocks on one of three square yards of summit, sat down facing east, took three breaths, and was surprised to see a condor soar by, not 20 feet from where he sat. He focused on the flight of the condor for over an hour. During that time, it flapped its wings just twice, probably to adjust to the thermals rising out of the valley. It was a flight meditation that gave Gordon a profound sense of connection to the landscape.

Mt. Kilimanjaro, altitude 19,341 feet, dominates the African plain of Tanzania. Gordon pondered the facts about the pre-history of the area. Part of our hominid heritage is found below Kilimanjaro on the vast wooded grasslands of the Great Rift of eastern Africa. *Australopithecine* primates lived here 3.4 million years ago. They breathed the air, mated, had babies, sat around campfires, watched stars, and made tools. It has only been during the past 150 years that we have become aware of their presence, as revealed from numerous archaeological digs. At Laetoli, an archaeological site not far from Kilimanjaro, three pairs of hominid footsteps were discovered embedded in volcanic ash. Analysis shows they were made by a male, a female, and a youngster. They were dated at 3.3 million years old.

Looking around on the crater rim of Kilimanjaro, Gordon saw three volcanic cones, each one higher than the next. Beyond the highest was another, Uhuru Peak, the highest point of the crater rim. It took him 45 minutes to hike up to the summit. Once there, he found a large sign mounted on logs and encrusted with ice. Written in English was a declaration: "Congratulations. You are now on Uhuru Peak, Tanzania, highest point in Africa. 5,895 meters."

He sat down below the sign, looked east, and decided to stay the night. It was cold but he had dressed for the weather. At 5:49 a.m., the sun emerged on the horizon. Gordon sat cross-legged in a lotus position. There were no clouds to the east, but morning mist hung in the valleys to the west. It was all so brilliant. He felt the antiquity of the mountain and the hominids who once dwelled below it three million years ago.

K2, at altitude 28,251 feet, is the second-highest mountain in the world. Located at the center of the Hindu Kush Range of the Himalaya, it is considered by many to be the most difficult mountain in the world to climb. There are no easy routes. Ninety-one climbers have died on the mountain; 377 have succeeded and lived to tell their story.

In August of 2008, a group of 25 climbers attempted the summit. Eleven perished when large blocks of an ice serac cascaded down on seven of them. It obliterated their trail and fixed ropes, preventing the remaining four from returning to their camp. They died of exposure and from being swept off the ridge by avalanches.

Gordon arrived at the summit as the sun rose. He pulled out his yoga blocks, sat down on them, and breathed a sigh of relief. He'd started his summit bid at 2:30 a.m. from camp, 1,400 vertical feet below on the Abruzzi Ridge. It was easy at first, then the angle became steeper and the huge hanging serac that defined the upper ridge confronted him. He needed to go left around it. Once beyond it, the slope angled up to the summit crest. He climbed quickly through the bottleneck below the serac by using the trail and the fixed ropes left by other climbers. Arriving at the summit, he could look into vast China plains and look back into a sea of mountains in Pakistan. The view encompassed the most rugged mountain landscape in the world.

Ten thousand feet below him, the Baltoro Glacier, where his base camp was located, collected its tributary glaciers and continued for 39 miles into Pakistan. It terminated just a few miles above the town of Skardu. No other glaciers, except those in Antarctica, were longer. Other significant summits lay below him: Trango Towers; Gasherbrum I, II, and III; Broad Peak; and Muztah Tower. The Concordia could be seen 16 miles in the distance where the Baltoro and the Godwin Austen Glaciers merged. Galen Royal called this place "In the Throne of the Mountain Gods."

Before leaving the summit, and to complete his meditation, he envisioned the events that took place on July 22, 2018, when a Polish mountaineer, Andrzej Bargiel, completed a solo climb of K2. A support team worked with him to assist his successful climb by using a drone modified for high-altitude flying. It helped define his route up and down the mountain. What happened next at the summit, however, is what pushed the limits of mountaineering. He stepped into his skis and skied the precipitous slopes down to base camp, located 11,000 feet below on the Boltoro Glacier. It was a remarkable feat of concentration, focus, stamina, and skill. One simply puts the adrenal fear produced by the body on hold and meditates on survival.

Mt. Everest, altitude 29,035 feet, was named after the British surveyor, Sir George Everest, who discovered the mountain in 1841. It was first climbed in 1953 by Sir Edmund Hillary, a New Zealander, and a Tibetan sherpa name Tenzing Norgay. It has become a mecca for mountaineers, trekkers, and others seeking fame—or discovering something about themselves. It is also a graveyard. More than 300 climbers have perished while attempting the summit or returning from the summit.

The most famous of those who perished were George Mallory and Andrew Irvine. When last seen on June 9, 1924, they were about 800 feet below the summit. A cloud enveloped them, and they disappeared, never to return to base camp. Were they successful at climbing Everest? It is an enigma that has never been answered. Finding Irvine's camera could tell the rest of the story.

Gordon arrived at Everest's summit in mid-June, two days after the last climber had left for the South Col on June 8th. It was the only summit on which he used oxygen from a tank that he was carrying on his back. Being in the death zone above 26,000 feet required extraordinary amounts of energy just to stay conscious. It made for an awkward meditation on yoga blocks.

He could not sit on the actual summit because of a survey pole, as well as the collection of stone and metal amulets and an assortment of flags set there by climbers. But Gordon was compelled, like so many others, to leave his own amulet on the summit: an Icelandic cross made from soapstone. While placing it next to other objects, he found a Celtic cross. The Buddhist prayer flags were tattered by the recent hurricane-force winds of over 100 mph. In the distance, monsoon storm clouds moved up the valleys and began to engulf the peaks.

Gordon knew it was time to return to the South Col, then to Camp III, across the Cwm Valley of snow, climb down through the treacherous icefall to basecamp, then hike out to Lukla, fly back to Katmandu, and return to Idaho.

Mt. Everest on the Nepal/Tibet border. Image retrieved online, copyright-free, photographer unknown.

Back in Idaho, Gordon returned to enjoy the summer solstice on the summit of Mt. Borah and the warm high-altitude sun with calm winds and mares' tails clouds. He brought a string of prayer flags home with him from Nepal, which he anchored between two rocks near the summit. He stood watching Sanskrit wind prayers float off the red, blue, yellow, and green flags. They fluttered into the upper Big Lost River basin and hovered over Thirsty Dog Cabin. Then, they turned into sage-grouse that walked among the sagebrush sea.

Elkstone Cabin was where, numerous times, the author rolled out his yoga mat and brought out the singing bowl with incense holder. The ambiance of this special place in the Idaho mountains was the foundation of the Seven Summits Meditation practice—even in the snow. Photos by Richard Howard.

The Numb Tongue
of Mr. Walker

I HAD A GOLD MOLAR CAP REPLACED ON MY back lower mandible on March 18th. Five hours after the procedure, I noticed that my tongue felt numb as though it was still under the influence of the pain suppressant. My dentist called during the evening, as that was his way of giving extra-quality dental care. He asked, "Are you doing OK?" I briefly mentioned the numb tongue condition. I said that I would call him back in the morning at his office if the condition persisted.

Well, I didn't, and I let it go until Thursday, March 26th. That was the first time I bit my tongue, drew blood, and hollered a lot of nasty swear words that I hadn't heard in years. I was in an elevator with five other people. All of them instantly had their cell phones out, ready to call 911 about the berserker on the elevator. I managed to calm them down even though I was frothing blood at the corner of my mouth.

On Friday, March 27th, I phoned Sage Dental and talked to Monica, a dental assistant, about the numb tongue condition. She arranged an appointment for me to see the dentist on Monday, March 30, at 10:50 a.m.

On March 29th, the numb tongue condition continued unabated. It had been 11 days and by then I could add to the initial symptoms, and describe some of the side effects.

The tongue was numb on the right dorsal and medial areas of the tongue. It did not exhibit any discoloration. The ventral epithelial layer was sensitive to toothpaste when brushing my teeth, so I used a smaller amount of toothpaste, which relieved the discomfort. The numbness was more noticeable at night and in the early morning . . . probably because this is when I brushed my teeth and examined that area of the tongue for any changes.

Another annoying symptom of the condition was random biting of my tongue, which happened about three times a day. This momentary event was extremely painful for 10-15 seconds. I had detected one bruise or lingual hematoma on my numb tongue but no puncture wounds.

When that happened, I restrained myself from hitting walls, cupboards or doors, and throwing coffee mugs through windows. Well, I threw one coffee mug on the cement driveway in front of the house. It was most satisfying. The neighbors who were out for a morning dog walk looked aghast and confused. I didn't bother to give them an explanation.

After visiting the dentist again, he told me that one in about 60,000 patients has this issue after a painkiller is injected into the mouth muscle. This may result in a nerve being pinched or severed by the needle, which produces a localized numbing of the mouth, mostly in the tongue and cheek. This is no joke. He told me it should gradually disappear in about six months.

On September 27th, I noticed a slight swelling of the lymph node under the right mandible. It also was slightly sensitive to the touch, but otherwise was not noticeable. I thought that the numb tongue condition had metastasized into the lymph system and that there would be rough times ahead. The positive in all this is that my numb tongue symptoms diminished and I could fully taste the hoppy malts of a Sockeye IPA.

By December 27th the numb tongue condition was no longer evident. No random biting of the tongue, no pain, no numbness. My tongue returned to a normal behavioral spectrum of tasting food and keeping my mouth free of food particles, which helped me taste and chew food—and talk—which I like to do when I haven't seen friends in a while.

The dentist was right: in six months, the condition would diminish or fully disappear.

I didn't sue the dentist.

Too Many Notes:
The Brilliance of Wine Labels

I N THE MOVIE *AMADEUS*, THE EMPEROR OF Austria attended the premiere opening of a new opera composed by Mozart. The composer was asked what he thought of it. The emperor leaned toward the court musician to seek an opinion. The court musician whispered back in the emperor's ear, "Too many notes." This sent Mozart into a tantrum, to which he replied, "An opera has no more and no less than all the notes it should have, Your Majesty." But the comment, "too many notes" became a part of history associated with the opera. Mozart's reply was swept into the dustbin.

Wine labels often contain notes about the contents of the bottle. Some labels perfectly describe the taste of the wine. Other labels are too flowery, or do not resonate with the taste of the wine in the bottle: there are just "too many notes."

Gordon examined several dozen wine bottles at Trader Joe's, Costco, Albertsons, and Whole Foods Market to develop an appreciation of wine label descriptions. He found no wine label descriptions to be the same—almost like human fingerprints or short stories by an original author.

It became apparent to him that there are talented writers behind some of these short narratives. He pondered whether one could make a living writing descriptive wine labels. There are authors out there who may have tried but quickly ran out of material. Other authors might have realized that to succeed at this profession, it might be best to have a regular day job. No one has yet to receive a Pulitzer Prize or the Carnegie Medal for Excellence for being best creator of wine label copy. No university offers a Master of Fine Arts degree in this category. The University of California at Irvine, though, did hold a two-day conference about marketing wine, during which an English professor spoke for an hour about developing wine labels. There is no web page that rates the creativity of wine labels. Amazon Books does not sell wine label books. Yet, thousands—maybe millions— of wine labels are read each day by wine lovers as they shop for their favorite Merlot, Riesling, Malbec, or Chenin Blanc.

So, here are some wine labels by unknown authors that will impress you. Some are serious, some are funny, and some . . . well . . . have too many notes.

160

Petite Sirah goes literary.
Powerful titan, arms, reaching for the sky, earthbound devourer, open your eyes.

Throw off your blankets, the day has begun, indulge yourself in warm Lodi sun.

Take what is given, the world is your own, enjoy your dominion, you sit on the throne.

Stand and be noticed, grapes without peer. Instruct the others what they should fear.

Raise up your standard, proclaim your rights, answer to no one, conquer with might.

Hail the victor, the king without flare, salute your new master with trumpet notes of victory . . . Petite Sirah.

A Merlot dives into history.
The heart of the prohibition era and wine's darkest hour was when it was deemed illegal. It was also the year our winery first planted vineyards in California and farmed grapes that were sold to friends and neighbors. Story goes some of these grapes might have been used to make wine. For those who dared to toil in the black market of winemaking, field blends were the wine of choice and a crowd favorite at speakeasies across the country. Crafted from

a blend of varieties, our limited edition delivers dark, rich, fruit flavors, alluring spice notes and a deep, full-bodied palate in the style reminiscent of the prohibition era.

A California Red delves into mythology.
This wine is an homage to our family's Welsh roots. The Goddess Rhiannon is a figure of power and mystery in Celtic mythology. Associated with horses and magical birds, she represents the contrasting qualities of change and steadfastness — an interesting parallel to the winemaking tradition of creating distinctive blends. From each unique harvest, our winemaker creates a wine that expresses a consistent personal style and character. Rhiannon is a delicious blend of Petite Sirah, Syrah, and Barbera with luscious cherry and notes of berry aromas. When enjoyed in the company of good food, friends and family, you may even describe the taste as divine.

The five senses make this Argentina Malbec a favorite.
I smell with one nose, an ancient black rose, a memory lingering, briefly exposed. I see with two eyes, through shadows and lies, a secret revealing, wrapped in disguise. I hear with my ears, three fallen tears, echoing softly, heightening my fears. I taste with my tongue, my panic's begun, four sides enclosed, melding as one. I touch with my hands, a sinister plan, five fingers discerning where I do I stand?

Way too many notes and the Malbec tasted awful.

An original White Vino Riesling from the South Hills of Idaho.
This fine dinner wine is a product of the South Hills Vineyard and Winery, just north of the Twin Falls County Dump. Our grapes thrive in the rich silt and loam adjacent to the potato fields, where they are tended to at least once a month by our part-time staff of one. The rumor that our wine is made by foot stomping with clean

socks in plastic buckets from the middle of August 'til the first of September is not true.

Note the bottle number: Bottle #24/7.

A light smooth red blend that will pique your interest, from Patterson, Washington.

This luscious red wine will pique your interest right out of the gate. Its color and aromas of ripe berries and dark stone fruits, flavors of plum and peach notes, balance in perfect harmony, giving way to a soft, velvety blush. *14 Hands* celebrates the spirit of the wild horses that roamed the Columbia River Basin. *14 Hands* celebrate these tough little horses that were revered around the West for their strength and endurance. The soils that once gave them their wild spirit now feeds our vines. Our *14 Hands* wines share with the horses a sense of intensity of this unbridled freedom.

A Dark Horse original red blend from Modesto, California.
It contains sulfites and has a government warning on the label. All wines are required by the federal Alcohol and Tobacco Tax and Trade Bureau (TTB) to have this government warning label.

Dark Horse Big Red Blend showcases deep flavors of dark berry and black currant, supported by tannins, hints and notes of dark roasted oak, and a long finish.

Angels and Cowboys, a 2019 red blend that goes beyond the norm.
There's a lover, a trailblazer, and a rulebreaker in all of us. Dare to indulge. Our propriety red is a bold and robust Zinfandel-based blend with a supporting cast of Syrah, Carignan, Petite Sirah, and Grenache. Supple on the palate with ripe fruit, dark spice and lengthy notes, driving finish. Vinted at Healdsburg, California.

From Dancing Crow Vineyards, a 2120 Sauvignon Blanc.
One cool, spring day in the shadow of Mt. Konicki, a family came
to lay out their vineyard, using straw to mark the vines. While
feasting during their midday lunch, they saw a murder of crows,
dancing around the straw, which made them laugh. Yet, when they
looked again, the crows and straw were gone. The family learned
two things that day: be wary of dancing crows, and what to name
their vineyard. Vinted in Lake County, St. Helena, California.

**From the classy Cupcake Vineyards in Monterey County,
a 2019 Chardonnay that is creamy, full of apples and lemons.**
This Chardonnay is crafted with grapes from California's esteemed
Monterey County. We barrel ferment our Chardonnay to achieve
a rich, creamy wine with flavors of apple, lemon, vanilla, and a hint
of toasted almond. Enjoy with crab cakes, charcuterie, or copious
amounts of sunshine. It's a *Cupcake* glass of wine you won't forget.

**A sophisticated Ponzi Vineyards Tavola Pinot Noir
from Oregon's Willamette Valley.**
This Pinot Noir is bottled by *Ponzi Vineyards* in Sherwood,
Oregon. Stop by the vineyards sometime or buy a case at your
favorite wine store. Tavola, the Italian word for table, is a sacred
place where family and friends gather, sharing simple food,
good wine, and honest conversation. In honor of preserving
this universal tradition, *Ponzi Vineyards* offer this approachable,
food-friendly wine. Innovation continues with second generation
sisters, Anna Maria and Luisa Ponzi, who maintain a winemaking
tradition of excellence and commitment to sustainability. This
Oregon winery has been a leading producer of American wine
for 50 years. Enjoy the Pinot Noir and if you see them, invite the
Ponzi sisters to your table.

For those flint nappers and atlatl-makers, this Cabernet Sauvignon made by Obsidian Ridge Wineries in the Red Hills of Lake County, California, will satisfy to the sharp point of perfection.
Obsidian, glassy black rock of volcanic origin, covers the steep slopes of *Obsidian Ridge Vineyard*. At 2,640 feet, our vineyard rises amid the Red Hills in a mountainous region of the North Coast, California. With incomparable red soils, and an altitude-moderated climate, our vineyard is one of the highest in the famous Mayacamus Range, and the result is a bold, structured, mountain Cabernet Sauvignon.

For those into the geology of wines, this Cabernet Sauvignon is for you.
The *Margarita Vineyard* estate stands alone and apart as the southernmost vineyard in the Paso Robles region, tucked beneath the peaks of the Santa Lucia Mountains and just 14 miles from the Pacific Ocean. Here, the vines unfold along a rare diversity of five soil types—ancient seabed, rocky alluvium, shale, volcanic, and granite—amid one of the coolest growing environments. The resulting wines express an unmistakable sense of place, with fine structure and deep flavors that resemble notes from a Bach fugue. This 2019 Cab offers rich, layered flavors of blackberry, black current, and cocoa with soft notes of supple tannins. Recommended pairings include filet mignon, rack of lamb, and spicy grilled pork chops.

Here is a sure-shot wine that is aged in bourbon barrels.
A red wine vintage 2019 that is fermented by traditions that are made to be broken. That's why our dark and jammy red wine is blended with select lots aged in smoky bourbon casks. When cracked, these barrels open after three months . . . and let's just say we know pretty quickly, we are onto something good. *Cooper and Thief* red wine is rich and warm, with vanilla flavors and some subtle spicy notes. It finishes with a smooth mouth feel. Bottled by *Cooper and Thief* Cellars Masters, Acampo, California.

*From the famous Yakima Valley, one must taste this epitome
of white wine.*
The 2020 Chenin Blanc by *L'Ecole N°41 Vineyards* has produced
this old-vine, crisp, and aromatic Vouvray-style Chenin Blanc
since 1987. This is a standout Chenin Blanc! With pronounced
aromatics which range from citrus peel to fresh stone fruit,
laced with white floral flourishes, it is vibrant and energetic.
In the mouth, flavors burst forward with tropical kiwi and guava,
completed by a snappy quince note. An exceedingly interesting
and tasty wine, its complexity persists to a vibrant finish.

Gordon decided he would collect 200 wine labels and create
an album of them. This story was a start. Maybe there would
be enough threads within the labels that he could write a novel,
film script, or play from them. It is comforting to know that
there is plenty of material for a project like this.

By the last count done in 2018, at least 8,391 wineries in North
America produce an average of four types of wine: red, red blend,
red varietal, and white wines. Therefore, this provides 33, 564 wine
bottle labels as source material.

So, Gordon thought, *better get crackin.'*

Letter from Reno

GENTS:

It's rare when I write letters rather than emails, but this is a rare story. From October 5th through October 9th, I attended the Great Basin Archaeological Conference in Reno, Nevada.

On my trip to the conference, I had the benefit of riding with a local rancher-turned-professional archaeologist from Kings River Valley, Nevada. He was a great travel guide, full of information and tales.

Among the prehistoric stories, he told me about Cave Springs, south of Orovada, and its 8,000-year-old occupation by Paleo-Indians. Go west of Cave Springs 81 miles and you'll be in Denio, Oregon, the northern tier of the Black Rock Desert. Then, there was the finding of a cheetah skull at Crut Cave on the east side of Lake Winnemucca, and the oldest dated petroglyphs in North America circa 9,800 BP on the west side. Finally, there were the baskets, and cached and dried Lahontan cutthroat trout in caves on the north end of Pyramid Lake in association with barbed spear points made from Bison horn circa 11,800 B.P.

While going through northeastern Oregon and south to Winnemucca, he told me the late 20th century tale of loner Claude Dallas. He learned first hand about Dallas when he was once confronted by a dozen lawmen searching his ranch buildings (without a warrant), looking for any evidence that Dallas may have been there during his escape from Bull Camp on the South Fork.

So, I'm sending you some pictures of interest from this most memorable trip: a few from Paradise and a few from Orovada. I took one photo at about 7:30 p.m. on October 9th, just at the edge of Jordan Valley, which had my heart pounding *was this Dallas?...* and a picture of very old petroglyphs at the Rusty Can site on the west side of Lake Winnemucca, circa 8,900 BP. The last one is of an atlatl of my own making and the "dart" to defend against imaginary ancestral enemies and to hunt imaginary camel, horse, bison, deer, antelope, and maybe mammoth.

By the way, the archaeological conference was superb. There is much synthesis in the trends and tangents of archaeological investigations these days in the Great Basin.

All the best, Richard
October 10, 2016

Letter to John Rember

JOHN, YOU NEED TO KNOW THAT I STARTED reading *MFA in a Box* while flying to Indonesia. The flight takes 20 hours and 36 minutes (LA to Taipei to Jakarta). Four hours into the flight, I begin to read the introduction: "*MFA in a Box* is not a *How to Write* a book. It's a *Why to Write* a book." Two hundred and twenty-five pages later, the Epilogue begins with "Writing Travel." I arrived at this point in the book eight days after returning from Indonesia. During that time, I filled two 5" x 8" legal pads of notes and impressions about the book . . . not about my trip to Java, Bali, and several other islands.

There was so much I found in common with your writing and career path (except mine was in anthro at Idaho State and wildlife biology at Utah State). The notes I took would have been written in the book margins, but they weren't, because it was a borrowed book. Marilee Marsh would not appreciate her book being marked up with notes written in Java, or in yoga studios, or in Hindu and Buddhist temples. When I got home to Boise, I went to the *Boise Weekly* office. They took my request for you to contact me.

Late one night while catching up on emails, there was your reply. It was just like the last scene in the movie *Contact*, where Jodie Foster is looking up in the dark sky, holding grains of sand in her hand. *Rember replied to my request.*

I had a ton of emails to respond to when I returned from my trip. In my email queue, your reply to me about *MFA in a Box* appeared between an email from Davey Jones from Fisherman's Fleet in LaPaz, Mexico, tantalizing me to go on yet another fly-fishing odyssey, and an email from Debbie Arkle from the Idaho Conservation League, encouraging members to join ICL outside on one of their many hikes this summer. The email from *Boise Weekly* to you describes a "message from a walk-in." Yep, I walked into *Boise Weekly* to send you a message because I was compelled to write to you about your MFA book.

So, with this short description about email messages and provenance, I want you to know there was a lot in your book I could relate to. Mostly, about growing up in Idaho and struggling with the destiny of where one is born—and into which family one is born—and which family members get to share the experience of growing up. But then, a pattern emerges at the end of each chapter with your rules and points to live by. They weren't Ten Commandments delivered from a high deity that were written on gold tablets. No, just good common sense points that summarize some of the wisdom and righteousness you have distilled from your experience of riding in the saddle in bona fide wilderness areas, contemplating Idaho sunsets, and teaching writing courses. Yes, and a whole lot more.

I can't continue too much further for now. The local fireworks are crackin' and boomin' outside. It has become a real distraction. Let's plan to meet on August 29th in Stanley, say between 5 and 8 p.m. at the Stanley Museum. We can start with a discussion about back-country experiences and then ease into *MFA in a Box.*

All the best, Richard
July 4th, 2014

Writers on the Wind

SHERRY, GREETINGS FROM ELKSTONE CABIN in snowy Long Valley, Idaho. I read with great interest your email from last week about the sojourn to San Francisco and Berkeley. Having your daughter along with you to share stories and make new adventures around both cities must have been quite special.

Good to hear that you are back at the writing desk and shaping new avenues for your characters in the *Celtic Circle* series of novels. With some of the horrific news events coming out of France, Belgium, and now Ukraine, this may give you pause to rewrite some sections. Perhaps not. We will read about unexpected tangents the families take in *Celtic Circle* that are independent from today's events; then on to the arduous task of editing the wake of your writing efforts. Hope you have smooth sailing as you enter the ocean of edits.

My own attempts at writing have been on hold. It's been a windless sea with no islands in sight. I've managed to develop a table of contents for ten short stories, but then this only includes their titles and not the hard work of key-stroking the stories onto a zip drive. After New Year's, I lived through lost weekends and days when I watched it snow, read books, viewed movies, chopped wood for the stove, and took long walks with Cali, my dog. Few words have been written.

I'm returning to Boise next week for a few days to attend the Idaho Writers Guild luncheon and a discussion group about the Boulder White Clouds Wilderness expansion. Will stock up with groceries and return to Long Valley. Then begin again to shovel snow, chop wood, and take long dog walks with Cali. Maybe I will find a strong westerly wind in the sails.

Hope all is well, Richard
April 1, 2017

IV: Sagebrush Sea

"Thunderhead Over the Boise Front" by Rachel Teannalach

Malicious Woman
Who Lived in a Shoe

"THERE WAS AN OLD WOMAN WHO LIVED
in a shoe. She had so many children, she didn't
know what to do ..." *Obviously.*
—From *Mother Goose*

"So, what do you know about her, and did she really
change forever those people's lives?" I asked. The 80-year-old
man coughed and squinted, then looked at his gin and tonic.
"Let me drink one more of these and I will tell what I know.
It isn't very pretty."

"Whew! Are those drinks stiff and refreshing! It makes an
old man feel like going dancing tonight."

"So, this is the story about the malicious mother who was
married four times, had 11 children by her own efforts, and
raised three stepchildren because they were brought into the
family. She did terrible things to those husbands she cast away.
She was by any means, "an old woman who lived in a shoe," even
when she was just 27, and grew even older by the time she was
32. She should have died when she was 50, but lived to be 66.
That's the short story," he said.

"There are 35 more years behind this that have bothered
me for a long time. For all I know, maybe I could have changed
the destiny of a dozen people if I had taken my son and her
with me to work at the lumber mill in British Columbia?"

"Well, I didn't," he said. "You know some real-life stories
should never be told, since they come out makin' one think what
would have, could have, or should have happened."

The old man coughed again, and said, "The Docs told me
that this malicious parent syndrome could get better with age—
or get worse—but she needed to go tell them about it. They
couldn't force her to do it, though. She stayed worse—and
poisoned her children with hate too."

He recalled, "She grew up in Muncie, Indiana, a daughter to a rich father who made his money farming and raising dairy cows. Her mother was a sweetie to all of us who worked for the old man. She would come out to where we were plowing fields around lunchtime in her red Hummer. She would bring us fried chicken, potato salad, and lemonade for lunch. It was a real treat."

He continued, "She made it special for us. The word got around that he was an OK guy, and so was his wife."

Then he said, "I first saw their daughter when she was 12 years old. She would come with her mother where we were plowing fields. She was a pretty thing with blue eyes, brunette hair, and big for her age. She had a cute smile and dimples that would make you smile, there were so many of them. After that, she would come out occasionally with her mom and intently watch the men planting and tilling the fields."

"Later on, when she was 23 and visited the fields, she would just stop work. She would wear light-colored summer dresses and tennis shoes. She was tall for her age, maybe 5'-10", with a thick build. The lunch break with fried chicken, potato salad, and lemonade got took to another level. I'd hear a few of the other guys say, *Boy the chicken is good, but what's for dessert?* Or more directly, *It would be nice to have her join us for dessert.* I'd tell the guys, 'Cool it, eat your lunch, and get back to work in 15 minutes.'

"You know, I just can't go on with this because it brings up such terrible memories, kind of like I would imagine someone sufferin' from that combat disease.

"Guess you'll have to catch me another time when I can talk about it," he said. "I'm going to drink another gin and then go dancin'. Want to join me?"

The Dark Forest
with No Name

THIS IS A STORY ABOUT TWO ALZHEIMER'S victims. My name is Gordon Walker and I'm an an author. My wife is Elaine. Jim is my brother-in-law. Both Elaine and Jim passed from Alzheimer's (ALZ). Her story is a memoir I wrote. Their story is a eulogy for both of them. Both Elaine and Jim were highly-educated people who endured the agony of losing their memories, their abilities to read, write, enjoy the symphony, canoeing, gardening, quilting, or book club friends. They also lost orientation to their neighborhoods and lost their recognition of loved ones, to the point where their eyes no longer held brightness and their bodies expressed no joy. These are part of a long list of ALZ hallmarks. They render victims as if they are alone on a frozen lake on a very cold overcast morning in late January; skating with no skates; ice fishing with no bait and no hook tied to the line; or no bonfire onshore to keep warm.

While we can read about the clinical aspects of this disease in hundreds of medical reports that have been published in journals and medical books, this story is formatted as a memoir written by a caregiver who experienced firsthand the long path that his wife took into a dark forest—a forest without green meadows, without springs and brooks, without sunshine—only fragments of light.

Elaine's doctor told her that she could no longer drive a car. She frowned at being told this. She'd driven a car since she was 16, and now she was 76. It was disheartening to learn than she didn't pass the Montreal Cognitive Assessment Test (MoCA) with a score of 15, but rather scored only 13 on it. Had she passed the test, it would have meant another of year of being independent and able to drive around town and sometimes to McCall. I conferred with the doctor about the MoCA test. It was the doctor's decision to tell her that she had Alzheimer's and, therefore, she could no longer drive. All of this had been carefully orchestrated with Dr. Koehler two weeks before taking Elaine to the clinic.

Even before she lost her license, though, there were signs that tau protein tangles and beta-amyloid plaques within her brain were beginning to interrupt the normal flow of neuron messages. An incident occurred 12 years ago, when she told me while at a seafood restaurant in Portland that if I went out fishing the next day, she was flying back to Boise. I would find the door to our home locked and could find another place to live. It was so totally irrational and out of character that I took her seriously. I didn't go fishing.

I thought about that incident again 12 years later as Elaine and I walked to the parking lot after the doctor told her that she could no longer drive the car. To her, this was totally irrational: the doctor and her husband, they just didn't understand. To make it even worse, I sold her car three weeks later. She plotted to have a friend buy another car for her, and she wouldn't tell me about it. She would hide the car at a neighbor's house who lived two blocks away.

So, I began to write a memoir. What follows are raw entries that are dated to provide a timeline to the present.

August 2, 2018

Elaine had an appointment with Dr. Koehler on August 1st. It was the appointment to give her some preliminary tests to determine if there were any memory issues. The tests didn't result in a specific diagnosis, but the doctor set up another appointment for her on August 20th to do a CT scan of her brain and administer some more extensive tests. He sent a note home with Elaine that requested her spouse join her at that appointment. To summarize the message from the doctor, "This will begin a dialogue that will be more constructive for all of us."

On August 2nd, Elaine and I drove to the cabin. We took Sage, our Border Collie, with us too. Sage had carved some significant wounds on Elaine's arm with his claws . . . about seven of them. It was an innocent action on his part. Dr. Koehler examined them and gave Elaine a super-grade Neosporin salve to put on them. In three days, the wounds healed.

Anyway, we got to the cabin, settled in, had lunch, and began to watch the news. Elaine suddenly said, "Is this the first time Sage has been to the cabin?" I patiently said, "No, he has been here before." She said, "He seems very calm about being here." It was the 12th time he had been to the cabin since we had gotten him, and Elaine had been with him at least six of those times. This was a glaring example of the short-term memory lapses she frequently exhibited.

During the four-day stay at the cabin, she again asked me this same question five times: "Is this first time Sage has been to the cabin?"

Elaine was pleased to be at the cabin and was comfortable watching her favorite videos like *Call of the Mid-Wife* and *Downton Abbey*, *Wallander*, and *Everest* . . . repeatedly.

August 16, 2018

To: Dr. Koehler
From: Gordon Walker
Subject: Elaine Williams-Walker

This is the first letter I've sent to you about Elaine and the possible issues with her memory. I trust this letter will be kept in strict confidence between you and me, my son Owen, and my daughter Alissa.

I know Owen had separately visited your office in July and talked to an office assistant about the concern we have for Elaine. This was a few days before she was scheduled to meet with you for her semi-annual health checkup. Your brother did the checkup, and we don't know if he was aware of our concern. He may have not talked with the office assistant who Owen spoke with. To our dismay, the next checkup was scheduled for January 2019. Alissa pressed Elaine to see you much sooner than next January. Due to some scheduling conflicts on our end, we have now made the appointment for August 1st at 11:20 a.m.

I do hope with your examination and analysis, we can help
Elaine with this memory dilemma. She still has a vivid long-
term memory, but short-term memory seems to be failing her.
—Gordon Walker

August 18, 2018

This morning I made reservations for us to stay a motel in
Netarts, Oregon, in mid-September. Elaine was thrilled that
had done this. Several times today she asked me, "When we are
going? How long will we stay in Oregon?" We have made it a
family tradition for the past 30 years to go to the Oregon coast
at least once a year to get our "ocean fix."

September 2, 2018

Our plans to go to the Oregon coast are finalized. We will travel
to Netarts, Oregon, located directly west of Tillamook. We will
be able to spend our days on the coast at the Terimore Motel,
Room 14. Elaine is always happy when she gets her annual
"ocean fix."

Elaine continued to query me several times a day about
when we would be going to Oregon and how long would we be
there. I would repeat the itinerary and the dates, "We leave on
September 11th. The first night we will go to Hood River and
stay at the Westcliff Motel. Early the next day we will travel
through Portland to Tillamook, and then to Netarts. We will stay
at the Terimore Motel until September 18th. Then, the next day
on the 19th, we will drive back to Boise."

Elaine liked to hear the trip details but got lost in them
and asked again and again what the dates were. She would get
irritated at me if I told her that the dates are on the calendar.

September 11, 2018

Finally, the day arrived. We packed our luggage, Sage, and his
dog gear, and left for Oregon. I did all the driving. We had an
uneventful trip to Hood River. When we got there in the late

afternoon, Elaine wanted to sleep. I took Sage for a walk along the Columbia River. We had a good evening. We went into town and ate at our favorite restaurant, took a walk around downtown, returned to the Westcliff Motel, and went to bed.

This was Sage's first time staying at a motel. When he heard other people closing doors or walking outside our room, he barked loudly. This happened about 12-14 times during the night. I didn't get much sleep. I thought about all sorts of things we needed to do to correct his behavior. We left early the next morning, not wanting to hear from the motel manager.

When we arrived in Netarts, the weather was overcast, with blustery winds that pounded the ocean, and the misty rain kept us moving fast to get our gear inside our motel room. So we decided to wait out the storm before taking a walk. We turned on the TV and the film *Everest* was playing, so we watched it. Two minutes into the film, Elaine looked at me and asked, "Have you seen this film before? I haven't." There was an honest, sincere tone to her voice. "Yes, I've seen this before," I replied.

I was more than mildly shocked at her question. We have a copy of this video in our library at home and another copy at our cabin. We've watched it seven or eight times together. Elaine had watched the video herself 15-16 times during the past year.

After the storm, we took a walk on the beach at Cape Lookout, where, when the kids were youngsters our family had spent many summer vacations camping. Years later, we brought them back as adults with their own kids to enjoy the beauty of the place.

Each day we took walks on the beach. Elaine smiled the most beautiful smiles, and her hair blew in the wind just as I remembered her 30 years ago when we first came to this place.

We watched the tide ebb and flow at Netarts Bay. We tossed the Chuckit! ball numerous times for Sage. Elaine regularly took her "meds." We only drank three bottles of wine during the time we were there, and no whiskey. Her attitude improved each day. There were no "down-days"—just "down moments"—that soon passed. The trip had been a real "tonic" for Elaine. Sage adjusted to the night noises and by the fourth evening, there were just a few barks from him and a lot of tail-wagging when he would greet guests and visitors. Most people couldn't resist petting Sage. He would catch little dog bones in mid-air when they were tossed to him.

September 23, 2018

Elaine would not sit down with me to and have a sincere talk about her visit to Dr. Koehler's office. There were a dozen times when I hinted that we should talk about this important family issue. She would avoid the hint.

A friend whose relative has ALZ, suggested I buy an erasable note board so that Elaine could refer to it rather than asking me questions all the time. I bought one so we could write down various activity dates. She could refer to the board instead of asking me all the time, "When is this going to happen? What date would guests arrive? Who are we going to see?" The questions were incessant each day. During the previous three weeks, this pattern became noticeably more frequent. She rarely referred to the erasable note board. When I asked her to look at the note board instead of directly answering her questions, she became visibly disturbed. She would pout to me about making her life miserable. Here are a few examples:

• Our dog Sage has a grooming appointment on September 30th. Beginning early last week, Elaine began to ask me two to three times a day when, and at what time, Sage was to be taken to the groomer. Now, for the past few days, her questioning pattern has increased to three or four times per day.

• Elaine kept asking me, "When will Alissa bring Sage home?" Alissa had taken Sage to our cabin located near McCall, Idaho, for three days. I was patient and told her that Alissa texted me that she will bring Sage home on Monday. I said, "Alissa will call us when she is back in Boise, and then we can go over to get Sage." Again this morning she asked, "When is Alissa going to bring Sage back to us?" Once again, I told Elaine that she will call us when it's time to go over to her house and pick up Sage. It will be some time shortly after noon. She exclaimed, "I'm never going to let Alissa take Sage again!" Finally, Alissa called, and Elaine and I picked Sage up without any fanfare.

• I continue to do most of the cooking, and I am getting good at it. She appreciates that I do this. There are times however, when she gets frustrated about either not having enough or having too much for dinner. I always cook enough for second helpings for both of us. I'm concerned about the amount of wine and, sometimes, the Maker's Mark whiskey she consumes in a week. A fifth of Maker's over a three-week period and four to five bottles of wine during a ten-day period is excessive.

183

• She is adamant about watching TV shows during dinner, while I prefer to eat outside on the patio table and enjoy the evening temperatures. We used to do this often and talk about the day and discuss family trips or plan birthdays or just laugh about small things and enjoy the evening. This doesn't happen anymore. Clearly, we are growing more distant in our relationship.

September 24, 2018
This is yet another example of short-term memory lapse that Elaine exhibits frequently: every day or sometimes twice or three times a day. Yesterday afternoon she went grocery shopping at Albertsons Market. Elaine purchased a tube of dinner rolls, those that are popped open and baked in the oven. She baked them for dinner that night, and we ate two rolls for dinner. The rolls were delicious with butter and jam. I stored the rest of the rolls in a bread bag labeled "Trader Joe's." The next morning, she came out to the kitchen. I was drinking my tea and reading the newspaper. She picked up the bread bag of dinner rolls and said, "Oh! Where did we get the dinner rolls? They must have come from Trader Joe's." I just listened. I did not correct her or comment.

September 28, 2018

I'm very tired of having to deal with Sage and his daily needs. If you love Border Collies, addressing their daily needs is quite pleasant. However, I only like him. Elaine loves the dog. He is a great companion dog for her.

But I feed him. I take him for walks. I clean up the dog bombs in the backyard. I buy him food. I arrange for him to be groomed. I let him outside, I let him inside. I fill his water bowl every day. I pet him. I take him out and run him through the sprinklers. I throw Chuckit! balls for him while in the park.

Today, I tried holding him back from going to the front door when someone rang the doorbell. I twisted to catch him and strained my calf muscle . . . hurt liked hell. I swore and cussed because I was in pain and agony. I took an Aleve and sat down. I thought about getting up and leaving the house for the evening. I just didn't want to be a part of the dinner routine with Elaine and Sage. I was really stressed out.

October 2, 2018

Elaine totally screwed up the cable TV the other day and we had to have a cable guy come out and straighten it out. She reassures me that she knows how to navigate through the channels and command buttons, but continues to call me to help her out.

Elaine surprised me when she said she wanted to go to the Land Trust of Treasure Valley dinner and auction. She has never gone before. I've gone every year for ten years to support their mission, which is to buy and manage lands for the Boise Front so that we all have trails to hike and bike on throughout the year. While I go every week on a long hike, Elaine has not hiked with me in over a year.

October 25, 2018
Dr. Koehler:

First, I want to thank you and your staff for finding time to
reschedule Elaine's appointment with you. It was essential that
you examine her and give her the MoCA test.

I appreciate your discussion with Elaine about the results of
the MoCA test and telling her that she could no longer drive a
car. This was a very delicate moment for you, Elaine, and me. She
did not respond well to your message. As soon as we left your
office, she growled about taking the MoCA test, and about
you telling her she couldn't drive anymore. She said that she
never wanted to return to your office again. This reaction was
not surprising. I believe it is symptomatic of her condition, and
not directed at you, Dr. Koehler. She thinks the world of you
as a doctor, and she later told me that.

Just last week, October 18-22, I drove us to Vancouver,
Washington, to see our son and his family. She did quite well
during the entire trip, except for one issue. About 2:00 a.m. on
October 20th, she woke up in our motel room with severe burning in her throat and incessant coughing. The symptoms were so
alarming, I thought about taking her to an emergency room at
a nearby hospital. I went to WebMD online, however, and read
what might be the possible diagnosis: esophageal acid reflux.
Fortunately, we had some Pepcid® in our portable med bag.
I gave her two chewable tablets, and within 15 minutes she
had stabilized with no more symptoms except for a raw throat.
WebMD recommended some chamomile tea or warm water
and a gargle. Again, we were fortunate. I went downstairs to the
motel dining room at 3:30 a.m. and found a coffee and tea table.
Looking through the selection of tea bags, I found two chamomile
tea bags. I made some tea and brought it up to her. She drank all
of it, and by 4:00 a.m., she was feeling much better. A few minutes
later she fell asleep.

In the morning around 8:00 a.m. at breakfast, I asked how she felt after the acid reflux attack during the night? She didn't remember the episode and said she felt fine. The rest of the visit with our son and his family went well. I'm very relieved and pleased that we did this trip now and not six months from now.

Another incident occurred, however, after our return to Boise. We needed to be at the airport by 7:30 a.m. to meet Alissa and her husband Alex, who were returning from their vacation in San Francisco. Elaine started fussing about going on a trip almost as soon as I woke her up. She reluctantly got in the car and asked me several times, "Why do I have to go on this trip?" Just as we were getting to the airport, she said, "I don't want to go, and I will remember this forever that you made me go on this trip." I tried to convince her we were just picking up Alissa and Alex. Fortunately, when we arrived at the airport, she got out of the car, and we went into the airport to meet Alissa and Alex, with no further talk about going on a trip.

This journal entry summarizes how it's gone for the past few weeks since we visited your office. Elaine has not driven the car since she last saw you. She has reduced her alcohol consumption. She takes her meds regularly, but I need to remind her each time during the day. We have taken some drives through the city to see the fall colors of leaves. I'm seeing a counselor who helps me to address the challenges of being a caregiver. Each day, I make a point to find something that both Elaine and I can enjoy or laugh about. This helps us both. So, overall, we are doing OK.

—Gordon Walker

December 12, 2018
Elaine stopped making quilts in May 2018. She was a quilter for 19 years and did extraordinary work. She worked briefly this October and November with other quilters on their projects, but on none of her own.

Her sleep patterns have changed since last fall when she would get a good seven to eight hours of sleep and take a short

½-hour nap during the day. Elaine now will sleep during the night for seven to eight hours, but then will "nap" for another three to four hours during the day . . . almost every day.

Her diet is OK. Lately, for the past few weeks, I've been doing all the preparations for dinner. I've changed the diet to include fish, mostly salmon, and salads with cabbage, beets, carrots, lettuce, and Italian parsley. I've found a lot of joy in cooking for Elaine these past few weeks. She's been so diligent about preparing meals for me during the 40 years of our marriage. It's about time.

187

January 20, 2019

The month of January was full of tragedy and triumph for Elaine and me. We enjoy eating vegetables from our garden, and shopping for a better diversity of food at Fred Meyer and Albertsons grocery stores. I cook dinner most of the time, using several kinds of olive oil, which we have come to prefer over corn and canola oil. Our meats include chicken, salmon, pork, and beef (mostly salmon and chicken). I became good at rolling chicken in panko bread crumbs and then frying it. Yum!

We prefer a modest salad of shredded iceberg lettuce, red beets, diced white onion, green, yellow and red peppers, slivers of carrots, with Trader Joe's organic coleslaw dressing. For dessert, we enjoy Dairy Queen (DQ) Dilly® Bars or Klondike® bars from Albertsons. Wine and ice water are our usual beverages with dinner.

The evening of January 24th, I served dinner about 6:15 p.m. It was a pleasant one, full of talk about the pictures of our family that are set on two tables in the dining room. Two hours later, I went to DQ and bought Dilly bars for dessert. I came home and got settled in my comfort chair. Elaine was sitting across from me in her comfort chair, eating her treat. I asked her if she liked the dinner I had cooked and served for us—which was just two hours before. She replied, "What dinner? Did we eat dinner tonight?" Her response surprised me.

February 17, 2019

Here is the most recent update about the "negative milestones" for Elaine since my last journal entry.

She starts the day by having her coffee and reading the paper. About a half-hour later, she takes her first drink of the day. It is usually about four ounces from a newly-opened bottle of *Ménage à Trois* red blend wine. By the time the day is over, she has finished the bottle of wine. Usually about one hour before supper, she has a drink of Maker's Mark Whiskey, too.

This pattern of drinking and the progression of other negative milestones became a discussion the other night with two friends from Pocatello. Vivian is a retired registered nurse. When she heard me talk about Elaine's ALZ condition and her amount of drinking, she insisted, "You need to confront Elaine right away about driving privileges and tell her that she will need to have her driver's license and her car keys taken away. There are expensive liability issues to consider. If she had a bad accident, your situation would become much more complex. You would be confronted by law enforcement, insurance agencies, medical providers, and court hearings."

I explained to Vivian that we had already taken the license and keys away from her seven months ago. I told Vivian that the moment was full of tension and resulted in Elaine never returning to Dr. Koehler's office. Elaine had also heaped a lot of verbal abuse on me for the loss of her driving privileges.

July 15, 2019

My contributions to this journal are sporadic. The last journal entry was made February 17, 2019. It's been about a year-and-a-half since we began to notice changes in Elaine's memory and behavior.

It is now mid-July 2019, and her repetitive behavior is becoming more severe. For example, if we are planning to go to the cabin on Friday, and it is the Monday prior to leaving, she will ask me eight to nine times a day when we are going to the cabin. She also will ask who is staying at the cabin, when in fact no one is there other than us. She has illusions that someone is staying there. She gets disgusted with me for not letting her know who is staying at the cabin, however, if someone will be at the cabin, I let her know days in advance. Ten minutes later, she forgets that we even talked about someone staying there.

Some new incidents have occurred that I haven't witnessed before. She asked me the other night whether my dad was still alive. I gently told her that my dad passed away in 1992.

Recently, she was writing a text message to Alissa and asked me how to spell "wow." I told her, and she thanked me as if this was a normal question.

One evening, she walked down the hall to the bathroom. A minute later, I heard a yell and went to see what happened. She had tripped while trying to go to the bathroom and fell into the tub. She hit her head on the side of the tub which produced a gash about two inches long. It was bleeding a lot but it wasn't deep. I took a washcloth and made a compress, got the bleeding to stop, and then helped her to the bedroom so she could lie down on the bed. By the next morning, she was doing OK. The area around the head wound was a little swollen, but it was not infected. It healed within a few days and didn't require further attention.

November 31, 2019

This is my journal entry about Elaine that covers October 3rd through November 31st, 2019.

On October 10th, I took Elaine to a friend's *Celebration of Life*. He was a valuable colleague to both of us. It was the last event we attended together.

I actually have taken Elaine to five other events between October 10th and November 29th. We arrive at the events, but then she refuses to participate. She will stay in the car or sit on a bench at the event venue. When I last attended a conference in

Pocatello, she remained behind in the hotel room. In years past, she would have gladly joined me at all of these events for the entire time.

On October 18th, we drove to Vancouver, Washington, to visit our son and his family. We stayed in a motel nearby his home. Each day we would visit with the family. I enjoyed it immensely. So did Elaine, but she found reasons to leave early and return to the motel. Here are some examples:

• On a field trip to the Oregon Museum of Science and Industry (OMSI), at a movie, or at restaurant, she would last about a half-hour and then want to leave. This has become a common pattern whenever we go out.

• On November 4, 2019, I noticed other negative milestones. I do nearly all of our meal preparation. It is daunting for Elaine to follow a recipe. If she does any cooking, I need to monitor it. She will leave pans on the heating elements for an hour or more and burn the ingredients. Now, when I leave the house and she is at home, I take the knobs off the stove and hide them. She is challenged by storing food in the right place. I will find cooked food (such as leftover chicken and rice) in the cupboard and not in the refrigerator. Putting washed dishes away is confusing to her. Several times, I've discovered that she stored a full load of unwashed dishes in the cupboard.

• Writing checks to pay monthly bills or composing a thank-you card by herself is no longer possible. If I work with her very closely, she can write out a check but she has immense trouble doing so. When financial or credit card statements arrive in the mail, she opens them, but finds them bewildering. She hands them to me and asks, "What is this? Do I need to write a check?" She needs help writing notes and thank-you cards: composing, spelling, dating, and sealing the envelope.

• When I take Elaine to a grocery store, she has trouble using the right credit card or debit card to pay for groceries. She generally doesn't want me to help her shopping, so I shop for groceries on my own. I make two grocery lists, one for her and one for myself. I will find what is on my list and put it in the shopping cart. She gets creative and I will find only two or three items in her cart that are on the list. The rest of the items are of little use or we already have enough at home. Elaine is very sensitive to criticism, so I don't say anything to her and will go to another checkout counter to pay for my groceries. It is painful to watch the grocery clerk help her find the right card and to insert it properly in the credit card machine. Sometimes she shows three or four cards to the clerk at the checkout stand before the right one is found and inserted.

• Elaine remains persistent about returning her car keys, saying, "It would be better to sit in jail rather than being cooped up like a chicken in this house. I need my car keys so I can do things . . . go to the store and visit friends." Her statements are accompanied by a rapid burst of expletives directed at me. I've tried to remain calm—no shouting back or escalating the situation during these episodes. I really don't know any techniques to calm her down.

• Sometimes I put my head in my hands and cry. This stops her for a short period. I've tried redirecting the conversation by asking, "What's for dinner? Should we go out shopping? Shall we go for a walk with Sage or go visit a friend who lives several blocks away? Can I turn on one of your favorite TV shows? Or, let's go rake leaves." Sometimes, I pick up my cell phone and suggest she call her brother, our son, or my older sister in Lawrence. It helps—but only for a very short while.

November 31, 2019

Elaine has a very pleasant side to her when she is having a good day. When she is around friends, she stumbles with her memory lapses but never exhibits outbursts. Most of her friends know she is having trouble with dementia. They are cordial and kind; and roll with it. They treat her with respect. These good times are becoming less and less frequent as we head into the deep fall season, particularly when I'm alone with her at home or driving around with her in our car.

Where do I go from here? We are at a crossroads. I have visited six senior living centers that have memory care services. I don't believe this is an option just yet. Rather, I would prefer to find an "In-Home Care" service.

January 18, 2021

It has been over a year since I last updated this memoir about Elaine and the terrible progression of her ALZ condition. What follows is a summary of negative milestones that we have both suffered.

In early February of 2020, I completed all the preparations to go to Nepal for a 10-day trek into the Annapurna Sanctuary. This was a pilgrimage that I had wanted to do since I was in my 20s. It was going to be my last major adventure because I am on the edge of being too old to take this type of trip. I told Elaine that I had found someone to stay with her at home, since I would be gone for 22 days.

To train for this 10-day trek into and out of the Annapurna Sanctuary, I would walk the greenbelt or hike in the foothills. One night as I finished walking nearly five miles along the Boise River Greenbelt, I returned home to prepare dinner for us. Elaine half-yelled at me and told me I wasn't going anywhere. She said she refused to be taken care of by strangers while I was on this Nepal trek. I begged her to reconsider since she had been fine with this trip up until now. The more I begged, the more adamant she got, refusing to have anyone stay at the house.

192

The next day I canceled all my arrangements. I canceled airline tickets, stopped home-care for Elaine, and advised the trekking company that I wasn't going. I asked them to find a good use for my non-refundable deposit. I was very distraught and stressed.

Two days later I developed a virulent head cold. It was so bad, I thought I might have the flu—even though I had received my influenza shots four months prior. It was a Friday night, so I went to the emergency clinic at my primary care doctor's office. After determining it was not the flu (two variants were present in the Boise population), the physician's assistant took an EKG and showed concern. My heart rate was up around 130 bpm and wouldn't come down after I rested for 15 minutes. He sent me to St. Luke's Hospital for emergency heart care and to have a CT scan done to determine if there was any heart damage.

Later that night, the docs at St. Luke's ER determined there was some minor damage to the top ventricle. They put me on two drugs, diltiazem extended-release, a heart modulation drug, and Eliquis,® a blood thinner. A week later, a heart specialist examined me and confirmed what the ER docs had determined. He recommended I schedule a conversion procedure which would reduce my heart rate back to normal. I told him to give me four days to think about it.

Within that four days, the world was turned upside down with the Covid 19 virus pandemic. I was told that I couldn't have a conversion procedure done because the hospital was going to need all the operating tables and beds available to care for Covid patients. Two years later, I'm still taking the two meds.

March 2021

We both got our Covid 19 vaccine shots. Later, the booster. Returning to Elaine's condition, she stopped taking all her meds over a year ago, in February of 2020. She refused to eat breakfast most days. In the late afternoon or early evening, she would exhibit the "Sundowner's Syndrome," where she would become verbally abusive to me over the smallest incident. These episodes of abusiveness would last from 5 to 25 minutes, which have increasingly become more frequent this past year. They are very troubling to endure. No amount of reasoning will quiet them.

Elaine became convinced that her mother and my mother were still alive. She started hearing Alissa and her son talking, when in fact they were not there. She heard the cell phones ring or the microwave buzz when there was no sound to be heard.

She gets confused about Alexia, a friend who passed away in November 2020, and whether she is dead or alive. Sometimes, she asks me to call Alexia so she can talk to her. Her repetitive behavior is at an all-time high. She repeats stories about her brother and mother; my mother; and familiar objects in our living room such as plates, cups, pictures, and lamps.

I watch her closely should she start a cooking project. She gets angry at me for hanging in the kitchen and watching her. Many times when she starts something in the kitchen, I must finish it and clean up the mess. She eats healthy foods, but she rarely will eat much of it. She still likes Klondike ice cream bars for dessert. She hasn't the stamina to walk more than half a block. I take her on rides two to three times per week, and we take Sage with us. Daily, I take him for walks, but she declines to go with us. Elaine refuses to take a shower if I ask her to do so. Alissa comes over to the house to give her a shower twice a month. Alissa is so assertive that Elaine does what she demands, and then she will take a shower.

As to sleeping arrangements, on most nights, Elaine sleeps half the night in our bedroom, then she moves into her sewing room which has a comfortable bed and sleeps there the second half of the night. Sometimes if Elaine's snoring bothers me, I will get up and sleep the remainder of the night on the couch. But here is another ALZ milestone: she will not let me sleep on the sewing room bed. She goes into a terrible rage if she catches me sleeping there so I sleep on the couch to reduce the tension.

Elaine no longer watches TV shows. She gets very confused as to what is happening. When she asks me to explain what is happening, she becomes even more confused. She turns off the TV after five or six minutes. Just a year ago, she would enjoy watching full-length features.

April 2021

I hired a wonderful woman from a local in-home care company that specialized in the care of dementia patients. Sheila cared for Elaine twice a week for two four-hour shifts. This gave me some relief. For the first three weeks, Elaine was resistant to having this stranger in the house. When Sheila would arrive at the house, Elaine would run down the hall and lock herself in her bedroom. Thirty minutes later, she would come out and sit in her favorite lounge chair and brood.

Gradually over a five-week period she began to talk to Sheila, and she ate the delicious food Sheila prepared for lunch or dinner. After six months, I had to let Sheila go. They had become good friends, and it was a heartbreaking decision that I had to make, but caring for Elaine was overwhelming me. I needed to place her in a memory care facility.

May 2021

Our daughter, Alissa, found a medical clinic that offered house calls. It was a revelation to me that a clinic today would have staff that would do this. Fifty years ago, this was a common practice, but I thought that the only way to get medical care these days was to go to an outpatient clinic or a hospital.

I scheduled an appointment and met with a doctor and nurse at our home. Both were highly-trained in assessing geriatric diseases. They confirmed her ALZ condition and advised me what lay ahead for Elaine. They predicted that I would soon be overwhelmed with Elaine's daily demands, and that within six months she would be required to live in an assisted care home.

December 6, 2021

For months, I researched many care facilities to find the best place for Elaine. On December 6th I brought her to the door of the BrightStar Care home. The home has a maximum capacity of ten residents. They offer full-time care, with prepared meals and daily medicine monitoring. Each resident has a private bedroom, too. It is a sunny place, located in a neighborhood not far from our home.

While expensive, I was certain this was a good place for Elaine. A lot of our friends confirmed my decision. During that first month, Elaine adjusted to her new living situation. I did my best to make her feel comfortable, even installing a bird feeder outside her bedroom window.

January 28, 2022

Elaine hit two more memory loss milestones. First, during one of my visits to her BrightStar home, she confronted me with the question, "What is *mycelium*?" Recently, she had talked to my sister, Fran, via cell phone. Fran wanted to know what mycelium was, and Elaine didn't know what to tell her. So, I called my sister and together with Elaine, I told them it was the root of mushrooms that fixed nitrogen and other essential elements. These fine-hair roots that are found in the soil are intertwined with other plant and tree roots, and form a symbiotic relationship. Hearing this explanation, Elaine just stared out the window.

It was a sad moment. It brought me to tears. When Elaine was a biology teacher, she taught her students about the detailed structure and function of mycelium.

During another visit, Elaine asked me how the household at 2415 South Channel Road was. I rolled with the question and told her that the house was just fine. But we moved in 1985 from this house, which was located on four acres of pasture and had an artesian well and a trout pond. The South Channel house was demolished in 1990 to make way for a subdivision that has since engulfed the four acres and the adjacent 600 acres of pastureland. It was another sad moment for me.

Elaine continues down the path into that dark forest with no name . . . staring out the window.

February 21, 2022

Sage and I drive twice a week from home, a short distance to the BrightStar house. I leave Sage in the car while I go in—and find Elaine in her favorite chair. The folks at BrightStar are helpful and courteous. I call ahead an hour before and let them know I'm coming for a visit so that they can get Elaine out of bed or move her into the visitor's room. They comb her hair, pull it back and tie a red ribbon bow in it, wash her face, and put some light makeup on for her, including maroon lipstick and dark eyebrow pencil. The caregivers at BrightStar dress her in brightly colored clothes to dignify her appearance so that when I arrive, she feels better and manages to smile. I kiss her on the cheek and whisper in her ear that, "I love you." Sometimes, I bring a bouquet of flowers and wine for Elaine. I pour her a small glass full of Malbec or her favorite red blend that she likes cooled and not served at room temperature.

The sunroom at the BrightStar house is for visitors. It has big picture windows to the backyard veranda, and is more private because they can close it off from other activities in the home. It has comfortable chairs and a big sofa. It's a good idea to occasionally lock the doors for greater privacy, since other patients might come in to say "hello," then sit down, and then start talking to you or others which will distract a visit. In one case a patient, who once was a doctor, tried to use his stethoscope to take my pulse. He mentioned that he had many other patients he had to see that afternoon, and then looked at his watch as though expecting the next patient to come through the door into his office. Without locked doors to enable more private visits, it can become a Mad Hatter's tea party.

I asked the caregivers at BrightStar if it was acceptable to bring Sage into the house. By now, this dear Border Collie friend of mine is five years old. He likes beer, retrieves Chuckit! balls at the park, and learned how to open the refrigerator door to get at the leftovers from Thanksgiving. (I had to invent a Velcro tape lock which wraps around the door to prevent him from taking inventory and raiding the refrigerator.) The caregivers signal me that it is OK to bring Sage into the sunroom for a visit. He wags his tail and puts his front paws on Elaine's lap. They both seem happy to see each other. She pets him several times and I coax him off her lap with a dog treat bone. We stay for another ten minutes—not talking, but just sitting there together. Elaine has her eyes on Sage. After ten minutes, she asks me what the name of this dog is. I go up to her and kiss her on the cheek and ask her, "Who do you love more? Do you love Sage or do you love me more?" She smiles at me and says, "Sage, of course." The visit ends and Sage and I go to the parking lot and return home.

198

April 11, 2022
It's my birthday today. I was born in Pocatello 79 years ago. I stop by to see Elaine for a short visit and share a muffin and a glass of milk with her. She is listless and has not slept well this past week. Still, I manage to get a smile from her when at the end of my visit, I ask her, "Who do love more, me or Sage?" She tells me, "Sage of course." I kiss her on the cheek. As I'm going out the door at BrightStar house, one of the caregivers tells me, "Gordon, you always make it a good day for Elaine—and for us—when you come to visit. Come as often as you can." Some who share a similar situation to me have decided it is best for both married partners to live together in an assisted living place so that they can be close to their spouse. I have instead elected to remain at our home that is is only a few minutes away from BrightStar. I can quickly get there should I be needed for any emergency.

April 16, 2022
A BrightStar caregiver calls. She tells me that a nurse who monitors Elaine's health each week has sent her to St. Luke's hospital due to very low blood pressure and hyperventilation. I go immediately to the hospital where they have taken extra-ordinary means to monitor and keep Elaine from passing out.

I stay with her for five hours. With the treatments, she is
stabilized and intubated with some liquid food and energy
drinks. She remains in the hospital for three days and then
is transported back to BrightStar house. She rejoins the
other patients and behaves as though nothing happened.
I asked Elaine if she remembers being in the hospital for
three days. She doesn't remember.

    I talk to the nurse who ordered Elaine's transportation
and stay at St. Luke's hospital. I review with the nurse and
the caregivers at BrightStar that Elaine is not to be given
extraordinary care again. This is based on a discussion Elaine
and I had with our lawyer four years earlier when neither of
us wanted extraordinary care, and stated that clearly in our
notarized wills. We believe there is a time and place where
the body works with the mind and the spirit to shut down the
body pulse and take one's last breath. One takes the first breath
of life when they are born and the last breath when one dies.
Extraordinary means doesn't have a place in this mystical process.

May 16, 2022
The geese that are nesting on the roof of a garage next to the
BrightStar house have hatched their young. Nine pint-sized
goslings are running around on the roof. It's a 12-foot drop
to the ground. An hour later all the goslings are on the ground
and mother goose guides them between the two buildings, and
then crosses Steven's Street to the canal. Whew! They all made
it without being run over by a car or getting caught in the claws
of an itinerant cat whose owner leaves the garage door open all
day so the cat/pet predator can wander the neighborhood to prey
upon quail, songbirds at bird feeders and goslings that can't find
the safety of a canal or pond.

    Elaine smiles at this when I tell her that the geese are
safe. She tells me she wants to see Sage. I bring Sage into the
BrightStar house sunroom. Sage puts his front paws on her
lap and curls his head in her lap as Elaine pets him around the

head, down along his neck, and shoulders. They remain this way for five minutes. Sage never sits still for five minutes. It's not characteristic of Border Collies. He steps down from her lap, I attached his leash to his neck collar. The visit is over. Elaine smiles when she tells me without asking her that she loves Sage more than she loves me.

June 29, 2022

Today is Elaine's birthday. Alissa and I agree by text to meet at BrightStar house in the afternoon. We bring a birthday cake, candles, ice cream, and of course, Sage is also with us. The caregivers at BrightStar tell us that Elaine is having a tough day. Her blood pressure is down again. She ate very little for breakfast or lunch. She did take a few sips from an energy drink.

Elaine lights up as she is wheeled into the BrightStar sunroom since she can now only walk a few steps. She sees Sage and he runs up to her and puts his front paws in her lap. She pets him and we tell her it's her birthday. She asks, "So how old am I?" We tell her, "You are 79 years old but you look ten years younger!" She smiles as we light the seven candles on the cake. She hasn't the strength to blow them out. She tries twice. We blow them out for her but don't bother to cut the cake. She wouldn't eat any nor would she like the ice cream. We sing happy birthday to her and she smiles while she is still petting Sage.

Ten minutes passes without any of us saying much but just enjoying the moment and sensing gratitude by sharing this day with Elaine. The visit is over. Elaine is wheeled by a caregiver down the hall into her bedroom. On our way out Alissa suggests we give the cake and ice cream to the caregivers to share among themselves and with the other patients. The caregivers are all smiles as we hand them the seven-candle cake and vanilla bean ice cream.

July 4, 2022

I get an urgent call from the BrightStar house. It's not a caregiver, but the hospice nurse from Capstone Medical Clinic.
She tells me that Elaine's vital signs are very low and that if
I can, I should hurry to BrightStar as soon as possible. I tell her
that I will be there in five minutes.

I arrive and knock on the door. A caregiver answers the
door and escorts me down the hall to Elaine's bedroom. Another
caregiver is standing in the bedroom. The hospice nurse is at
Elaine's bedside sitting in a chair, taking her pulse. She turns
her face to me and says, "Elaine will be gone in a while." She
stands up and beckons me to sit down in the chair beside Elaine.
I reach and hold Elaine's hand. It is warm but not a robust warm
of a healthy body. Her head is lying at an angle away from me,
almost resting on her shoulder. She draws quick shallow breaths.
Her face looks grey. Her eyes are not focused. She doesn't
acknowledge me when I hold her hand, or say "Hello Elaine,
I love you."

The hospice nurse tells me that Elaine lungs are filling with
fluids because her bodily functions can no longer sustain proper
circulation. She asks me, "Is it ok to give her a shot of a relaxant
that will ease the pain and panic of not being able to breathe
regularly?" I tell her, "Yes, give her the relaxant."

This is on the edge of no extraordinary means, but years
ago in our will we did allow for relief of pain during the process
of dying. The nurse steps away and returns with a syringe and
the relaxant. She takes Elaine's arm and presses the needle
into her. There is no use in trying to find a vein for they have
collapsed, but there is enough circulation to carry the relaxant.
Her desperate breathing eases and becomes more regular.
The hospice nurse signals to the caregivers that they should
leave the room.

She tells me, "They will be down the hall if we need anything. These last minutes, or maybe hours, will be ours alone to
share." Fifteen minutes pass, and I notice while looking out the

window, that five species of birds are feeding at the birdfeeder just outside Elaine's bedroom window. When I have visited Elaine these past few months, I've never seen so many birds at the feeder.

"What divine provision is this? Or has July 4th become a day when fledgling birds have discovered the bird feeder as a source of easy food and to hell with the worms in the ground?" I take it as a providential sign seeing the birds and thinking about all the good times Elaine and I have shared.

Suddenly, I notice her hand is cold and I look at her face. Two more short, shallow breaths and Elaine is gone. Passed over the great divide. Her mouth is open as if to take another breath or to say goodbye or to tell me about the birds. I kiss her on the cheek one last time. My tears are silent and I sit with her for another ten minutes before going out to tell the hospice nurse and the others that Elaine has passed.

The hospice nurse returns to Elaine's bedroom. I follow her. She inserts the stethoscope into her ears and places the scope on Elaine's wrist. There is no pulse. She tries the carotid artery on Elaine's neck. Still no pulse. She turns to me and confirms that Elaine has passed. She tells me I can stay alone with Elaine for another hour. Or, if I would prefer, she will call the hospice men to come and get Elaine and to take her to the Bowman Funeral Parlor.

I tell her, "This is what I want done. First, you can tell them to come now, but it will still them take twenty minutes to get here. Second, I want Elaine to stay wrapped in this quilt. Third, I want this picture of Sage placed on top of the quilt. I will secure it with some scotch tape. Both are to remain with her until she is cremated at Bowman."

The nurse agrees with my requests and assures me that they will be conveyed to the hospice men and to the people at Bowman Funeral Parlor.

The hospice men arrive twenty minutes later. They unfold a gurney with a black body bag on top and place Elaine in it along with the quilt and picture of Sage. They zip it up, role Elaine out into the hall. Then they return to the bedroom and dismantle the electronic bed, the oxygen generator, and take them out to the truck. They return to wheel the gurney out to the truck. I witness all of this and am still crying silent tears.

The hospice nurse and caregivers surround me and hug me and tell me that Elaine is in a better place and is not suffering from Alzheimer's, or hunger, or from shortness of breath. I look out the bedroom window one last time. The birds have gone.

August 10, 2022

It's been just over a month since Elaine has passed. Two weeks ago, Alissa urged me to plan for Elaine's Celebration of Life. She did not want this to linger into the fall months when she would have to return to work at her high school. Owen felt the same way. So, I planned to have the celebration at Bowman Funeral Parlor where Elaine had been cremated. They placed her ashes in two jars that were decorated with hummingbirds. Owen and Alissa had different ideas and pushed my plan off the table. Their plan was to hold the Celebration of Life at the Stone House next to the Ram Restaurant, along the Boise greenbelt. It's just a few hundred steps east of the BSU football stadium with its blue turf football field: the place where Elaine spent many days watching the BSU Bronco football team combat other teams to win games and titles and conferences and bring home trophies. She shared the celebration of these victories with Gene, the Athletic Director for BSU.

The emails and text messages went out to invite friends and neighbors to attend Elaine's Celebration of Life on August 10th from 4:00 to 7:30 p.m. Elaine's quilting friends were so lovingly creative. To honor Elaine, they gathered 18 quilts that she had made, and a few that the quilting friends had made. Alissa handled all the food and catering services at the Stone House. Owen took care of a guest book, candles, celebration cards, and wildflower seed packets for the tables. Together, they selected photos from many photo albums—some were over 30 years old.

With these photos, they created a beautiful video of Elaine's life that was shown during the celebration on four TV screens inside the Stone House.

The quilts were displayed outside for all to admire, over the iron fence that separated the Stone House guests from the public who walked along the greenbelt. The quilts were a wonderful display of color and pattern that reflected Elaine's life.

Over a hundred people attended this event to visit with us as well as others. Some had not seen each other in 20 years. Everyone was there to toast to Elaine's engagement with life. One of my close friends told me that this was the best Celebration of Life she had ever attended, and that she hoped her family would give her one just like it.

There were so many highlights of this celebration. The undeniable fact, though, was a display of love for a woman who touched so many during her life.

Elaine was a living statue of life. As a mentor, she brought positive tangents to people's lives. She gave us two wonderful children, Alissa and Owen, who share in those tangents. The last round of wine was served at 7:35 p.m. with those who remained to toast Elaine one last time. Some walked out the door to their cars. Others walked home on the greenbelt path along the Boise River, smelling the lush, vibrant green cottonwood forest.

A family chorten above the Salmon River in the Sawtooth Basin.
The storm clouds are a metaphor for the "Dark Forest with No Name."
Photo by Richard Howard.

A Dark Forest Eulogy for Jim and Elaine

Through the dark forest they walked.
There were no meadows, brooks, or streams.
No sunshine, no moon, no stars. But soon,
they crested the great divide and walked into the
valley of mystical light.
The canoe was there waiting for them,
paddles in the canoe.
Athabaskan drummers beat out a slow cadence
while singing songs of the spirit for Jim.
Boise State Marching Band drummers beat out a rousing
roll while singing the Blue Turf football fight song for Elaine.
Lapping waves at Redfish Lake shore
stirred the mirror reflection of the Sawtooth Mountains
into intense colors of blue and white, green, orange and red . . .
the colors of Tibetan prayer flags.
And so, we waved goodbye to Jim and Elaine
as they paddled their canoe gently into the tranquil sunset.

Bonneville Point thunderstorm. Photo by Richard Howard.

Mortality Storms

GORDON WALKER OF BOISE, IDAHO, PASSED over the "Great Divide" on Thursday, December 21, 2027, at his Elkstone Cabin near McCall, Idaho. Gordon was born April 11, 1943, in Pocatello, Idaho, to loving parents John and Lilly Walker.

He graduated from Pocatello High School in 1960. He was an athletic student who was on the high school ski and tennis teams. He attended four universities: University of Idaho, San Francisco State, U. C. Berkley, and Idaho State University. He received his Bachelor of Arts Degree in Anthropology in 1969, studying under Drs. Earl Swanson and B. Robert Butler. He went on to graduate school in anthropology at the University of Tubingen, Germany, but returned to the United States. He had an epiphany and turned to wildlife biology as a course of study.

Mentors who contributed to his studies were Professors Edson Fichter and Charles Trost of Idaho State University. He entered Utah State University, earning a Master's Degree in Wildlife Ecology in 1974, working under Dr. Michael Wolfe.

He was then employed by the Bureau of Land Management as a raptor biologist at the Morley Nelson National Birds of Prey Conservation Area near Boise, Idaho. After two years with BLM, he was hired by the U.S. Fish and Wildlife Service. He worked in the Service's Boise office, where he was assigned to various projects throughout the western United States, coordinating recovery programs under the Endangered Species Act (ESA) for a variety of species, including mountain caribou, grizzly bear, bald eagle, peregrine falcon, and the northern Idaho ground squirrel. He was a Certified Wildlife Biologist, as decreed by The Wildlife Society, and won numerous awards for his work in the field of wildlife conservation. Most notably, the Axline Award for Environmental Activism was presented to him in 2009 by the Idaho Conservation League for his work on sage-grouse conservation.

Gordon enjoyed climbing the peaks of the Northwest, downhill skiing at resorts, backcountry skiing in the Sawtooths, and fishing freshwater rivers for steelhead trout and salmon, and the Baja waters for dorado and striped marlin. He was a fishing guide in Alaska for four summers, where he worked for Dennis and Cheryl Harms, owners of Alaska Trophy Safaris. *Some of the best of times . . . for intense adventure.*

He was introduced to falconry by Tom Smith and Joe Platt when he was in his teens. This led to lifelong friendships with Morley Nelson, Scott Sawby, Doc Mullins, Frank Renn, Charles Schwartz, Ed Pitcher, Bruce Haak, Phil Bucher, Bob Collins, Paul Mascuch, and numerous other falconers throughout the United States and Europe. He was a member of the North American Falconry Association and a founding member of the Idaho Falconry Association.

He never lost his interest in anthropology and was active in the Idaho Archaeology Society. He initiated the development of an atlatl exhibit, curated at the Museum of Natural History at Idaho State University. Gordon traveled with his wife, Elaine, to distant lands in Central America, South Africa, Australia, Turkey, and Europe to visit prehistoric sites, and he accumulated an extensive anthropology library.

Gordon found a great way to conclude his life experiences by writing a modest book titled *Never Give Up on the Sagebrush Sea: Stories from an Idaho Native*, published by Elkstone Press in 2014. It can be found on Amazon Books as a paperback or in Kindle format. *Never Give Up on the Sagebrush Sea* is a memoir of sorts. One of the best stories in the book, titled "Moving Tables at The Flying M," is about his biologist friends Roy, Dan, Bill, Dave, Herb, Sam, and about ten others who met on Tuesday mornings at The Flying M Bistro in downtown Boise. This "Fusion of Fishers" provided him with some of the best of times during his retirement. The Covid epidemic derailed the Tuesday morning high-level coffee conferences. "Guys' Night

Out," held at one of the many city parks, became a rework of the coffee conferences at The Flying M. The group brought their own chairs, beer, and chips. Most wore masks and kept six-foot distances from each other . . . for a while. When everyone got Pfizer shots (or whatever) and boosters, they regrouped again and tried brewpubs, such as The Clairvoyant and the White Dog Brewing Company. They both had excellent pilsner beer, which is what Gordon preferred—and so did his border collie, Sage.

209

Gordon published another book titled *Stormy Waters on the Sagebrush Sea*. Gordon always had a vision to have one of his stories scripted into a film. He went to book conferences organized by the Idaho Writers Guild and pitched his short stories to scriptwriters from the West Coast. No one seemed interested. So back to his writing desk, Gordon would start "playing the triangle," as he liked to describe his writing efforts.

He remained active in his retirement as a member of the Idaho Conservation League, the Land Trust of the Treasure Valley, Advocates for the West, Save Our Salmon, Baroque Symphony Orchestra, Idaho Falconers Association, North American Falconers Association, the Osher Institute at Boise State University, and the Idaho Writers Guild.

He enjoyed the love and affection of his family. Gordon is survived by two wonderful, energetic children, Alissa and Owen. Also, he is survived by Linde, Owen's wife, and their children Byron and Jillian—all wonderful people. Daughter Alissa married Alex on June 23, 2018, at Elkstone Cabin under a stunning aspen arbor and a perfect cobalt-blue sky. The marriage was witnessed by 168 people and concluded with the best party ever. To Alissa's credit, she started their son Easton skiing just before he turned two years old. Gordon's sisters, Gunda and Frances, outlived their younger brother. They were all lifelong friends.

He will be missed by relatives and friends. Look for him as a falcon soars overhead or when a fish rises from the riffles.

A *Celebration of Life* will be held at 3:00 pm on Tuesday, April 11, 2028, at the Cathedral of the Rockies in Boise, Idaho.

In lieu of flowers, memorial donations can be made to The Archives of Falconry at The Peregrine Fund's World Center for Birds of Prey, 5668 West Flying Hawk Lane, Boise, Idaho, 83709, or to The Idaho Conservation League, P.O. Box 844, Boise, Idaho, 83701.

Manhattan

A WALK WITH JILL THROUGH THE Mountain View Cemetery in Pocatello began with a cobalt-blue sky overhead. She wore her bright-green and orange-flowered London dress. Our friends and relatives were buried at Mountain View for their long rest. Most of their headstones were intact, but a few had fallen over or the letters had worn thin due to the weather elements. We straightened the headstones and wrote over the letters and numbers that had worn thin, using a black permanent marker. It helped us to know that they were being cared for in this world—and hoped that they would guide us in the next world when the time came.

A red-tailed hawk soared overhead and landed in one of the huge 100-year-old cottonwood trees. It saw us but was more focused on a tree squirrel running along a branch 40 feet from the ground. In 23 seconds, it was over. We saw the squirrel dangling from the sharp grasp of the hawk's talons. Another cycle of life witnessed while walking in the cemetery.

We returned to my red Toyota truck and decided to go watch the sunset. Our friends and relatives joined us in spirit. Eventually we came to the trailhead of Cusick Trail on the west bench of Pocatello. We took the three-mile trail to the top of Kimport Peak. There, we witnessed the sunset and more. Five elk walked slowly out from a grove of aspen trees and began to browse. A migrating goshawk circled overhead. The sunset colors were shaded tones of Tibetan prayer flags: blue, red, yellow and green, with the final color being orange like monk's robes. We saw our chakra colors in the setting sun. It became love and light for us as we gazed across the Snake River plain and witnessed the diminishing red hues on Big Butte in the Arco Desert.

Jill and I drove back to Pocatello, reflecting on the enchantment of Mountain View and Kimport. Looking at the Big Lost Range across the Arco Desert, we decided on a camping trip near Double Springs Pass north of Mackay. Before leaving the city, we picked up our two children: Sven, who was 16, and Tamarack, 14. They had been staying at Ben and Lucy's house.

We arrived at basecamp late at night. Camp 10 is a developed campground for hikers who intend to climb Mt. Borah. Camp 10 is named for the average number of hours it takes climbers to climb this highest Idaho peak. In 20 minutes, we set up our REI tent and all got toasty in our sleeping bags.

The next morning, at 5:00 am, we began our climb to the Mt. Borah summit. Four hours into the climb, a snow cornice and highly exposed rock scramble challenged us. There was high danger of slipping, which could send us on a 300-foot slide onto a lethal scree slope of rocks. I unfurled our blue and yellow climbing rope. Jill belayed me across the cornice while I cut steps with my ice ax. There was enough extra rope that Jill, Sven, and Tamarack followed in my steps with the safety of a belay. The slope angle decreased after climbing the rocky ridge, and we hiked to the summit. We rolled out a string of Tibetan prayer flags and secured them with rocks. We watch the flags flapping in the wind, shedding prayers down the western slope toward Thirsty Dog Ranch, which was owned by friends who had recently passed over the "Great Divide."

On the way down, we stopped 200 meters above tree line and built a rock chorten. It tied together our friends in Mountain View cemetery, Thirsty Dog, and others who had perished in Vietnam, Iraq, Syria, and Ukraine.

By 4:00 pm, we returned to Camp 10, ate dinner, and then drove to Mackay in the red Toyota truck. On Saturday night, we saw a rodeo. Then we went to Honest Jon's Bar to hear a western band. Like Vegas, "What happens in Mackay, stays in Mackay." The owner let Tamarack and Sven in the bar even though they didn't come close to meeting the 21-year age requirement. They sat at the table with us at Jon's Bar. Tamarack whispered a sweet message in my ear, and I went to talk to the band members.

They all nodded, and said, "Sure, hell yes! Bring her up here." Tamarack confidently stepped onstage and sang *Home On The Range*. The crowd roared with approval and wanted an encore. She brought the house down with the last notes of *You Are My Sunshine*. Afterwards, free beer for us and Shirley Temples for the kids.

We went back to Camp 10 and got cozy in our tent. We awoke the next morning to a cool yellow and orange sunrise. Then we cooked a breakfast of eggs, hash browns, toast with cherry preserves, Pom juice, and green tea. We packed up our gear and drove to Shoshone, Idaho, where we bought the Manhattan Café. It was a cherished family dream.

The family bought the Manhattan Café in Shoshone, Idaho, and settled in with ranchers, cowboys, farmers, BLM staff, Mormons, and Methodists. The café thrived and was visited by politicians, hunters, fishermen and tourists throughout southern Idaho. Photo by Bob House.

Lost Weekends
at Elkstone Cabin

IN SEPTEMBER OF 1999, ELAINE AND I DROVE by a log cabin on Carefree Lane. We were hunting for a possible purchase of land or a house that was in the vicinity of McCall, Idaho. A lot of people have dreams to own a cabin in the woods or a second home that could provide a sanctuary and respite from the pace of everyday life.

We passed by an old cabin and barn that sat on a long driveway. The place was unkept and appeared to be unoccupied. Encouraged by our friend Wayne, we decided to return to the property for another look. We walked around the cabin and barn and tried to rethink the possibilities of purchasing the place. The visit still didn't excite us.

We found an old real estate flyer for the log cabin in the mailbox, and contact information for the realtor, Jean. Later that September, we met Jean at the "Carefree Cabin." Jean shared some history about the place and noted it had been vacant for about 18 months. The former owner had moved to Challis and had lowered the price for a quick sell. It had originally been listed for $189,000 but the asking price had been dropped to $144,500. This piqued our interest because it was closer to what we had budgeted for a second property. The property needed a lot of work, though! Overgrown bushes climbed up into the solarium that was attached to the south side of the cabin. The barn smelled moldy, and was unsanitary—mostly from mouse droppings. Around the perimeter of the property, a decaying wood post-and-pole fence needed removal. Inside the five-acre perimeter, there were piles of rubbish, discarded fencing, old tires, piles of horse and mule manure, and weeds.

Once we were inside the cabin, though, there were features that lit a fire inside of us. We wanted this place. On the first floor, pieces of bright black obsidian were embedded in the stone walls. The carpentry work on the walls and floors was custom. From the second-story window, looking east, there was a view of Jughandle Peak, where sunrises would light up the bedroom on that side of the house. From the west window, there was an unobstructed view of the Chokecherry Hills, where we could imagine enjoying beautiful sunsets. The "kicker" for me though, was the flat Oakley flagstone floor in the living room. Elk hoof prints were stamped in the grout. This unique feature immediately spurred my idea for a new name for the place: Elkstone Cabin.

Jean explained to us that the 1,500-square-foot cabin was built with high-altitude lodgepole pine logs, probably harvested above 6,500 feet north of McCall. This meant they had high-density tree rings and were much more stout and stronger than trees that had grown at 4,500 feet near Smiths Ferry, just 45 miles south of McCall.

We bought Elkstone Cabin on October 9, 1999. Wayne was the first to congratulate us. He knew the former owner. Two weeks later, Wayne received a phone call from Jim, the former owner of the cabin. He told Wayne that he had "sellers' remorse" and asked if we would consider selling the property back to him for more than we had just purchased it. We declined the offer.

Moving forward, our work was cut out for us. We had to learn how to care for a log structure, repairs, surrounding grounds maintenance, and more. We dedicated that fall season to cleaning the cabin and barn. We cleared vegetation from inside the solarium. We repaired and replaced door latches and rusty plumbing, and purchased a new refrigerator. Our heat source was a Vermont Castings Defiant stove, located in the kitchen. To our delight, the stove also had a warming shelf with the iconic dragon under-brackets that this Vermont Castings model was known for. Electric baseboard heaters upstairs and down would supplement the stove, so we were confident that we would be warm through the winter.

By late November, there was a foot of snow outside the cabin door.

A few months later in February, the snow had piled up five feet. We had acquired our cabin in one of the hardest winters in the area since the 1950s.

Thankfully, it held together without any serious issues. We were challenged, however, with plowing the 80-yard-long driveway clear of snow so that we could drive to the barn where we parked our truck to protect it from those cold winter nights. At first, our new Honda snowblower was adequate for plowing four-to-eight-inch snowfalls off the driveway. When heavier snows came, we hired the reliable IdaHoe plowing company known locally for doing a great job clearing snow with a heavier-duty D-4 front-end loader. By late March of each year, there would be piles of snow 10-to-12 feet high from the snow plowing, which might remain until mid-June before melting.

217

We made trips from Boise to McCall annually, at least five to seven times to do repairs, mow the lawn, remove garbage, fill the propane tank, shovel snow, and drink beer. We called it "recreational main-tenance." If it went beyond this, we would drink whiskey . . . and wonder why we ever bought the place.

Twenty-three years of owning Elkstone Cabin has provided grist for stories about our

Winter at Elkstone Cabin. Photo by Richard Howard.

cabin and the many memorable events that took place there. Skilled plumbers, electricians, propane stove specialists, carpet layers, and two carpenters worked to help us keep the cabin in good shape.

They all recalled stories about helping to build the place in 1973 with Jim, the original owner, who wanted only the best craftsmen to do custom work on every aspect of the cabin. Our friend Wayne was Jim's friend, and he too helped to build this log home that would easily last a hundred years. The craftsmanship was indeed superb from aspects: the foundation, logs, wiring, pipes, lights, stone, gravel, glass, and paint. It all combined perfectly to give a very special life to our Elkstone Cabin. It's now 47 years old—and counting.

A steel- and wooden-post corral is attached to the barn, built to keep horses and mules. Our neighbor Sam, a fire control officer for the Payette National Forest, who lived down the road, had a horse named Dilly. He bought Dilly for his 12-year-old daughter Kate. His wife Khris was a wildlife biologist for the Payette, Forest, who rode both English and western saddle styles and was passionate about competitive riding. They asked us if they could stable Dilly in our corral and barn for a monthly rent. Soon, Dilly was living at Elkstone Cabin Stables. Dilly (the filly) was easy to ride and responsive to the bridle, which allowed them to excel at the competitions nearby.

Each Friday night, Khris and Kate would come over to the cabin, load Dilly into a horse trailer, and drive over to the riding stable. They would stay through the weekend to practice and compete in English saddle dressage, sport jumping, and western barrel racing. Khris and Kate often returned with trophies they had won during these events.

They won numerous ASPCA national Maclay points at these competitions, and elsewhere in the Pacific Northwest, which qualified them to compete in the 2008 National Equestrian Show in Lexington, Kentucky. Kate, at age 17, trailered up Dilly and along with her mom. drove Sam's Dodge Ram truck

to Kentucky for the horse show. As a registered and qualified
trainer, Khris entered Kate in the national junior competition
for women under 18 years of age. Kate competed well in the
national championship competition. By the end of week, she
was ranked 10th nationally, and earned first place in the western
junior division. She won a boatload of ribbons there, and was
honored as the best and fairest junior competitor of the National
Equestrian Show.

It was just great to hear about this. We were proud to think
that in some small way, the spirit of Elkstone Cabin contributed
to this success. Kate went away to college that fall after graduating from McCall-Donnelly High School. Dilly was dutifully
cared for by Sam and Khris.

One morning in late October, Sam phoned. Dilly, at 14
years old, had died in the Elkstone Cabin barn. Probably, the
hard competition shortened her life or maybe the hard McCall
winters taxed her body. Sam asked permission to bury their
beloved horse just north of the corral at our Elkstone Cabin,
which had been home to Dilly. We agreed, of course.

A week later, as we were driving down the road to the
cabin, we saw where Dilly had been laid to rest. At one end of
the grave was a two-foot-high cross and some fresh flowers in
a vase. We got out of the truck, walked to the grave, and read the
inscription that was attached to the cross on a brass plaque:
Dilly. Kate's Horse Friend. B. 1994—D. 2008.

Kate wasn't able to come home from college until Thanksgiving vacation. When she did, she came over to the cabin
grounds where Dilly was buried. Every day—sometimes twice a
day—she brought flowers and cried at Dilly's gravesite. Before
Kate returned to school, we invited she and her family over to
enjoy a salmon and elk steak dinner with us. Kate and Khris
recalled stories about Dilly. By the end of the evening, after
dessert and several rounds of Maker's Mark® whiskey, we
were all in tears.

Elkstone Cabin became a weekend destination for
friends and acquaintances throughout the year. I placed a

leather-bound journal on the counter near the cabin front door. We encouraged people to write a few lines in the journal about their stay at the cabin. Over the years, we have had 41 guests, some who have stayed multiple times and rebook months in advance. There also were a few guests who appreciated our cabin, but never returned because it was too "rustic" for them.

Sometimes we hosted big parties on weekends when friends could get away from Boise. Guests would bring their BBQs along for feasts. The smell of roasting BBQ chicken, sirloin steaks, corn wrapped in corn leaves, Idaho baker potatoes, and green peppers satisfied huge appetites. We kept chokecherry, blackberry, and strawberry-apple pies warming in the kitchen stove until ready to be served. A grand fire would burn in our outdoor fire ring. Adirondack and green camp chairs were placed around the fire. Sometimes party-goers would shoot fireworks displays on July 4th or December 21st, the winter solstice. Guests would enjoy themselves at these parties until midnight or the early morning hours, and then folks would wander off to find a bed, sleeping bag, tent, or truck camper to sleep in until morning.

We also hosted ski parties with eight or ten friends at a time, who would stay at the cabin over the weekend during mid-February. Everyone was good at skiing and enjoyed hitting the slopes at Brundage for the day. Sometimes it was so cold that a few sips of Maker's Mark® or schnapps hit the spot during short ski breaks. We would return to Elkstone Cabin, clear snow from around the fire ring, and build a huge bon fire. Everyone brought a dish to share that would be warmed up in the kitchen and served inside the cozy cabin. The more hardy souls would eat their dinner sitting around the campfire in four feet of snow. This enhanced the enjoyment of the feast, the wine, the whiskey, and the night sky. Sometimes, we heard the howl of coyotes.

We kept an aluminum canoe at the cabin. It wasn't used much, but on occasion we would throw it on top of the truck, tie it down, and travel to the north shore of Payette Lake.

There, we would launch the canoe and paddle for three miles up the North Fork of the Payette River. It was a superb outing, especially in the fall, when we would glide over dozens of spawning kokanee salmon and sometimes, get a glimpse of a deer—or better yet—a moose, around the river bend. The river was almost always crystal clear, except in the spring when tannins from the pine trees would color the river a light brown.

I tried other rivers and a few lakes with this canoe, but preferred to take my 16-foot Alumaweld drift boat, nicknamed the *Otter*, that was stored safely in the cabin barn. I could oar down the Salmon, Clearwater or South Fork of the Snake Rivers and fish for steelhead, salmon, or trout. Sometimes I would put the 9.9 hp Johnson motor on its transom and explore lakes, trolling Wolly Buggers behind the *Otter* for lunker trout.

Many special events occurred at Elkstone Cabin, but perhaps the most memorable was our daughter Alissa's wedding. We began preparing for her wedding three months before the big day. Everyone had their eye focused on June 23rd. While the planning was intense and the logistics were demanding, there was no end to the enthusiasm we all shared. The guest list was supposed to be kept at no more than 90 attendees. When we asked Alissa how many RSVPs she had received, she replied, "168." Whew! That was a big crowd of friends and relatives.

We selected a nearly-level spot in the back field for the ceremony, which we mowed and watered to thicken the grass. A wedding arbor was made from aspen trees that we harvested from a nearby grove, and we hung beautiful flowers from it. We arranged all the chairs for wedding guests as though it were an outside church, split equally on two sides with an aisle down the middle for bride, groom, and the wedding party. Wildflowers in the field had reached maximum bloom just a few days before.

The big day dawned with a sunny sky, occasional broken cloud cover, and no chance of high wind or rain. June 23rd was perfect in every way.

The ceremony began with the bridesmaids. They wore bright red dresses and slowly walked down the stairs from the second-floor veranda to the lawn, around a row of pine trees, and to the aisle of chairs outdoors. They stopped and stood near the reverend's podium and aspen arbor, and faced the seated wedding guests. The bride followed and joined her bridesmaids. On the other side of the podium was the groom with his groomsmen, also facing the audience. A sound man had set up a superb music system with speakers that could reach out to everyone who attended the celebration. "Here Comes The Bride" soon faded to quiet, and Reverend Allie invited everyone to stand. She recited a decree about love and marriage, then invited the groom and bride to place rings on each other's fingers. Four minutes later, she finished the ceremony by saying, "the groom may kiss the bride." It was a special moment for bride and groom, parents, relatives, friends, and Sage the Border Collie. A year-and-a-half later, the bride and groom were blessed with a baby boy. They named him Weston.

The dinner party that followed the wedding was over-flowing with unrestrained joy. The open bar lubricated the party, and we also filled a canoe with ice, beer, and soft drinks. The buffet was splendid—a perfect complement to the festive beverages. Guests were so happy that they were inspired to make raucous dinner toasts. Music livened the celebration, while guests danced under the aspen and pine trees. The food, drinks, dancing, laughter, and gaiety energized everyone at the wedding, from the smallest kids and young people to the older adults. We heard so many times, "What a wonderful occasion this was! This was the best wedding they had ever been to," and more similar compliments. And so, it was a fine, fine weekend for this wonderful wedding celebration.

Elkstone Cabin also provided more private moments for us all. I have spent many hours there writing stories. I positioned my desk on the second floor near the west window, and could look out the south window for birds and deer; the west window for storm clouds and sunsets.

We always strung Tibetan prayer flags from the pine trees to the aspens on the west side. I would take occasional pauses walking from my desk to the outside veranda, and watch the colorful flags waving in the wind from the second floor. The prismatic colors, Buddhist symbols, and Sanskrit writing on the flags always gave me further pause. It made me think of the Annapurna Sanctuary in the Himalaya mountains, or the sagebrush sea in the Pahsimeroi on the east side of the Lost River Mountain Range.

Often, I would roll out a yoga mat on the second floor of the cabin, and arrange my yoga blocks, tension strap, and singing bowl for a practice or meditation. Sometimes I would do this for five minutes and sometimes for an hour. It nourished my imagination and invigorated my body and soul.

Afterwards, I was able to walk back to my desk, turn on my computer, and write 1,400 words in one sitting. Writing demands contemplation, discipline, and courage. After completing a story, I knew that I had achieved all those qualities.

Other days, I would just take long walks with our dog Sage and breathe in the peace of the property.

It was good to know I could rely of the beauty and serenity of Elkstone Cabin and its surroundings: my base camp during all seasons.

Elkstone Cabin is base camp for the author. It demands maintenance year-round, but it is cool and comfortable in the summer and toasty warm in the winter. Photo of the cabin and property in 2018 by Richard Howard.

Yoga Nuns
of the Treasure Valley

GORDON WALKER ROLLED UP HIS BLUE yoga mat, and collected his yoga blocks and black tension strap, and stuffed them into a Trader Joe's bag. He grabbed his warming blanket too. Gordon then walked outside to a full spectrum of colorful fall leaves on the trees and from those that had fallen to the ground. It was mid-November in Hyde Park, Boise, Idaho.

This Sunday morning practice with yoga guide Darcy Midday had been vigorous, tending toward vinyasa. The True North Yoga Studio located just three blocks east of Hyde Park provided some of the best highly-skilled yoga instructors in the Treasure Valley. Each Sunday morning Gordon would drive from his home in east Boise to the North End.

He would practice for an hour with Darcy, Martha, or Jennie. Afterward, he would visit his favorite bistro, *Certified Kitchen and Bakery* on the west side of 13th Street in Hyde Park. Rather than drive this morning, he walked the three blocks to Hyde Park. While walking, he thought about his newest mission in life, inspired three weeks earlier while grabbing a bite to eat at the bistro. He would visit ten yoga studios in the Treasure Valley. True North was first, then Yoga Tree, followed by Hollywood Market Studio, the downtown Boise YMCA, and six others.

Morning practice with Darcy and nine other men and women began with the clear tones of a Tibetan singing bowl struck twice. Following Darcy, they sat silent with hands pressed together at sternum level while sitting in a lotus posture. They drew in three deep breaths through the nose and exhaled through the mouth.

Darcy then led her class through a sequence of positions, culminating in the high point of the practice, the Eagle pose.

The practice included other challenging poses, deep and shallow breathing moments. The closing meditation phase was open for ten minutes. The first minute was taken up with class recitation of "Om" and "Zu," with alternate deep and shallow breaths. The remaining minutes were for introspection, with focus only on one's breath, tending toward the final stage of *samadhi*. The practice ended with Darcy striking the singing bowl once and we all bowed ours heads, speaking the ending salutation, "Namaste."

Her yoga sequences encouraged us to focus extraordinarily well. After each pose, she subtly half-smiled, with the sweet sound of inhaling and exhaling of cleansing breaths. Darcy's bright blue eyes sparkled like mountain lake waves in the afternoon sun.

This reflection caused Gordon to think about recent and distant yoga memories that he treasured. After retiring from the company, which in his line of work was often referred to as "The Farm," he needed to re-center. So he began to practice yoga.

Then, he recalled his introduction to yoga when he was only 16 years old and was still in high school. That was 60 years ago! A progressive store in downtown Pocatello, the *Intermountain Bookstore*, once carried many arcane

The yoga teachers of Treasure Valley are dedicated to a way of life that is transformative. They demonstrate this wisdom and compassion every week, every month without waver. Web Photo courtesy of MUUV Studio.

and esoteric books. Gordon sometimes visited the store, mostly because his older sister worked there part-time.

One day, while visiting the store after school, he found a new shipment of books stacked by the counter that hadn't been yet been put on the shelves. He was attracted to a book with a black cover, entitled, *Hatha Yoga: The Report of a Personal Experience,* by Theos Bernard. The book was $38—an expensive book for the time. Gordon had never heard of yoga but it sounded mysterious, which appealed to him. He asked his sister, who was behind the counter, "Do you know anything about yoga"? She said, "No, but you might take the book over to the reading table and look through it. Perry Swisher, the owner of Intermountain encourages his customers to do this."

Gordon cracked open the book and saw pictures of the author in weird poses. Before long, he was engrossed in the first chapter of the book. From 1941 to 1943, Theos Bernard, then a PhD candidate at Columbia University in New York, spent two years in India and Nepal at ashrams studying yoga, the physical discipline of breath and body exercise. The book was a result of Bernard's dissertation, which was published in 1944. The book had 64 pages with 34 full-page black and white pictures of various hatha yoga poses demonstrated by Bernard. Captions under the photos identified the poses both in Hindi and English.

To quote from Bernard's book,

> "*Hatha Yoga* is a discipline involving various bodily and mental practices but central to them is the regulation of the breath. Hatha is derived from two Sanskrit roots. *Ha* (sun) and *tha* (moon) or the breath from the right nostril being the sun breath and from the left nostril being the moon breath. Yoga is derived from the root, *Yuja* (to join); therefore *Hatha Yoga* is the uniting of these two breaths. The effect is believed to induce a mental condition call *samadhi*. This is not a mystical or imaginary state but one that the actual condition can be subjectively experienced and objectively observed."

The book was to become a part of Gordon's permanent library. It was one of few books that he seldom loaned out to other people. If they wanted to read the book, he would invite them to his place. Hatha yoga became a practice that would intermittently return to Gordon as a discipline in his life.

The first time, this happened during his undergraduate college days when he was on a ship full of students crossing the Atlantic Ocean to Europe. The teachers on the ship wanted to know if there was anyone who could teach a yoga class. This was in 1965, when the cultural fascination for India, Nepal, and Tibet was gaining some interest in the west. Gordon volunteered. The first morning of the class, 34 students showed up on the second deck of the ship. Ten more students heard about the class and attended the second morning of the class. By asking some questions and conducting physical tests, it was obvious to Gordon that few in the crowd were familiar with hatha yoga. They had youthful enthusiasm and a desire to learn, though. Within five days, and two practices held per day, Gordon brought 44 students to a new level of awareness about hatha yoga before they landed at Le Havre, France.

His interest in yoga returned again when he was in graduate school at Utah State University. A rogue teacher taught a night class about yoga and its relationship to Buddhism and Hinduism. This noncredit course was outside the regular curriculum. The teacher asked Gordon to demonstrate hatha yoga postures, which piqued his practice of yoga again. Since there were no yoga studios in Logan, Utah, in the early1970s, Gordon would practice at isolated places around the university or at his student apartment. This lasted about a year, but then other school activities and his MS thesis field work became a priority.

Then, five years later while on assignment in Indonesia, before he retired, Gordon looked for yoga studios during his spare time. He had heard that Indonesia was a popular yoga center. He traveled to Ubud, Bali, a city only two hours by air from Jakarta, the capital of Indonesia. By chance encounter, the hotel he was staying at in Ubud was just two blocks from The Yoga Barn: School of Sacred Arts Studio. Gordon spoke with the owner, who told him that Ubud was known as a yoga center for Indonesians, Australians, Europeans and others from North America. Gordon stayed an extra week there to practice at the studio.

The studio was crowded and it offered a variety of yoga classes. Gordon selected several and attended them twice a day, one in the morning and one in the evening. The studio had four halls. Each hall opened to striking combination of jungle vegetation and rice fields where stark white, black-billed egrets hunted for food daily. Each hall had well-polished, chestnut brown teak floors. The yoga teachers were mostly Australian but the studio invited special touring teachers from all over to make their presentations.

One such unusual event was practice led by a Tibetan monk from Darjeeling, India. Gordon attended this practice with 28 other yoga students at 8:00 pm. It began as an asana practice for the first half hour. The next hour was a deep dive into the intense sounds of 14 Tibetan singing bowls, 5" to 24" in diameter, arranged in a circle. The monk asked the practitioners to lie down on their yoga mats with a yoga block under each person's head. The concert of singing bowls played by the monk lasted for ten minutes. Then another concert began, in which he asked everyone to slowly walk around the circle of singing bowls and strike each one as they passed by it. Instead of cacophony, the harmony of tones that emanated from about 10 students striking bowls at the same time was incredible.

The practice then ended, with students returning to their mats, meditating on their breaths with closed eyes. He came around to each person, and rather than using the bowl striker, he ran two fingers around the rim of a 15-inch bowl, which caused a ringing sound that varied in pitch.

The four practice halls at Yoga Barn in Ubud Bali, Indonesia, had polished chestnut brown teak floors. Each opened to a mix of jungle vegetation and rice fields. Photo by Richard Howard.

The bowl was held above each person's head, then to the side and chest, and finally above the head for about four minutes. This induced such a deep meditation for Gordon that he described it as an out-of-body, or near-death experience. As the monk moved on to the next student, Gordon was drawn back from the column of light to his yoga mat in the studio.

After he retired, Gordon experienced a rekindling of his interest in yoga. One of Gordon's hatha yoga instructors in Boise, Jennie, said, "Keep yourself active with yoga or you will rust." That statement hit a cord with Gordon.

He has continued the practice for many years now, in studios and sometimes in his own way at Elkstone Cabin, his base camp near McCall, Idaho. Not Zen, Tibetan Buddha, India Buddha, or Hindu practices, but Gordon based his meditative concentration based on reading about Revelation Sutras, the oldest wooden hand press documents (~ 800AD) in the world. His meditations had become a central portal to focus his energy.

First, he counts backward from 30 to one with a breath drawn in and a breath exhaled out with each count. Stepping into a deeper state after each number counted, Gordon let his thoughts drop away so that his inner mind could surface. Soon he was committed to being a granite stone sitting quietly. The first picture emerged of him sitting in a lotus posture on top of the first of seven summits that he visited during this meditation. Gordon was so inspired by this experience that he wrote a short story about it, the "Seven Summits Meditation." The concept came to Gordon at a visit to the Certified Kitchen and Bakery but he later composed it during a six-day writing marathon at Elkstone Cabin.

At Elkstone, Gordon practiced this meditation and the associated asana positions. He revisited the meditation sitting on the banks of the North Fork of the Payette River listening to the sound of rapids from the high flows of spring runoff. He also practiced it while rafting the Hells Canyon of the Snake River Canyon with Elizabeth and Jon; alone overnight by a campfire in Bobcat Cave east of Howe, Idaho; and camping near Grasmere,

Owyhee County, Idaho on the sagebrush sea under a perfect night sky full of stars.

Gordon was moving into another phase of his yoga practice, spurred by recent life experiences, but also by discussions with his yoga teachers, where he began to question the physical body, the complexity of the brain, and mysteries of the mind. It also came from practicing hatha yoga in many venues, reading books, and pondering the meaning of spiritual essays. Instead of a quest for mystical experiences, (a universal trait found across most cultures and throughout history), he found it more productive in his personal synthesis, to read more about the topic of near-death experiences (NDE). Neuroscientists have focused for years on exploring the anatomy of creativity, the source of consciousness, and near-death experiences.

Of the three, Gordon discovered that NDE has been the most easily identified and studied. In 1986, Dr. Melvin Morse collaborated with other scientists at the University of Washington and in Chile. They discovered that NDEs could be induced by electrical stimulation of the Sylvian fissure, which is located in the right temporal lobe just above the right ear. Fundamental to this discovery were interviews of patients who had experienced NDEs. Common to all experiences was a recollection of intense light and love. Living, dying, near death experiences, mysticism, and origins of the mind's energy are interrelated, but they are also personal and individualized experiences.

For instance, the source of reported intense light may forever remain a mystery; and maybe it should. But those who experience the light say that it is more than just light. Some say that it wraps them in an intense warmth of caring that they have never felt before: it has a mystical quality to it. Other NDE phases that are reported, such as entering a tunnel, being out of the body, witnessing the living, talking to relatives that have passed, having little desire to return to the body, are also significant and extraordinary.

The yoga teachers Gordon knew and respected practiced in the Treasure Valley, McCall, and Riggins were a metaphor in Gordon's mind: "Yoga Nuns" who fulfill a need in the community. All instructors had 300-hour or 500-hour teaching certificates; some 1,000-hour certificates. All of them offered services in other areas of human health like Reiki therapy, Ayurvedic medicine, and personal counseling. They attracted resolute students who practiced under them—some becoming inspired enough to obtain their own yoga teaching certificates. All are well-read and often suggest significant references to students. A few titles include: *Yoga Anatomy: An Illustrated Guide to Postures, Movements, and Breathing Techniques"* by Kaminoff and Mathews; *Meditations on Intention and Being: Daily Reflections on the Path of Yoga, Mindfulness, and Compassion* by R. Gates; *How to Meditate: A Guide to Self-Discovery* by L. LeShan; and *Living With the Himalayan Masters* by S. Rama.

Then there is the *Yoga Journal*, perhaps the best periodic publication for teachers and students alike. This journal's combination of pictures, essays, and diversity of subject matter offer a smorgasbord of high-bar editions ten times a year. All of the yoga nuns are well-traveled and keep journals or blogs about where they've been, what they've discovered, and what revelations they've had.

India is usually the top destination, but so too are Nepal, Thailand, Indonesia, Mexico, and even Alaska. The workshops and retreats they create become a temporary sense of place which imparts a significant memory for those who attend and participate.

How such wisdom and life experience comes to these yoga nuns who are mostly at such a young age is not a mystery. They are dedicated to a way of life that is transformative. Still, they demonstrate wisdom, compassion, humbleness, and sense of presence that is far beyond their physical age, every week, every month without waver. They are the breath of the sun and the moon. *Samadhi, Om Zu, Namaste.*

Gordon Walker, with his blue mat and Lululemon blocks, has practiced yoga in studios, and in many places outdoors, including Bali (top), Pocatello, Idaho (middle), and the sands of Cape Lookout along the Oregon coast (bottom). Photos by Richard Howard.

Highways, Clams, and the Doors at Cannabis Corner

W E PREPARED FOR OUR ANNUAL ROAD trip that spring to hunt for clams. Four friends were planning to join us in Long Beach, Washington for the clam hunt. Elaine and I, and our clamming buddies, kept close watch on websites and weather forecasts to determine when it was best to "go to the coast." We scrutinized the Washington Department of Fisheries website about the clam season, which gave us information about limits, red tide warnings, tide tables, and other important data. We particularly looked at the daily razor clam limits, which usually were set at 15 clams per day.

This was serious business. Our gear showed it, too. We were fully loaded with aluminum clam guns, a shovel, chest waders, five-gallon buckets, knives, Teflon cutting boards, sweaters, hats, jackets, and extra clothing.

Soon, we were on the road. On our way from Boise to Long Beach, we stopped over at Hood River, Oregon. There, we stayed at the Westcliff Lodge, a place we always knew we could trust for excellent accommodations for our group and our dogs. That night we ate a quick dinner and then scrambled for last-minute shopping items.

The next morning, breakfast at the Egg River Café in Hood River fueled us for the day. It started perfectly as we looked out the restaurant west window at a grand view of Mt. Adams, a 12,280-foot volcano that was first climbed in 1854. The local Native American Chinook Tribe called it *Klickitat*, meaning "beyond." We gazed out the window at the snow-covered volcano and leisurely perused *The Oregonian* for news we had missed and possible clamming updates. Although we were not in a hurry, we soon took to the highway. We headed toward the "Bridge the Gods," which crosses the Columbia River from Oregon to Washington. It's a classical steel truss cantilever bridge, built in 1926, that is 1,856 feet long.

From Interstate Highway 84 in Oregon, we entered
Washington State Highway 14. We had planned a spur-of-
the-moment stop in North Bonneville, Washington. Our
curiosity had gotten the better of us from an ad we read in
The Oregonian that morning about a small business there.

"Cannabis Corner" at 420 Evergreen Drive was advertised as the only commercial pot shop in the nation owned and
operated by a local government: the town of North Bonneville.
This tiny Washington hamlet is a "one-horse town" just north
of the Bridge of the Gods, along banks of the Columbia
River. There is one gas station, one hotel, and one pot shop.
Its municipal government supports one sheriff, a part-time
mayor, and 11 other staffers—including six who work at
Cannabis Corner.

Washington State law requires that all taxes on cannabis
sales from privately-owned shops must go back to the state.
To skirt around this, the good folks who live in North Bonneville
passed "a public development authority" initiative that allowed
profits from a city-owned pot shop to be returned to the town.
The State of Washington did not challenge this, so North

Bonneville collects cannabis sales profits and uses them to benefit the town's infrastructure and to pay its employees. The mayor of the town was so proud of this venture that his car license plates read "MJMAYOR." With an annual budget of $1.2 million, the Cannabis Corner sales profits nearly doubled the town's income. It also secured robust health insurance and a 401(c) retirement plan for the town's employees.

The clam diggers walked through the doors at Cannabis Corner, where they were greeted by a friendly and knowledgeable employee behind the counter. Slim, Nicknamed "Gossamer," told the group that he was 23 years old, and was a Borah High School graduate. He had moved to North Bonneville from Boise. He had never held health insurance and said he sure hadn't even thought about saving for retirement. When the Cannabis Corner explained their 401(c) program to him, he said that he simply glowed inside thinking about kicking up his heels when he would turn 62. Slim said that he woke up smiling everyday, ready to go to his job as a "Bud Manager" at Cannabis Corner.

He educated the clam diggers about the dozen or so types of buds under the glass counter in display trays. He was proud to say that all were grown in Washington State. He recommended 10%-strength buds if they hadn't used pot in a while or had never tried it before. But if they had, then he recommended the 30% buds. They would keep them feeling good for several hours. Slim also was obligated to give the group a copy of the Cannabis Corner mission statement:

> We are pleased to offer exceptional cannabis products
> for responsible adult consumption while maintaining a
> high level of ethics, professionalism, and customer service.
> Serving as a model to other communities, we are helping to
> revitalize the local economy and promote economic growth.
> We strive to be an exemplary employer, a model business,
> and ensure that all profits are used for the benefit of
> the community."

Fascinated by all the products for sale at Cannabis Corner, the clam diggers spent over an hour there. It was overwhelming.

The store sold 16 types of buds, pre-rolled joints, five different oatmeal cookies, eight flavors of gum drops, dark chocolate candy bars (some with nuts and cranberries), nine shapes and flavors of Bonbons, and five soda drinks. Every product was clearly labeled, identifying the various potencies of cannabis in each.

The clammers were like kids visiting Cramer's Candy Emporium at Bown's Crossing in Boise, that boasts a similar variety, with ten flavors of sorbet ice cream, 25 chocolate Bonbons, and 15 varieties of soda drinks including root beer sarsaparilla. One store sold a sugar high—the other store sold a "maryjane" high.

The clam diggers made their purchases and thanked Slim, alias "Gossamer, the Bud Manager," for his help. We were ready to get to Long Beach. The hunt would soon be upon us.

Two hours later, we checked into the Merry Maids Motel and Cottages in Long Beach, situated just 106 yards from the coast by a sand dune. We purchased groceries and returned to our cottages so that we could prepare our dinner feast of BBQ salmon garnished with lemon and dill, peppered and buttered mashed potatoes, French-cut green beans, Pilsner beer, and red wine. Because we needed to be on the beach during low tide at 5:30 the next morning, we went to bed early, and repeated that same schedule the whole trip.

Under the clam hunt regulations, each hunter could have 15 clams per day. Among the six of us, that meant our limit was a total of 90 clams. Clam hunting was glorious. We limited-out on razor clams each day after about three hours of hunting. The real work began after the hunt, though. The clams had to soak for two hours in five-gallon buckets of fresh cold water. After that, the clams were ready to be opened, cut, sliced, and diced, and then stored in one gallon baggies. The Merry Maids Motel and Cottages provided 12-foot-long clam-cleaning counters by Cottage # 14 for their guests. There was a freshwater hose nearby to rinse the clams. For the last step, a big dumpster was on-site where we dumped about 40 pounds of fragmented shells into it.

Starving after our early-morning hunt and prep work, we drove to Teri's Restaurant, two miles south of our cabins, for a quick breakfast. We savored hearty breakfasts of eggs, hash browns, and buttered whole wheat toast, plus oatmeal sprinkled with brown sugar, walnuts, and cranberries. We drank coffee, and more coffee, while we talked about our morning hunt (that we also shared with about 200 other people who were also hunting clams on the beach).

On our second day, the Washington Department of Fisheries told us that there were 5,280 people hunting clams along the 16-mile Long Beach shoreline.

Our clamming group was deeply satisfied knowing that we had harvested our limit from the sand and sea. We reflected on how Native Americans may have felt when they harvested clams 250 years ago along these same shores of the Pacific. Everyone in our clam digger party harvested their full limits in three days: almost 270 clams. Another impressive count: we packed 28 one-gallon freezer-bags full of clams.

We dined on two bag-fulls the last night at our campfire party on our last night near the cabins in the protective cover of a sand dune. It was a successful clam safari, surely one that this party of clam diggers would remember for years.

Oh, yes . . . about the campfire party. . .

We collected a huge pile of driftwood to burn and laid it inside a ring of stones. Then we set our portable camp chairs around a big ring of stones. We greased #8 iron skillets with olive oil and laid them on wooden planks, and placed our cooking utensils and flatware nearby. We dragged our big ice chests, full of our items for the feast, including clams, sirloin steaks, iceberg lettuce, blue cheese salad dressing, Yukon Gold potatoes, butter, and salt and pepper.

In one of the ice chests, there was a white tray with a few more items: three types of pot buds, loaded oatmeal cookies, and two dozen special Bonbons that we had bought at the Cannabis Corner stop.

Ahhh . . . the sun had set, and most of the other guests had finished their cabin stays. We pondered, "Well, here we are. We have the beach, the night sky, the stars, and the sea—all to ourselves now. More than enough to enjoy our last night."

With a good Malbec wine from Indian Creek Winery, we toasted to the clam gods who provided us with such abundance. We then set out to prep our special hors d'oeuvre: minced clam dip with tortilla chips. We chopped clams and

red onions, added some lemon juice, and threw the mix into
the big skillet. Then, we added 10% buds, and fried the whole
combination. It was delicious—made all the better by the buds.
The clam dip, wine, and calming sound of ocean waves lapping
nearby set our mood perfectly. We consumed our dinner as we
watched the campfire flames loft into smoke and drift away
with the breeze. We rested a bit, and then headed toward our
dessert, consisting of "the North Bonneville" oatmeal cookies
and Bonbons. We slowly coasted along some more—maybe for
an hour—maybe more.

The embers of the fire were low but still radiated heat
to ward off the April night chill. Everyone wrapped up in
homemade quilts or Pendleton blankets. We were all in a relaxed
post-dessert state, ready to hear a bedtime story.

The story was "Gossamer Wump," a tale about a master
musician who played an essential orchestra instrument, the
triangle. We learned that Frank Morgan wrote, narrated, and
recorded the story in 1950 on a Capitol Records 78-rpm album.
Here is the story of Gossamer Wump:

> *Gossamer Wump was born on a farm. He had
> one green and one blue eye. His shock of brown hair never
> looked combed because of the all the cowlicks. He owned
> a dog named George. Wump's first words sounded as if he
> was clucking like a chicken. Later, after six months,
> he learned to crow like a rooster and bark like a dog.
> One day when he was older and in town for a visit,
> Wump heard a marching band. He liked all the instru-
> ments but his favorite was the triangle. He was so
> impressed that he decided to learn how to play it.
> He packed up 27 peanut butter sandwiches, his dog
> George, and went to the big city to learn how to
> play the triangle.*

He was fortunate for the music professor, Cuddy Nutty Dump, who said that he had room for just one more student in the group. Wump practiced for six years under Dump. He became a star pupil.

However, one night while playing the triangle in a local band, he accidentally hit the bandleader, Gaylord Gallop on the head. It sounded so good to Wump that he played the entire piece on Gaylord's head. Gallop was so mad by the end of the piece that he insisted Dump get rid of Wump—or he would quit the music school.

Wump was so sad as he walked down the street after leaving Dump's music school. But then he heard an orchestra playing in an auditorium. He went to listen and noticed the orchestra did not have a triangle player.

So Wump talked to the director of the Washington Pot Symphony(WPS), Stanislaw Hudnut. Hudnut wanted to hear Wump play before hiring him. Wump played his best and most difficult piece for Hudnut. When he finished, Hudnut said, "My boy, with my symphony orchestra, you will play."

Gossamer Wump was thrilled about this new start in his music career. After eight concerts, Hudnut gave Wump the opportunity to play a solo accompanied by the WPS. The music hall sold out all the tickets to Gossamer Wump's solo concert. There was a loud applause when Hudnut walked out to his director's podium. There was an even louder applause when Wump walked out and stood there by the podium bowing to the audience. Hudnut raised his baton and the music began.

However, when Wump went to play his triangle, his pants fell down. He pulled them up again and continued his solo accompanied by the WPS. They fell down again and so he pulled them up. This continued for nine measures of music until a woman in the audience started to laugh, then a big fat man started to laugh, and then a little boy started to laugh. Soon, everyone was laughing . . .

The now *very* relaxed clam hunters who were sitting around the campfire eating Bonbons also laughed ... and listened on to the story ...

> *Wump was so embarrassed he ran off the*
> *stage, out of the auditorium and down the street.*
> *He didn't know what he was going to do now that*
> *his music career was in shambles.*
> *But an older gentleman approached Wump*
> *who had heard him play the solo with the WPS.*
> *He was impressed with Wump's talent.*
> *The man owned Cramer's Candy Emporium.*
> *He gave Wump a job driving an ice cream truck.*
> *Today, one can hear Wump playing his*
> *marvelous and melodious triangle while selling*
> *ice cream, cookies, and Bonbons for Cramer's that*
> *is located at Bown's Crossing in east Boise.*
> *"Arf! Arf! Woof! Woof!"*
> *"Oh, poor George," exclaimed Wump.*
> *"I forgot to let him out of the suitcase."*

Epilogue

This vista makes one committed to never give up on the stormy waters of the Sagebrush Sea. Photo of Big Southern Butte, Idaho, by Devin Englestead.

Salmon River Destiny

WATER IS IMPORTANT TO ALL OF US, like breathing and sustenance.

Reflect on how water has been treated in the hands of our society.

Water in the springs and tributaries of the upper Salmon River of Idaho is not like ditch water used for livestock.

This water hasn't been manipulated by dams, canals and mines— though that becomes its destiny.

This water was beckoned from the sky and is handled by the granite, basalt, and sedimentary rock of the Sawtooth and White Cloud Mountains.

From its tributaries, it creates a liquid highway that supports the totemic Chinook and sockeye salmon that have been here since before the Pleistocene.

We are losing the cycles of the Chinook, sockeye, and steelhead. There are people with deceit on their minds who would like it that way.

There are wild strains and hatchery domestics of salmon and steelhead.

The domestics are being handled by managers, changing their seasonal migration patterns and restricting their genetic codes.

But the wilds are being cared for by the elements of evolutionary progress.

In their 960-mile journey from Buoy 10 at the
Mouth of the Columbia,
> up over four dams on the Columbia River,
>> up over four dams on the Snake River,
>>> then turning east into the Salmon River,
one can hear audible sounds of relief as wild strains and the
domestics too, make their way into the headwaters after
this epic journey.

Each species begins its spawning frenzy in cold clear water,
dropping eggs between quartzite stones in the shallows of redds.

This powerful cycle of migrating fish, coming home to spawn,
should influence us to give back to the river—to treat both with
respect and awe, while bearing witness to

the Sawtooth granite backbone of our respective origins.

. . . or soon we will be living with ghosts.

> *—Elkstone Cabin, McCall, Idaho*
> *October 30, 1999*

*This short essay was inspired after building a rock cairn–chorten on a
Salmon River tributary in the Sawtooth Mountains. The chorten was
for my good friend Gary Smith. Gary was a wilderness ranger for the
Sawtooth National Recreation Area from 1975 to 1977. Tragically,
at the age of 46, he was struck down with multiple sclerosis. He died
in April of 1988.*

We cherish this powerful cycle of salmon returning to spawn on a tributary of the Salmon River at Dagger Falls . . . or soon we will be living with ghosts. Photo by William H. Mullins.

Consider the Sagebrush Sea

BOBCAT CAVE NEAR ARCO, IDAHO, has 21 pictographs that are part of the ancient stone library found across the Snake River Plain.

Ten miles south of the cave, a nuclear glow from three atomic reactors may become a replacement for our oil and gas addiction.

Thirty miles north of the cave, a snow plume cascades into the clear, frigid air from the summit of Borah Peak.

Five miles east of the cave, a flock of sage-grouse fly urgently to escape the mortal stoop of a gyrfalcon.

Eight miles west of the cave, thunderheads pour a column of rain into a thirsty basin of sage.

About the Author

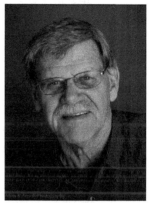

R ICHARD HOWARD is one of those rare Idaho native sons. Born in Pocatello to a prominent medical doctor and a nurse, he was raised with a rich heritage. His parents and sisters all claimed notable achievements in various history, science, writing, music, and academic endeavors.

Richard has published scientific papers, short stories, essays, and poems. His first book, *Never Give Up on the Sagebrush Sea*, was published in 2014 by Elkstone Press. Many of his stories, essays, and poems were inspired by his extensive travels in Europe, Australia, South Africa, Central America, and Indonesia.

Richard Howard.
Photo by Allan Ansell.

The fictional short stories in *Stormy Waters on the Sagebrush Sea* are a deeper attempt by the author to reveal more of his personal history, while addressing themes relevant to the cross-currents of the Northwest and our Nation.

For over 20 years, Richard nurtured his sense of adventure through mountain climbing in the western United States—especially in his favorite Idaho ranges: the Sawtooth Mountains, the White Clouds, and the Big Lost River Range.

He practiced falconry during a time when the sport attracted outstanding men and women who made significant contributions to international raptor conservation. He often took his hawks or falcons and his dog into Idaho's sagebrush sea in pursuit of wild game. He still enjoys witnessing the hunting flights of falcons or hawks with friends who are perhaps the most highly skilled falconers in North America.

In pursuit of an education, Richard obtained his under-graduate degree in anthropology at Idaho State University. He worked for the Smithsonian Institution on archaeology digs in the Midwest, and then returned to work on digs in Idaho. His mentors include Drs. Earl Swanson, Max Pavesic, and B. Robert Butler. His focus on rock art and the atlatl introduced him to professionals in the field, where he gained numerous insights about human prehistory.

Other significant mentors, Drs. Charles Trost, Edson Fichter, and Michael Wolfe, guided him through the field of wildlife biology. He obtained his Master's Degree in Wildlife Ecology at Utah State University. His master's thesis was a seminal work on the life history of the ferruginous hawk in southern Idaho and northern Utah.

In another season of his life, Richard worked four summers as a fishing guide in Alaska. There, he witnessed firsthand the value of clean rivers—unimpeded by dams—with an abundance of fish in the rivers and huge numbers of migrating caribou.

Continuing his love for the outdoors, Richard established his core career as a fish and wildlife biologist with the U.S. Fish and Wildlife Service. He worked primarily in the Northwestern United States, but also was assigned to work details in Canada, Mexico, and Washington, D.C.

After he retired, he started his own business, Biosage Consultants. He provided environmental consulting services for wind and solar energy projects and integrated green housing developments.

Richard enjoys classical, folk, and blues music and embraces the performing arts scene found across Southern Idaho. There is always hope in his heart that, one day, one of his stories will be film-scripted and made into a movie. He is fascinated by the unfolding drama of environmental trends—and political responses to those trends. He continues his interest in anthropology as a member of the Idaho Archaeological Society, and he attends regional and national meetings on the prehistory and origins of humans and their migrations.

Elkstone Cabin, located near McCall, Idaho, is his "base camp." From there, Richard writes from his desk, as he witnesses the passage of the seasons.

— Elkstone Cabin, McCall, Idaho
April 11, 2022

Elkstone Cabin, near McCall, Idaho, June 2008. The author has spent much of his time writing books, skiing, hiking, fishing, and hunting there. It is his "base camp." The cabin was named for the elk footprints that are embedded in the grout of the Oakley flagstone floor. Photo by Richard Howard.

McCall, Idaho

Printed in the USA
CPSIA information can be obtained
at www.ICGtesting.com
LVHW020147260823
756141LV00004B/59